QUITE POSSIBLY ALIEN

QUITE POSSIBLY ALIEN

A FREEMAN UNIVERSE NOVEL

PATRICK O'SULLIVAN

dunkerron press

A Dunkerron Press™ Book.

Copyright © 2014, 2021 by Patrick O'Sullivan

PatrickOSullivan.com

Illustration © Tom Edwards

TomEdwardsDesign.com

ISBN-13: 978-1-62560-020-2

ISBN-10: 1625600208

This is a work of fiction. Names, characters, dialogue, places and incidents are either the product of the author's imagination or are used fictitiously, and any resemblance to actual persons, living or dead, business establishments, events or locales is entirely coincidental.

Dunkerron Press and the Dunkerron colophon are trademarks of Dunkerron, LLC.

1

The Freeman merchant vessel *Last Stand* plunged into normal space with a shudder. They'd missed the destination coordinates by a considerable amount but Bosditch was used to that. If he had money for a decent piloting computer he wouldn't be anywhere near this middle-of-nowhere handoff, and he damned sure wouldn't be smuggling people.

The only good thing about making deliveries in the void between Prix Canada and Sizemore was that it was hard to bump into anything or anyone by accident. Bosditch was hours early for the drop and he had time to look around. He needed every second.

Bosditch's fingers stumbled over the newly replaced sensor rig. The new rig had full immersion capability, not that he knew how to use it. It still seemed alien, half the size of the old rig and gleaming in the semidark, the outline of the old console on the deck sole a distinct terminator between what was and what had been.

It felt strange, stepping over that line. Like he was walking on a new deck, one where there weren't any footworn paths to follow.

The sensor repair had topped the list, right above the rail gun, then the cargo capture rig. Once all that kit worked again he'd have options. He wouldn't be reduced to dropping containers down gravity wells and ferrying Huangxu corpsicles past their genetic slave lords.

Only half the overhead luminaries worked, and half of those were half black. He'd been working in twilight for so long that he'd barely noticed it until now. The new sensor rig stood out amongst the remaining consoles, sturdy low-tech units that had felt his father's hands, and his grandfather's before that. He ran his fingers over the controls and wondered how long it would take for the new unit's control labels to wear away. If he hadn't grown up on the *Last Stand*, he wouldn't know how to operate most of the gear on board. His fingers didn't know what they were doing with the new console yet. They would learn, though.

They had to. There were people who depended on him. Getting caught wasn't an option.

Display after display of data rolled by, nearfeed sensor data from the almost now, farfeed data from the recent past. It was odd he hadn't heard from engineering.

He flicked his gaze to the environmental control station. Everything that wasn't shorted out was glowing green. Bosditch decided the frying-electronics smell permeating the bridge was left over from the old sensor rig.

He tapped the communications console alive.

Then he tapped it dead again.

He'd been warned.

You couldn't single-hand a merchant vessel, but you could short crew her if you had to. Bosditch hadn't liked the way this deal smelled from the get-go. He'd needed both Anders and

Lenoch in engineering to have any chance of getting in and out of here alive. What he didn't need was a crew full of witnesses.

Or victims. He hadn't even heard of the vessel he was transferring cargo to, but he didn't like the sound of it. *Sudden Fall of Darkness.* It wasn't in the registry database but that didn't mean anything. Neither was *Last Stand.*

Bosditch cursed under his breath as he scrolled methodically through the sensor log. A real sensorman with a full immersion rating was as much a luxury as an honest career. Bosditch could wish all day and it wouldn't change a thing.

It was blasted hard to concentrate. He kept imagining all the things that could go wrong. He hated this part of the job, hated it with a passion both wide and deep.

Once he finished running the logs, he'd call down to engineering. He'd hired on the pair of engineers knowing what they were, and knowing it had been a decade since they'd been off world. If there was anything wrong they'd report in.

Otherwise, Merchant Bosditch, mind your own end of the stick.

Lenoch had even insisted that he sign a document to that effect.

As if his word wasn't good enough.

Bosditch's finger hovered over the comm stud.

It retreated.

He had his own work to do.

A little more discipline as a lad, and he wouldn't be getting a headache crawling through the sensor logs line by line.

Self-control. That's what the almighty Merchant's Academy said he lacked.

If that were all he lacked, he'd rejoice at such good fortune. Bosditch's gaze drifted toward the comm stud and then back to the sensor log.

Did he miss something?

No. He didn't miss anything. No need to scroll back. There was truly nothing. Nothing out here at all.

Bosditch let his breath out slowly.

This run wasn't as bad as some. At least this time he knew whose cargo he was carrying, and why.

What is it?

Who is it for?

Those weren't questions Bosditch asked. Not even of his wife. Maybe after they'd been married for a while longer, but then again, maybe not. With a little luck there wouldn't be more jobs like this. There wouldn't be any need-to-know standing between them, and they could both get on with a decent life together. Bosditch was born too old for this. And Adderly? She deserved better.

The comm squawked just as Bosditch was reaching to key it on.

"Bos, we've got a bit of a problem." Lenoch sounded distracted. "There's a—"

The proximity alarm sounded.

Bosditch gripped the piloting console as the ship rang with impact, the command bridge resonating in diminishing pulses. He managed to keep his feet under him. He ran his shaking fingers through his thinning hair. *Last Stand* shuddered again.

He bent over the localspace display and adjusted the gain.

Bosditch scanned the command consoles.

No alarms.

Their own sensor shadow and that was it.

The superluminal drive was offline and idling. If it were powered up, they'd be in their own isolated universe, where nothing could touch them and they could touch nothing.

He reached for the comm stud. "Are you girls all right?"

No answer.

It was a long, cold trundle down the spinal mast of a

Freeman vessel. They were running incredibly light, just twelve Freeman Freight Expeditors clamped on, self-powered cargo containers strung in a precisely balanced load along the mast.

The FFEs were all showing solid connections to the mast, they were all showing environmentals powered up and within tolerance. The cargo was intact. Bosditch did not want to jam himself into a mastcart and suffer the coffin ride to the engineering end of the mast.

"Anders? Lenoch?"

Bosditch checked the comm circuit.

It appeared active.

"Come on now, ladies, answer up."

Someone needed to stay on the bridge.

And someone needed to check on his crew.

There wasn't anyone but Bosditch. And there really wasn't any choice.

He hadn't lost a crewman in twenty years of knocking around the wider world.

They were in the middle of nowhere and the probability of something else slamming into them was perishing low. He hoped.

"I'm coming, girls," Bosditch said. "If you can hear me, hold on."

And if you can't hear me, I'm coming anyway.

There was a click on the comm, the sound of a finger on the stud, a rustling sound.

"No. Don't—"

"Anders?" Bosditch said.

Silence.

Bosditch didn't stop running until he gripped the mastbay ladder with both hands and swung his feet free for the long slide down.

To think he did this for fun when he was a kid. The old ones like his gran would shake their heads as he rocketed down the ladder, not slowing until his feet touched the deck sole, and then just barely slowing as he balled up and jammed his now man-sized bulk into the tiny railed mastcart designed for the wee bodies of Huangxu-engineered slaves.

Bosditch slammed the hatch and tongued the controls alive.

He hadn't considered hygiene when he was a boy.

Now the idea stuck in his mind as he settled his chin into the receiver and gazed down the long mastrail.

He wondered who had used these controls last.

He hoped it wasn't Anders. That woman had the tongue of a harpy.

If anything happened to her . . .

The mast of a Freeman merchant vessel was straight and strong as a merchant's word. It had to be to handle the load in normal space.

Bosditch found it always disconcerting the way the mastcart's viewport made the long carbon-composite cylinder seem to bend in an arc beneath him.

Bosditch counted FFEs as he passed.

Twelve containers of some valuable something, value that could be converted into hard currency that could in turn be converted into parts and labor, into a fully functioning merchant vessel that could go anywhere and do anything, the sort of vessel a man could be proud to bring his wife home to, could be confident he could start a family without having the wider world open up and swallow his future whole.

There were only eleven FFEs on the mast.

Bosditch jammed his tongue against the Go toggle as if that would do any good.

Mastcarts had only two speeds, on and off, and off didn't do any good at all, and on was painfully slow, slow enough that a man could inspect the welds and mastclamps on the FFEs as he crept along, the flat light of inspection luminaries bathing the pale containers in harsh and airless detail.

Half of those lights were burned out too.

Sweat wept into Bosditch's eyes.

The mastcart reeked, they always did, but this one positively ponged with flop sweat. Bosditch had torn the gasket this time. He could feel it. When he spied the black bulk of another vessel through a gap between FFEs, he knew it.

He stuffed his chin into the receiver with all his might and willed the cart to go, go, go.

The airlock cycled with the speed of drying adhesive.

Bosditch popped out and took off in a dead run for the drive-bay ladder.

Something was on fire, something electrical, and something . . . meaty.

Bosditch took the ladder two steps at a time, heart hammering against his ribs.

The drive-bay airlock was open, was melted open, still glowing a dull red.

Bosditch skidded to a halt and plastered his back against the bulkhead just outside the hatch.

"Do me first, you red-handed son of an Ojin parasite," Lenoch said. "I'm oldest."

"Do that, and you'll regret it, you Huangxu bootlicker," Anders said. "While you're gunning down my sister, I'll be on that valve over there. We'll see what raw plasma does to your fancy League armor."

Bosditch crept closer to the hatch.

"*Quite Possibly Alien*," Lenoch said. "Look at that, Andy. The arrogant pinholes plaster the name of their vessel all over their fecking goonsuits."

Bosditch chanced a glance into the drive bay.

There were two . . . somethings in League exoskeletal armor aiming weapons at his aunties.

"No one ever said pirates were smart, Lenny."

Anders held her arm across her chest, her forearm a red and roasted ruin.

She winced. "When Bosditch figures out what's up, he'll vent this whole damned compartment and slam *Last Stand* into superluminal space."

"I hope he does before these ignoramuses unbalance the mast with their club-fisted cargo handling."

Lenoch had always been the fierce one, the face of the family to the wider world.

Always, until Bosditch was old enough to shoulder that burden.

Lenoch's face twitched into a she-wolf grin. "If the mast snaps they all die."

Anders held her arm as if it belonged to someone else. "The pair of us were worse than dead on that fecking planet. Bosditch is a good man, and best he thinks about his fine young wife first. Better he not waste a tear for his ancient and obsolete kin."

"Truth, it's not sentiment we'll be wanting but vengeance," Lenoch said. "And Bosditch must live to see it done. Word of a merchant."

She spat onto the deck.

One of the guards shifted his footing.

The plasma rifle maintained its deadly focus on Anders.

"He will so do, Lenny. If he gets a move on before those other two get back here," Anders said. "He's a good boy."

"He is that," Lenoch said. "And a good man. I just hope he's still a quick one."

Lenoch turned as the sound of hullwalkers pounding against ceramic-composite deckplates echoed from behind the Templeman drive.

Anders darted her gaze toward the hatch coaming hiding Bosditch from view.

She glared and mouthed, "Go!"

Then her fierce gaze snapped into alignment with Lenoch's as two more suits of League exoskeletal armor appeared from behind the superluminal drive.

A mechanized voice boomed in the enclosed space. "We are taking the bridge, yes?"

The second of the pair spoke, a grating sound of metal on metal. "All we want is the cargo."

It might not even be a man in there at all, but a massive night-blue machine, far larger than the others, and scarred and dented from hard use. It held a weapon that seemed to meld into its arm.

Bosditch had to look twice.

A GRAIL gun. On his vessel.

"What of these . . . women, Commodore?"

"Do what you please with them," the largest suit said.

"It will be done. Yes, it will be."

Anders grinned. "Sonny, if you think you can do anything to us that hasn't been done before, you're in for a surprise."

"I think you will find the surprise is all yours, yes."

The smaller, hard-suited pirate extracted a box from a storage compartment on its armored sleeve. Something silver and blue writhed inside.

"Ixatl-Nine-Go. This will be very surprising, I think. Women are so amusing, don't you think, Commodore? Yes. Amusing."

"Leave no evidence," the commodore said.

It began to stride toward the hatch.

Toward Bosditch.

There was only one thing he could do.

Bosditch ran.

He was down the ladder.

He was in the mastcart, his tongue jammed against the Go toggle.

His heart pounded in his chest.

Anders. Lenoch. The last of Bosditch's kin.

He might yet be able to save them.

And if he couldn't?

He would avenge them. Word of a merchant.

He still had that. Merchant license.

No one could take that from him.

Bosditch blinked the tears away.

The mast seemed to curve beneath him as the mastcart crawled toward the bridge.

He counted FFEs as he passed.

The pirates had already removed three, and hard-suited work crews were beginning to unlatch a fourth.

Bosditch had to make it.

Had to make it for Adderly. For Anders and Lenoch.

For a future.

For vengeance.

Up ahead. They hadn't removed three FFEs.

They'd removed four.

From exactly the wrong places.

They were tugging on the fifth, oblivious to the tiny mastcart working slowly up the brittle surface of the delicately balanced mast.

The FFE ripped free.

The mast shuddered.

Bosditch cursed and kept the toggle pressed down.

There was no way he was going to be able to take this ship into superluminal space with that load. He'd have to wait until they popped all the FFEs now. The fools had left all the mass on the center of the span. It would resonate as the drive spooled up and that would be the end of it.

Bosditch passed another work crew.

These noticed.

These pointed.

These shouldered weapons.

The mastcart slid behind an FFE as Bosditch tongued the Stop toggle.

He wasn't going to make it.

Not this way.

He goosed the Go toggle until he was aligned with the FFE's inspection hatch.

He flicked the Field Lock toggle with his tongue and waited while the field window cycled up.

From outside it would glow blue, and bright, and impossible to miss.

It would take more than a handheld energy weapon to punch through that field. They'd need something bigger.

Like a GRAIL gun.

He'd have to hurry.

Bosditch popped the hatch and cycled the inspection lock.

Bosditch ducked inside the container.

He didn't want to question why he was smuggling people. Because once he did, he was liable to do something he would regret.

Like doubt his wife.

There were rows upon rows of cryo chambers, racked and stacked from deck sole to deckhead, all showing as active and occupied. A narrow aisle led between them from the inspection hatch to both ends of the FFE. One end of the container was a vast hatch for bulk loading and unloading.

Bosditch raced for the other end.

Something hammered against the FFE.

Bosditch's shoulders hunched when he heard steps overhead.

He sprinted toward the far end of the container and the master control panel.

He yanked the access hatch open, ignoring the controls that operated the mastclamps.

His fingers shied away from the other controls, the ones that programmed the cargo container for powered operation.

These containers had made the Freemen rich.

Some of the Freemen, anyway.

They were a smuggler's dream. Just program them, dump them into a gravity well, and haul asteroid out of the system. The FFEs would take it from there.

Or dead-drop them in the middle of nowhere, program them to proceed to a location that only you and your customer knew, and off you went.

Unless someone talked, someone associated with *Sudden Fall of Darkness*, and pirates got there first, before you could unload.

Pirates like the ones walking around on the FFE, trying to find a way in.

Quite Possibly Alien pirates.

Bosditch didn't want to believe the other possibility. That the shipper had talked. Adderly. His wife. He wouldn't believe that.

His fingers hovered over the controls.

Not Adderly. Never Adderly.

What was he waiting for?

A massive, armored monster shoved its way through the access hatch.

Exoskeletal armor. Exos, the League called them. Their technically superior boot on the neck of the world.

The nightmare raised its GRAIL gun and aimed it at Bosditch.

If Bosditch fired the FFE up without releasing the clamps it would shatter the mast and set off a cascade. Without Anders and Lenoch to control the reaction, *Last Stand's* drive containment field would begin to resonate. Undamped, the resonance would build in amplitude and frequency. When the strain became too great, the field would rupture. Universes would collide in a boiling knot of writhing gravity and one brief, bright spasm of light.

"Stand down or die," Bosditch said. "You are forewarned."

The commodore's metallic voice boomed in the cargo container. "I am informed, Merchant. You would rather shatter the world than surrender."

So. There was a Freeman in that thing. That was all Bosditch needed to know.

If it was human it could suffer.

It could die.

"I would rather live, and my crew as well. But if mine die, yours die." Bosditch's fingertip hovered over the drive control. "I said stand down!"

The GRAIL gun began to spool up. "All men die, little man."

"Take the cargo and leave us go," Bosditch said.

"I will take the cargo," the commodore said. "And you will go the way of all men."

Bosditch swallowed the lump in his throat. Adderly would have spared his crew. She would have spared him. This had nothing to do with his wife.

"Then we'll go together, *amadán.*"

Bosditch was forty standard years old and all but one of those years wasted.

Alone.

This was a hell of a way to live.

He couldn't bring a decent woman home to this.

Bosditch was a poor man.

And poor man's justice was better than no justice at all.

Every Freeman knew that in their bones.

The commodore was still scrambling for the hatch when Bosditch's finger found the ignition stud.

And stabbed.

2

"I'm not staring at her," Ciarán said. "I'm looking at her badge."

"Badges," Macer Gant said.

The lights in the zero-radial tramcar flickered as it bumped to a halt at Ringstop C. The doors opened and no one got on. There were just the three of them in the tramcar: the girl, and Macer, and Ciarán.

The tramcar was surprisingly clean, even by Trinity Station standards. The colorful seats were arranged parallel to the axis of the tramcar, so that passengers on either side of the narrow, carpeted aisle had to face one another.

Ciarán figured the tram was mostly Freeman tech. Other than the delicately sculpted sound baffles on the overhead, and the luxurious seating, and the elegantly carpeted sole, it looked just like the interior of a longboat underneath, which was no big surprise. Unless station tech was imported from the League or the Ojinate, it always resembled some scavenged part of a decommissioned longboat. The tram operators had installed an Ojin environmental unit, though. The atmosphere in the tramcar was chilly, and it smelled faintly of flowers Ciarán hadn't ever been able identify. The entire Ojin Sector of the station smelled that way. He figured if he closed his eyes and paid attention he could navigate between the Freeman, Ojin, and League Sectors of the station by scent alone.

Maybe someday he would try that. After he'd seen the wider world. After he'd been there and back.

Ciarán had ridden the Trinity Station tram exactly twice in four years, though he'd walked beside its guide rail every single day. Riding the tram was for the rich, or for those who didn't want their graduation uniforms sweated through on the long hike to Ringstop Zero. Ciarán had spent a week's food allowance on this, his second and final ride.

"She doesn't look old enough to have earned those badges herself," Macer said.

She didn't. Look it, that is. Only someone who had earned those badges would dare wear them on Trinity Station, though, the central trading station in Freeman space. Those were all Freeman routes. All except the one Ciarán didn't recognize.

The girl seated in the tramcar across from Macer and Ciarán didn't seem more than a couple of years older than Macer or most of the other students in Ciarán's academy cohort.

She had hearbuds jammed into her ears. The toes of her scarred hullwalkers tapped out a complex beat. Ciarán didn't recognize the dark blue utilities she wore, but that didn't mean anything. Except for Truxton Trading's standardized orange utilities, most of the merchant shipping companies didn't provide kit for ordinary spacers. Only bridge crew. The girl didn't have the look of an officer. Ciarán imagined she still remembered how to smile.

"She could be Pops' age for all we know," Ciarán said.

"Doubt it," Macer said. "No one lives that long on the long-hauls. Stick with the in-system work. You can still change your mind. Pops is an idiot."

Pops Howe was a rail-gun operator from Midpoint Platform who'd decided he'd had enough of manual labor. He'd enrolled in the Freeman Merchant Academy at forty-five standard years of age. Pops had been Ciarán's roommate first semester, thirty years Ciarán's senior and full of a thousand stories for every year he'd spent shifting cargo on Midpoint. Some of the stories might even be true.

Ciarán touched the Merchant Academy pip on his collar. He intended to ferret out fact from fiction for himself in less than a day. No way was he sticking with the in-system work.

The tram pinged and repeated the "doors closing" announcement in Freeman, in Trade, in League standard, in Ojin Eng. The girl leaned forward and studied her hand comp. Her dark shoulder-length hair swept forward and hid her eyes. She could be twice Pops' age if she'd spent every year circling a black hole's event horizon. The Huangxu Eng did that with some of their prisoners.

Pops said so.

"I don't recognize that one badge," Ciarán said. The others were local runs. Midpoint, Unity, Extraction Five, Ambidex, Prix Canada. Ciarán leaned forward to get a better look.

"Just ask her," Macer said. "Good chance to exercise your merchanty wiles."

Macer was an engineer, and he aspired to nothing more than earning a decent wage keeping Trinity-system tugs in operating condition. Ciarán and Macer had been comrades since they were kids. Once upon a time Ciarán would have been happy with the same outcome, knowing where the next meal was coming from, a steady girlfriend, a few brews and laughs, three days on, two off, and a trip planet-side every two score days.

Then he'd learned he'd aced the merchant exam, and later,

Pops jammed his brain full of stories of the wider world. Why not go see it all? He could always come home. Trinity Station wasn't going anywhere. Ciarán mac Diarmuid was.

What was that badge? He thought he'd memorized them all.

"I think I will ask her," Ciarán said. "Wait here."

"I'm not going anywhere," Macer said.

The tram lights flickered as it jerked to a stop at Ringstop B. The doors opened and a pair of Huangxu Eng stepped into the tramcar. Impossibly thin and tall, dressed in bright red skinsuits patterned with Imperial lions in gold. They might pass for human, but they weren't Freeman, or League, or Ojin, Eng or not Eng.

They couldn't look more out of place if they'd stepped on board naked.

Macer stiffened and tapped Ciarán's sleeve.

The Eng glanced around the compartment.

One of them eyeballed Ciarán's collar pip and grinned. They took seats on either side of the girl, towering over her even when seated.

She didn't look up, but her toe stopped its endless tapping.

The departure ping sounded. The door-closing announcement ran through its multilingual litany.

The Huangxu Eng to the girl's right frowned when the Ojin Eng announcement sounded.

The one to her left pulled a razorgun when the tram began its jerking motion, accelerating down the guide rail toward Ringstop A.

"Is that a—" Macer began, but Ciarán's elbow stopped his friend in midsentence.

The Huangxu Eng to the girl's left grabbed her hearbud cable and yanked. Tinny music sounded in the still compartment, battling the regular click of the tram across junction points echoing through the car.

The girl's gaze met Ciarán's. She didn't look frightened.

She looked angry.

"We're getting off at Ringstop A," Ciarán said.

Macer nodded. "Seems reasonable."

It was more than reasonable. It was sensible.

Ciarán smiled at the girl and let his gaze drift across the razorgun pressed against her ribcage.

A spacer's weapon, a razorgun fired knife-bladed disbursement rounds that would shred a body without penetrating a hull. Deadly at close range, that's what Pops said, but not so effective at even a modest distance.

If Ciarán could get between the girl and the Huangxu Eng, she might escape.

He would have to act, though, would have to time his actions with the jostling motion of the tram as it decelerated for Ringstop A. He'd shove the girl and Macer through the doors, then he'd be fast after them. The Huangxu Eng wouldn't kill a bystander on Trinity Station, not if they hoped to escape.

"When the car slows, get up and get off," Ciarán said. "I'll be right behind you."

The girl dipped her hand into her pocket and frowned.

"Right," Macer said. "These long-haul spacers can look out for themselves."

"They can," Ciarán said.

In less than one day, Ciarán aimed to be a long-haul spacer, apprenticed to a merchant or merchant captain on a nic Cartaí ship if he could swing it, a Truxton ship if that didn't work out.

He'd have to look out for himself. Until then he could rely on his comrades to pull him out of a bind, any bind he could manage to get himself into.

Who did this girl have to look out for her?

The tramcar began to decelerate.

"Give it over," one of the Huangxu Eng said in Trade

common, his accent nearly impenetrable. He held out his hand, palm up.

The girl began to ease her hand out of her pocket when the tramcar lurched.

Ciarán stumbled into the Huangxu Eng holding the razorgun and kept falling.

"Go!" Ciarán shouted to the girl as much as to Macer.

He had the Huangxu Eng's arm in his hands.

He jerked it up.

The razorgun discharged with a tearing sound.

The ceiling of the tramcar shredded, dropping insulation on Ciarán in a cloud of dusty scrap.

Ciarán was up, but the other Huangxu Eng had him by the ankle.

Ciarán kicked with his free leg and felt bone snap, and then he was free.

The girl stood in the hatchway, gaping.

Ciarán tackled her, slamming her out onto the Ringstop A platform just as the ping sounded and the multilingual announcement began its drone. The doors scythed closed and the tram began to accelerate away from the station.

The girl hammered Ciarán under the chin with enough force to snap his head back and roll him off her.

She was up, she had a weapon, and it was aimed squarely at Ciarán.

A nerve disrupter. Had to be.

Just like Pops described.

As Ciarán rose to his knees, she pressed the ugly muzzle to his temple.

The nerve disruptor had an ozone smell, like it had recently been used.

Her eyes blazed. "Tell me why I shouldn't scramble your brains."

"He was just trying to help," Macer said. "Don't—"

"Who asked him?"

She pulled the weapon away and rocked back on her heels.

"You morons, you—"

"Maura," a woman said. "Holster that weapon."

The girl's eyes blinked, and for a moment Ciarán wondered just what she intended to do.

"I will, Merchant Captain nic Cartaí."

The nerve disruptor disappeared into her pocket.

Ciarán stared at the badge on Maura's sleeve.

"Murrisk," he said. "Oh, wow."

Where they'd found a second-epoch League vessel. With a superluminal drive.

"You've been there?" There'd been some major disaster at Murrisk, and the whole system had been closed to trade more than a year ago, standard reckoning. If she'd been there, it hadn't been recently.

The girl stared at Ciarán. She had brown eyes shot with flecks of gold.

People passed behind her, glancing briefly then quickly looking away.

Don't get involved. It was practically the Freeman motto. The girl could be bleeding out on the platform and people would just step around. Or over.

It was crazy.

People were crazy.

"We both have," the other woman said. "Been to Murrisk. And back."

"Look, we're going to walk from here," Macer said. "Come on, Ciarán, we'll be late for graduation."

Macer took a step forward and tugged on Ciarán's sleeve.

Ciarán twisted so he could get a look at the other woman.

Blond hair cut shoulder length. Turquoise eyes, wide set, the sort that saw everything. Merchant captain's greatcoat, black, lined with red. Overseer's rod beneath her belt, the real deal, not an ironwood facsimile painted to look like the terror weapon.

"Nic Cartaí," Ciarán said. "That's what . . . Maura said."

"It is," the woman said.

Her gaze drilled into Ciarán. Seeing everything.

Ciarán felt his face heat.

Not a good reaction. Not in front of a merchant captain.

"Are you Caitriona nic Cartaí?" Ciarán asked.

She was too young to be Fionnuala nic Cartaí, matriarch of the nic Cartaí trading empire. The eldest nic Cartaí daughter looked more Ojin Eng than Freeman. That's what Pops said. He'd been known to be wrong, though. This woman was definitely Freeman, and appeared no older than the girl on the tram.

Not much older than Ciarán himself.

"She is my sister," the woman said. "You don't seem very rattled by your little adventure."

"It was all over so fast," Ciarán said. "Should I be?"

"Moron," Maura said. "It's not over. Someone has to pay for razorgun damage to the zero-radial tram."

Ciarán felt as if he'd been hammered in the gut. "I—"

"Can't afford to be rescuing damsels in distress," the nic Cartaí woman said.

"I can," Ciarán said. "Just not at the moment. I'll have to work out some sort of payments, I guess."

"Listen," Maura said. "If I'm ever in distress, I won't be looking for a snotty to rescue me. And I can pay for my own damage."

"As you should," nic Cartaí said. "You break it, you own it." She chuckled. "All of it. Including the messy bits."

Ciarán didn't see what was so funny. "I have to go. We're

graduating today, Macer and I. The Academy. I'll contact the stationmaster after. I'll tell her about the Huangxu Eng and—"

"No you won't." Maura glared at Ciarán. "Leave the stationmaster be. My contract, my tab."

"Maura," nic Cartaí said.

"I know. All of it." Maura grimaced. "What's your name, snotty?"

"Ciarán."

Maura sighed and pulled her hand comp out. "Your whole name."

"Ciarán mac Diarmuid," Ciarán said.

Maura stared at him, waiting for more.

"Trinity Surface."

Maura's gaze drilled into him.

All of it.

Right.

"Oileán Chléire."

"That's the back of beyond," Maura said.

"It's not so bad," Macer said. "The fishing's good."

Maura laughed. "I'll bet. They have flush toilets there?"

"Probably." Macer laughed too. "Someday."

Ciarán's face burned. "Look, we have to go."

"At least on the station you can go indoors," Maura said. "This is just so . . . precious."

"Maura Kavanagh," nic Cartaí said, "not everyone is born with a silver dagger in their pocket."

"They aren't, Merchant Captain. Some are born with it clenched between their teeth."

"Spare me," nic Cartaí said. "Merchant Apprentice mac Diarmuid, I thank you for rescuing my reckless navigator from Huangxu Eng hands." She fixed Ciarán with her gaze and smiled. "There is a shortage of heroes in the wider world. It is comforting to know we still grow them at home."

"She's a navigator?" Ciarán looked at Maura. A Kavanagh, and a navigator.

No way. That was officer territory, bridge crew, and first families, seriously out of his league. "Anyway, I didn't—"

"You did," nic Cartaí said. "Now you'd better hurry if you're to make your graduation ceremony."

"We will." Ciarán said. He stood. He was a lot taller than the Merchant Captain. Ciarán began to bow but caught himself in time.

He wasn't just Ciarán mac Diarmuid anymore. He wouldn't be in less than a day. He tilted his head, merchant to merchant. "Good launch, Merchant Captain nic Cartaí."

"Good launch to you, Merchant Apprentice," the merchant captain said.

Ciarán nodded to Maura. "Good launch, Navigator Kavanagh."

Maura winced.

She retrieved a handkerchief from her pocket and wiped it gently across Ciarán's chin. "Razorgun almost missed all of your dirtball-bred, bovine-boned bulk." She wadded the bloody cloth and jammed it into her pocket. "See you later, mac Diarmuid."

She looked like she wanted to heave.

Macer grabbed Ciarán's sleeve and tugged. The merchant captain and Navigator Maura Kavanagh headed in the opposite direction. "What did she mean by that?"

"I guess we both look pretty beefy by space-born standards," Ciarán said.

"You get used to the insults," Macer said. "It's the 'see you later' that has me worried. I'm telling you, Ciarán, no good will come of this."

"Probably not. But what was I supposed to do?"

"Stick with the in-system work. And mind your own

business. I've been saying it all along. But you're not going to, are you?"

"We'll see," Ciarán said.

First he had to graduate.

Then he had to petition for a posting.

There was a chance. Always a chance.

3

The compartment was bigger than a storage closet, an anteroom off the graduation hall, a low-G space blessedly devoid of objects to bump into. It might have been a conference room if it had any furniture. It didn't though, and that would have been strange on any other day. He figured the furniture was needed elsewhere, for some purpose he'd never know. There wasn't even a chair or leaning post in the compartment. Just Annie, and Macer, and him.

"Brawling, Plowboy?" Annie Blum wiped her thumb over Ciarán's chin. Ciarán winced at his mentor's attention.

"Ciarán doesn't brawl," Macer said. "He's too busy rescuing lost kittens. And damsels."

"Branching out, is he?" Annie said. "It's good to be flexible."

"Spare me the jibes, both of you," Ciarán said. "Is there blood on my uniform?" Ciarán ducked his chin to look.

"You're not kidding." Annie turned her attention to Macer. "Spill it."

Ciarán's best friend was bigger than Ciarán, but Macer had somehow managed to shrink to fit Trinity Station's standards of behavior. No one called Macer plowboy, or dirt-hugger, or farmer Seán anymore. Not if they wanted to remain standing. No one told Macer to step aside. Not twice.

"It's not my story." Macer's face clamped into a placid mask.

Annie Blum wasn't a Freeman. She was a blow-in, a League citizen, professor of linguistics, and as sharp a merchant as one were likely to find in Freeman space or beyond. She'd "adopted" Ciarán and Macer. She'd adopted most of the misfits, but the others eventually managed to move on. Only Macer and Ciarán were left. Annie Blum's special projects. She understood Freeman custom, knew it as well as any merchant captain. She was breaking the most central custom, asking about another's past.

Even the recent past was off limits.

"Someone was hassling a spacer," Ciarán said. "I got in the way."

"Does this someone have a name?"

"Everyone has a name," Macer said.

"Unless they have a model designation and serial number," Ciarán said.

Macer insisted on seeing everything as if it belonged in a Freeman box, part of a safe, in-system set of rules. Pops said the wider world wasn't like that. Not everyone had a name or deserved one.

"Look, I'm not going to play twenty questions with you," Annie said.

"One score questions," Macer said. "Technically."

"Nor will I engage in a stern chase for the facts," Annie said. "Now adjust your attitude. You are forewarned."

That's what Ciarán liked about his mentor. She knew the rules and picked and chose those she wished to use. "You are forewarned," was the formal declaration of intent amongst Freeman spacers.

It was easy to forget that Annie was as formidable an enemy as any on Trinity Station. She looked harmless with her curly blond gravity-length hair bound in a queue down her back. Pastel-blue eyes that blinked once and disarmed, wide-open irises that seemed to hide nothing. She was tall for a Freeman but short for a Leagueman.

Macer stiffened and nodded once. "I am informed, Merchant."

Exactly the right response. Then don't say another word if you valued your hide. That was the rule.

Annie pasted an innocent smile on her lips in public. Both Ciarán and Macer had been on the receiving end of tongue lashings that would shame a breakbulk foreman in private. An honest thirty standard years of age, so says Anastasia Blum. She'd only made one superluminal flight from Cordame in League space to Trinity Station. All the rest of her working life had been spent at the Academy, not even a trip down to Trinity's surface.

So she said.

So she volunteered freely.

Of course that all could be lies. Lots of people said it was, that it had to be. No one outlined their past in such detail unless it was fabricated.

Ciarán would like to be able to fabricate a past. Something glamorous. Something different than farmer Seán's second son, book smart, clay clinging to his boots when he debarked on the station, clay still clinging to his boots four years later as he tried to maneuver his gravity-grown bulk in the low-G of a Ring Zero waiting room.

This was a test. Everything was a test. All the Academy needed to do was turn on the artificial gravity generators for the ring and Ciarán could walk out and receive his diploma like a normal person. But they wouldn't. That wasn't the way it was done. Freemen were space-born. Real Freemen. The ones who mattered. The ones with interesting lives. Ciarán didn't have an interesting life. Not yet. But he would. *Count on it.*

"Count on what?" Annie said.

"Oh." Ciarán felt his face heat. "How many nic Cartaí merchant captains are there?"

"Over a hundred." Annie glanced at Macer. "Five score for you sticklers. Why?"

"He means how many are named nic Cartaí," Macer said.

"That is your spacer?" Annie's smile had disappeared. "Tell me no, I beg you."

"Freemen never beg," Macer said.

"That's the face of the story, boyo," Annie said, mocking Ciarán's and Macer's planetary accents. "Ciarán, who did you meet? Look at me now and spill it all."

Ciarán looked.

Annie rarely frowned. And she hadn't ever looked . . . official. Not with Ciarán and Macer.

He spilled it. All of it. He was almost done talking when the enunciator called a five-minute warning. Graduation was beginning.

"Finish." Annie crossed her arms and leaned against the compartment bulkhead. She did not look pleased.

Ciarán finished.

Annie let out her breath in a low whistle. "You could have been killed."

"I don't think—"

"No, you don't," Annie said. "But you're going to start. Soon. No good will come of this."

"That's what I said." Macer pointed a meaty finger at Ciarán. "I told you. We need to stick together. In-system work. Good pay. Pretty girls. The whole nine."

"No," Annie said. "That's not going to happen."

"It could," Macer said.

"No it couldn't," Ciarán said. "Not if I'm going to make a mark."

"You'll make a mark, all right." Annie shook her head. "Even if it's a stain. That nic Cartaí and that Kavanagh are odd-toothed gears."

"What—"

"She means they're black sheep, Ciarán." Macer grinned at Annie. "From the family but not of the family. Outcasts."

"I know what she means," Ciarán said. "I don't see—"

"That's Aoife nic Cartaí," Annie said. "*Quite Possibly Alien.*"

"She looked pretty fine to me," Macer said. "I don't think she's—"

"Her ship, Macer." Annie pulled out her hand comp. She tapped a few times and turned it around for Ciarán to see. "You want to sign on to that, Ciarán?"

The two-minute enunciator sounded.

The vessel in the holo didn't look like a standard Freeman merchant hull. It looked like a second-epoch League vessel with a Freeman Freight Expeditor mast grafted onto its black and knobby mass. There was a strange, bulbous lump aft of the primary mass. A superluminal drive, had to be, but not a standard Templeman unit.

"If she wants you then no one else will touch you," Annie said. "You've spit in the helmet big time, Plowboy."

"I don't understand. All I did was stop a crime."

"You might have stopped a crime. But you weren't playing on the side of the angels."

"I don't see how. The Huangxu Eng were—"

"I'd like to see inside that." Macer studied the image on Annie's hand comp. "That's not any configuration I've ever even heard of. Check out the mast. How are you supposed to load

FFEs onto that? You'd have to do it in a hardsuit. One container at a time."

"Trust me," Annie said. "It's a one-way ticket. Neither of you want to go near that hull. Not if you ever want to work on a decent ship again."

"You make them sound like pirates," Macer said.

"Then I'm getting through to you." Annie paced the compartment, her steps nearly propelling her airborne. "*Sudden Fall of Darkness* all over again. Blast it all."

She pulled a black box out of her pocket. She squeezed it and a single red gem glowed on its face.

"What is that?" Macer said.

"It's a scrambler," Ciarán said. League tech. Nothing they said in its proximity would make sense to the sensors monitoring every compartment on Trinity Station. Proscribed tech, and Annie was flashing it in public. Pops had one just like it.

"Listen to me, Ciarán," Annie said. "*Quite Possibly Alien* is Aoife nic Cartaí's ship now. It was called *Impossibly Alien* when they dug it out of the glacier on Murrisk."

"Oh," Ciarán said. "Pops told me about that ship. He said—"

"I don't care what he said," Annie said. "Whatever he said isn't half the truth. That ship is sentient. And almost certainly mad."

"There's no such thing as a sentient ship," Macer said.

"There's no such thing as a sentient Freeman ship," Annie said. "And that's not a Freeman ship."

"It's a Freeman merchant captain's ship," Macer said. "You said so."

"How do you know this?" Ciarán asked. He stared at the scrambler in Annie's fist.

"I came here on a brother ship. *Sudden Fall of Darkness*. Even brain-dead and refitted with modern tech the vessel was . . ." She visibly shivered. "Disturbing. You do not want to ship out on *Quite Possibly Alien*. You're not ready for that. Not yet."

"I won't, then," Ciarán said.

Annie watched Ciarán's face. "Are you going to settle for in-system work?"

Ciarán knew that look. His dad's face wore the same one when Ciarán told him he'd been accepted to the Academy. "I'm not."

"Then I hope they leave you be," Annie said.

"The navigator told Ciarán she'd see him again," Macer said. "She asked for his particulars."

The one-minute enunciator sounded.

When Annie looked at Ciarán, she seemed far more worried than she had ever done before. "Make me a promise, Ciarán mac Diarmuid."

"Anything," Ciarán said. "Anything but in-system work."

"Take your cat with you."

"I meant to leave her with Macer," Ciarán said. "She likes him, and—"

"Promise," Annie said. "Or I'm through with you."

"That's harsh," Macer said. "He hasn't done anything—"

"I'm not shipping out with those people," Ciarán said. "There are other options."

"I hope so," Annie said. "Now make that promise. Just in case."

"They may not want a cat on board."

"Blast, Ciarán," Macer said. "You can't possibly intend to sign on with pirates."

"He'd sign on with Lucifer if it meant he'd get to see the wider world," Annie said.

"That's—" Macer started.

"True," Ciarán said. He hated it, but it was true. "I promise. If they'll have her."

"Not good enough," Annie said.

"What do you want me to do?" Ciarán said. He couldn't make any demands. Couldn't set any conditions. He was a merchant apprentice. Almost.

"For once in your life," Annie said. "I want you to take a stand."

"Ciarán's not made that way," Macer said. "His mom—"

"I promise," Ciarán said. "Are you happy?"

"No," Annie said. "Are you?"

"I'm not."

"Go get your diploma." Annie flicked the scrambler off. "Afterward, we'll talk. If we can."

"Right." Ciarán straightened his uniform. "Right."

Macer glanced behind them as they entered the graduation chamber. "What just went on in there?"

"I don't know," Ciarán said. His guts knotted as he entered the compartment.

He couldn't tell if it was from the lack of gravity or the fallout from the conversation.

Probably both. He could think about that later.

He didn't dare look back.

He couldn't afford to.

4
___

Graduation was destined to be a fiasco. Ciarán knew what to expect—the evacuated core of Trinity Station set to low-G, the graduating classes arrayed in groups around the periphery of the nearly featureless sphere. They'd call his name and he'd shove off, swoop toward the center of the sphere, stop, shake hands, get his diploma, and then push off from the dais and sail on toward the posting compartment, through the hatch, and up to the consoles where he could log on and begin advertising for a posting. The instant he logged on he would be a merchant apprentice. No one could take that away. All he had to do was make it through the posting compartment hatch in one piece.

Nic Cartaí or Truxton. Those were the merchant houses he wanted to sign with. Kavanagh if he had to. Surely one of the Big Three would take him if he made a good showing here. His grades were good enough. Better than good, really, on everything but the physical tests.

Like this.

There were temporary clinging masts set up like stalagmites around the posting room hatch. Families clung to the masts, cheering their children on. Spacers clung on too, recent grads looking for a laugh, older hands trying to eyeball the merchandise before they began shopping for crew.

Macer was right about one thing. Long-haul work was dangerous, and there were always openings for new graduates.

Ciarán's family couldn't afford a trip to Trinity Station even if he'd invited them. He could have piggybacked a message on one of Macer's, but Macer's dad made it clear he didn't like running messages up to the mac Diarmuid place if he could avoid it. Ciarán's mom had been dead for a year before he even applied to the Academy, but he could just see his dad trying to cling to a pole in the unpredictable microgravity of an active port station's core.

Seán mac Diarmuid would get it right after one or two jaw-clenching tries, then he'd tell everyone around him how holding the clinging post was just like gripping a loy, or a slane, or a tusker, or any one of the other farm implements Ciarán hoped to forget about some day.

Macer managed to get through the whole process without making a fool of himself.

Ciarán pushed off with too little velocity and ended up dead still two meters short of the dais.

He ignored the laughing. He ignored the tossed lifelines from the crowd, every single one, waiting for the capture line to be thrown from the dais. The dean of the Merchant Academy shook his head and coiled the line. Ciarán was reaching for it when he was hammered in the back and shoved into the dais railing.

"Get on with it, Plowboy," Seamus mac Donnocha said. He gripped the rail and held his hand out for his diploma.

"Thanks," Seamus said to the dean, and then he was off, a lithe missile hurtling toward the posting compartment hatch.

The crowd went wild.

The dean pressed Ciarán's diploma into his hand. "It'll come, son," he said. "Give it time."

"I'm not sure I have time," Ciarán said. Seamus balled up and passed through the hatch like a god, unfolding in perfect synchrony with the increased gravity field in the compartment.

He waved to the cheering crowd.

"How's that kitten you rescued?" the dean said.

"I wouldn't call her a kitten," Ciarán said. "I'm not even sure I rescued her."

Maura Kavanagh clung to a spectator's mast. The others in the crowd cleared enough space around her that it was impossible to miss *Quite Possibly Alien*'s navigator.

The glares the Kavanagh officers on an adjacent mast directed toward the girl erased any doubt Ciarán had about Annie's assessment of his "rescue."

Maura Kavanagh was trouble.

"I imagine she's a handful by now," the dean said. "What'd you name her?"

Ciarán blinked. "Sir?"

"Your mong hu? Her name?"

"Oh." Ciarán looked at the diploma in his hand. "Plumpkin." He felt his face color. "Except it doesn't fit her anymore."

"No? She grow out of that name?"

"Sort of. Growing out of it, anyway."

"See? Give it time. Now shove off, son, there are others waiting."

The dean grabbed Ciarán's wrist and pulled him close. "It's better to hammer into the bulkhead than hang dead in irons, son. Shove off like you don't expect to come back. It's the best way to get where you're going."

"Yes, sir."

Ciarán shoved for all he was worth.

5

Ciarán's nose was probably broken, but if he kept his head tilted back he didn't think he'd get too much blood on the console. He typed his credentials in and waited for the console to respond.

"Awesome velocity, Plowboy." Seamus pushed back from his console. "Need to work on the vector, though."

"He barely missed." Macer swung into the seat next to Ciarán's. "The hatch is pretty small when you're man-sized."

"Moon-sized is more like it," Seamus said.

"It's all muscle," Macer said. "Want me to show you?"

"No need. Muscle's what they want on the in-system tugs. You'll both fit right in. Like meat in a roll-up."

"Ciarán's going out-system. You watch."

"He shoved off with enough boost. Too bad there was a bulkhead in his way."

"Too bad." Macer laughed. "Sure cleared the portside clinging masts of the rabble."

"Where'd they put you, Mace? Hullwalker on Pismire Trading's *Wormwood*?"

"Associate engineer, Truxton's *Tractor Four-Squared.*"

"Nice. Another farmer and his tractor united." Seamus flipped a yellow card through his fingers. "Maybe I'll require a tug. Truxton's *Golden Parachute.* Apprentice to Merchant Aengus Roche."

"Get all the roaches on one vessel," Macer said. "Makes perfect sense."

Ciarán leaned forward and studied his posting. *No way.*

He pressed cancel and entered his credentials again.

"What's wrong, Plowboy?" Seamus leaned over Ciarán's shoulder. "They assign you to a recycler shop on Midpoint Platform? You going to be bunking with Pops again?"

"Pops landed a Kavanagh berth," Macer said. "There's worse things than shipping out with an experienced hand."

"Experienced and wrinkled aren't synonyms," Seamus said. "You can enter your particulars a thousand times and it's not going to change anything, Plowboy. Somebody wants you bad."

Ciarán leaned his forehead against the console display. *This had to be wrong.*

He added the fact that he came with a cat or not at all and tried again.

Seamus's hand snaked out and pushed the commit button. A yellow card spat out the credentials chute. "How bad can it be?" He picked up the card. "You're top of the class for anything requiring a brain. Log a few hours in low-G and—"

"What?" Macer said. "They stick him in-system? It's not so bad, Ciarán. Like Seamus says, log a few hours in orbit and try for out-system work later. It'll be great. Really."

"Mother of Fate," Seamus said. "What'd you do? Kill those two Huangxu Eng?"

Macer was out of his seat. "What are you talking about, Seamus?"

"Haven't you been monitoring the newsfeeds? They found

two Huangxu Eng stuffed into a waste chute in the Ojin Eng sector. Blast, Ciarán. They posted you to *Quite Possibly Alien*."

"They didn't," Macer said. "They didn't."

"They did," Seamus said. "Apprentice to Merchant Captain Aoife nic Cartaí. Ciarán and his cat both."

"What are you going to do, Ciarán?" Macer tapped Ciarán's shoulder. "Ciarán?"

Ciarán's nose was bleeding again.

What was the point? He wiped his bloody hands on his uniform trousers. "I'm going to rename my cat. Then we're both going to report for duty."

On *Quite Possibly Alien*. With a shipload of pirates.

"We need to talk to Annie," Macer said.

"Man, you guys need to start paying attention to the real-time feeds," Seamus said. "Professor Anastasia Blum has petitioned for asylum in the League Sector."

"When would we have time to watch the news, Seamus?" Macer had Seamus by the collar. "Just exactly when?"

"Let go," Seamus said. "We're on the same side, Mace. We're both Truxton now."

"Calm down," Ciarán said. "It's not the end of the world."

"Oh, isn't it?" Macer said. "We've been a team since we were kids. How am I supposed to protect you when you're haring around space with a bunch of . . . bunch of . . ."

"Pirates," a woman said. "Wicked and fierce and thirsting for blood." Maura Kavanagh stood in the hatchway, a smile on her lips. "I'm here for the merchant captain's latest . . ." She waved her hand. "Amusement."

"Is that what this is for you?" Macer said. "Some sort of joke?" He let go of Seamus's collar and stood to his full height. It was easy to forget just how massive Macer was.

Maura Kavanagh stood her ground. "If I ever tell you a joke, you'll laugh." She stepped fully into the compartment and adjusted her footing. "Now stand down . . ." She peered at Macer's uniform tag. "Macer Gant. You are forewarned."

"Well, I'm not going to—"

"Enough," Ciarán said. He stood between Macer and *Quite Possibly Alien*'s navigator. Ciarán was a half a head taller than Macer but nowhere near as broad. Still, if Ciarán just stood still there was no way either one of them was getting around him.

"I need to get my kit. And my cat."

"Ciarán," Macer said. "You can't go with them."

"I can," Ciarán said. "I will."

"Been nice knowing you, Plowboy," Seamus said.

Ciarán looked at Seamus. A Truxton hand now. Like Macer. Ciarán nodded. "Thanks for the shove, Seamus."

"Anytime." Seamus studied Maura Kavanagh. "I mean that, Ciarán."

"You're not half bad, mac Donnocha," Ciarán said.

"I'm all bad," Seamus said. "And you know where to find me. If you need me." Seamus grinned.

"Ciarán—"

"Macer, I've got to do this."

"I know."

"Then stand down."

"Her first."

"She's my superior officer now. Don't make this any harder than it is."

"How exactly could I do that, Ciarán? I promised your dad—"

Ciarán turned. His friend's fists knotted again and again. "What?"

"I'd look after you."

"You have," Ciarán said. "Good job, brother."

"What am I supposed to tell him?" Macer said.

"Try the truth," Seamus said. "You'd have to kill Ciarán to stop him."

Ciarán wiped his nose. He flicked the blood onto Maura Kavanagh's hullwalkers. "Let's go."

"You'll polish those later," Maura said.

"I doubt it," Seamus said. "Ciarán isn't big on taking orders."

"We'll see," Maura said.

"You will," Seamus said. "I just wish I could be there to watch."

"I need to get my kit," Ciarán said. "And my cat."

6

"I'm not your superior officer." Maura Kavanagh paced alongside Ciarán on the long walk to the Arcade, one ringstop in from the Observation Ring. From time to time the zero-radial tram hammered past, pushing a wave front of frigid atmosphere.

"I know," Ciarán said. "But Macer doesn't. He's not interested in the commercial side of the house. He thinks in terms of chain of command."

"And you don't?"

"I . . ." Ciarán glanced over at the woman. The buffeting of a passing tram stirred Maura's utilities and rippled her hair. "Can." Best leave it at that.

"How much further is it? We passed the Academy three tram stops ago."

"Just to the Arcade. And anti-spinward a ways."

Maura stopped. "What? That'll take better than an hour."

"More like forty minutes unless we run."

"We're getting on the tram."

"You're welcome to," Ciarán said. "I can't afford it."

"You're a merchant apprentice on an interstellar vessel. Your pay will cover it. I'll spot you the fare."

Ciarán started walking again. "I have expenses."

"Like what?"

Cat food. But now wasn't the time to bring that up. "You know . . ." Ciarán shrugged. "The usual ones, I guess."

Maura sped up and walked backward in front of him, watching Ciarán's face. "Drugs? Gambling? Prostitutes?"

When Ciarán's face began to burn, she fell back in step with him and grinned.

"Not the usual ones, then. Farmer-boy expenses. Sending money home to the folks. Tithing to the church. A bolt of cloth for your sweetheart."

"You're mocking me."

"Of course. I'm a pirate. It's what we do when we're not plundering and pillaging."

"I think you're confusing pirates with barbarians. Pirates rob and murder."

"Like those two Huangxu Eng, you mean?"

Ciarán's heart missed a beat. "I wasn't . . . I mean . . . I—"

Maura shoved Ciarán in the back just as the tram began to slow for Ring Station H. "Run. We're getting on that tram."

"But—"

"On my tab, Ciarán mac Diarmuid. This time and this time only, you got me?"

"I understand, Navigator." Ciarán's legs didn't want to move.

Maura shoved Ciarán in the back again. "Then haul it, spacer. Double time. I'll be right behind you."

Right behind him. With a nerve disruptor in her pocket. Unless it was in her hand.

7

"You'll want to stay at this end of the compartment," Ciarán said. "This won't take a minute."

Macer, Seamus, Plumpkin, and Ciarán lived in a giant one-room apartment over Adrigole's Armory. It was long, and narrow, and only fit for habitation at one end. Seamus's dad had a deal with Merchant Adrigole and the station authorities, so it worked out well for everyone.

There were three sleep and study cubicles at the near end, above the firing point, and a battered couch, a scarred table, and a couple of folding chairs just inside the hatch. After hours they could drag them out into open space over the range but it wasn't after hours, and it wasn't a good idea to be anywhere near the down-range part of the compartment. Plumpkin's blanket was normally knotted up beside the couch. He'd have to shove Maura Kavanagh aside to take a look. There was a small head, and a kitchen in the far corner, more like a hotplate and microfridge, really, but Plumpkin never went over there. She didn't like feeling cornered.

"You live over a firing range?" Maura said.

"It's spacious and cheap," Ciarán said. His kit was already packed. He knew he was shipping out. He just hadn't expected it to be on *Quite Possibly Alien.* Or that he'd take the cat with him. Macer was going to look after Plumpkin. That was the plan.

She had to be in here somewhere, sleeping in the overhead, curled on her blanket in the corner. Really, she could be anywhere. Ciarán shouldered past Maura and took a look at the blanket.

No joy.

"Plumpkin?" Ciarán said.

"Is it safe?" Maura wandered around, checking the place out.

"Safe if you stay at this end of the compartment. Navigator Kavanagh, I wouldn't go down that way."

"I thought I saw something move. At the far end."

"There's nothing down there," Ciarán said. Just cat food. "Sometimes rounds come through the deck. When they're breaking the rules on the range. Even if you can't hear them firing below it doesn't mean they won't start at any minute."

"There's something dead down here. Something big."

"Don't, Navigator. Step back this way. It's not safe in that corner." Plumpkin didn't like people getting near her food. Not until she was done eating. Even when she'd been a kitten she'd been scary around dinnertime. Now she was scary all the time. Particularly around strangers.

"Ciarán mac Diarmuid, why is there a dead farm animal in your compartment?" Maura toed Plumpkin's dinner. "It's a cow."

"Calf." The briefest flicker of motion appeared behind Maura Kavanagh. Stalking her. "Navigator. Do not move. Do not speak." Ciarán stepped along the bulkhead toward the butt end of the compartment. Adrigole's wasn't too particular about what weapons the customers wanted to try out, legal or not.

Ciarán had more than three years to plot the patterns. The closer to the bulkhead he stayed, the better. "Plumpkin," Ciarán said. "Plumpkin."

The big cat ignored him.

Maura began to turn slowly.

Plumpkin's ears lay flat, held stiffly out to the side, her head low. The tip of her tail flicked once. Ciarán crept closer. He was almost there. Maura Kavanagh was much too close to Plumpkin's feeding station. Much too close.

Ciarán twitched when the firing began below, a projectile weapon of some sort, large caliber and nasty as sin.

"Plumpkin," Ciarán said.

The cat's adaptive camouflage began to fade, all of her attention focused on her prey. If a mong hu had a weakness it was this, the moment before they pounced, when they became fully visible in their natural colors.

Ciarán leapt the instant he could see the cat's white and orange swirl clearly.

They collided in midair, Plumpkin twisting, sweeping her diamond-tipped claws toward Ciarán's face in one fluid motion.

Her paw hammered into him, her claws retracted at the last moment.

The pair landed in a heap and then Plumpkin was on him, her raspy tongue flicking blood off the wound that had reopened on his chin.

Maura's eyes widened as she backed toward the center of the compartment.

"Navigator, you don't want to stand there. Get close to a bulkhead."

"That's not a cat. It's a mong hu."

"Mong hu are cats." Big, terrifying, deadly cats.

Terrifying unless they'd adopted you. Ciarán had long ago decided the choice to be friends was Plumpkin's, not his. She liked Macer. And Seamus, too, which had surprised him. But with Ciarán it was different. He was hers, and she was his. The thought of leaving her had gutted him. But there was no way a nic Cartaí or Truxton captain would take on a merchant apprentice with a cat in tow. Not, at least, a potentially lethal cat that answered only to the merchant apprentice and cost as much as three crewmen to feed.

Plumpkin glanced at Maura and growled.

"Please, get out of the center of the compartment. It's not safe."

"Now that's funny. And it's safe over there with that gene-modded killing machine?"

"It is. Please—"

A round punched through the deck a meter from Maura's feet, embedding itself in the antiballistic batting overhead.

She took two wide steps to her right and stood over the puncture. "There. What are the chances another round will strike in the same place?"

"Greater than zero. But it doesn't have to be the same place. Just close. Please come to the sleeping end of the compartment until the shooter pauses to reload."

"I think I'll stay right here."

The shooter kept squeezing off rounds at a rate of about one per second.

"You don't understand. The odds are that—"

"Sure I do," Maura said. "I'm a navigator. All we do is calculate the odds. All day, every day."

"Astronomically small odds. These aren't even—"

"Astronomically small with a Templeman drive. *Quite Possibly Alien*'s drive works . . . differently. I'll take a two percent chance of annihilation any day. That's a stroll on a pleasure deck."

It had taken Ciarán better than three years of measuring and calculating to compute the odds. Maura plucked a number right out of thin air. She wasn't far wrong.

"That's when firing on manual," Ciarán said. "When a customer switches to auto, all bets are off."

The firing stopped. Plumpkin growled again and ran for her blanket.

Ciarán knew that run. He pushed up with one hand and took off for the firing point end of the compartment just as the shooter below let loose on full auto.

Ciarán tagged six penetrations while Maura dusted antiballistic fibers off her utilities.

Plumpkin paced the length of the compartment and began chewing her dinner. She glanced up once or twice and growled at Maura.

"I like this place." Maura pointed at the three cubicles at the firing-point end of the compartment. "No one ever caught a round?"

"Macer. Standing right about where you were." Seamus could dance out of the way if an army was aiming at the deckhead.

"But not you or your calf-sized kitten."

"We have not."

Plumpkin finished feeding. She faded into the shadows as he watched.

He couldn't keep calling her by her kitten name. She wasn't the round ball of orange and white fluff she was when he'd found her cowering in a shipping container. "Plumpkin can hear the sound of a weapon being switched to auto. I'm just lucky, I guess."

"Of course. And thigh-high Plumpkin is just some lucky farm boy's friendly little pet."

"Wisp," Ciarán said. Plumpkin's new name. "I don't think she's Plumpkin anymore."

"I don't think she ever was." Maura glanced around. "You've been living here a long time."

"Three and a half years. Since Plum . . . *Wisp* was a kitten."

"And you get cows in orbit."

"Calves. Just one." Ciarán picked up his valise. "Macer's dad shipped up a pattern. A comrade cranks out duplicates in a macrofab. It's not cheap."

"And that's why you walk."

"It is. We can go. Plum . . . *Wisp* will follow as long as we go straight to your . . . our vessel." And as long as they didn't run across any farm animals on the way.

"How do you intend to feed that beast on a superluminal?"

"I have a copy of the calf pattern. And I checked my contract. The ship is responsible for feeding my cat."

"I don't think the merchant captain was expecting to feed a mong hu. Feeding one overgrown crewman is expensive enough."

Ciarán shrugged. "Then the merchant captain can release us both from the contract." And Ciarán could look for work on a decent ship. Pismire Trading was beginning to look pretty attractive.

"Unlikely. What happens if we run out of food for your little pet?"

"Nothing good. Maybe we ought to go now and see what Merchant Captain Aoife nic Cartaí has to say."

"Oh, I know what she'll say." Maura opened the compartment hatch. "Come on, Lucky. I want to see the look on her face. And yours."

Great. Another nickname.

At least it was a step up from Plowboy.

8

Aoife nic Cartaí met them at *Quite Possibly Alien*'s longboat berth. She smiled when she met Wisp. Judging from the looks they'd received along the way, Plumpkin was definitely Wisp now, pacing along at Ciarán's side like a mong hu out of a storybook.

The history of the big cats was intimately linked to that of the Freemen. If there was a symbol of Freeman independence and enmity toward the Huangxu Eng, it was a tie between the overseer's rod that Aoife nic Cartaí carried and the big cat brushing against Ciarán's thigh and dancing along on tiptoes at his side.

"I'd hoped you'd bring us luck, Ciarán mac Diarmuid," Aoife said. "I was expecting a ship's cat, and that would be fine enough."

"You're not going to dismiss us?" Ciarán said.

"By no means. What is your companion's name?"

"Plumpkin." Maura made certain to stay on Ciarán's right side, well away from Wisp.

"Wisp," Ciarán said. "As in—"

"Jack of the Lantern," Aoife said. "I see. Jack or Will would not do."

"She's a she," Ciarán said.

Aoife spoke into her handheld communicator. "Carlsbad, I need you." She knelt and held out her hand for Wisp to inspect. "All mong hu are male."

Ciarán knew that. They were designed as terror weapons, to be used against the Freemen by the Huangxu Eng. When the mong hu sided with the Freemen, the tables were turned. No females meant no self-replicating species. The Huangxu Eng were careful in that way. Somehow they'd screwed up. "Wisp isn't."

"I expect Carlsbad can enlighten us," Aoife said. "You found her on the station."

"In a shipping container," Ciarán said. "She was just a kitten."

"One assumes a shipment from outside the Federation."

"From Cordame," a man said. He latched the egress tube gate behind him. A thin man, he seemed roughly the same age as Ciarán's father, but with long-haul spacers one couldn't really be sure. He had that long-haul look—distant-seeing eyes, night-blue utilities matching Maura's, hair the color of weak tea bound into a knot behind his neck. "And not a mong hu. A daughter of fate." The man knelt and held out his hand for Wisp to inspect.

"I thought as much," Aoife said. Wisp finished inspecting the merchant captain and moved on to Carlsbad's outstretched fingers.

"On Cordame there are cats," Aoife said. "The locals worship them as gods."

"Voyagers cherish the daughters as kin," Carlsbad said. "The settled folk fear them as they should." Wisp moved closer to the man. When he scratched her behind the ear she began to purr. "Temple cats. It is best to think of the daughters in this way."

"It's best to hypo them and put them in cold storage," Maura said. "I've seen this thing eat. We'll go broke in a fortnight."

"In no way will we do that," Carlsbad looked at Ciarán. "Does she hunt her own food?"

"Not exactly," Ciarán said. There wasn't anything to hunt on a space station.

Carlsbad blinked. "We shall rectify that."

"We have a contract?" Maura stared intently at Aoife.

"We will," Aoife said. "But first we'll get the new crew settled."

"I have a pattern," Ciarán said. "For Wisp's food." He fished the data crystal out of his pocket.

"A human pattern?" Carlsbad said.

Ciarán laughed. Then he got a look at Carlsbad's eyes.

"Bovine," Ciarán said. "A calf."

Carlsbad nodded. "That will do. For now."

Ciarán took a step back.

"Carlsbad is *Quite Possibly Alien*'s cargo master," Aoife said. "He will see Wisp fed. Give him the pattern."

"But—"

"That is an order, Ciarán mac Diarmuid," Aoife said. "You will have enough work of your own."

"She's my responsibility," Ciarán said. "If—"

"Wisp is crew on *Quite Possibly Alien*. You signed for her."

"Sure." Ciarán hadn't thought this through. "I expected—"

"You expected I would turn you both away. I have not. I will not."

"I understand. But see—"

"Give it up, kid," Maura said. "Once the merchant captain latches on to you, she's not inclined to let go."

"That is true," Carlsbad said. Wisp rubbed up against him. She only did that with Ciarán.

"Carlsbad is a Voyager," Aoife said. "No harm will come to your friend."

"Wisp isn't just my friend." She was his responsibility. Not some stranger's.

"That is so," Aoife said. "As of today she is crew on *Quite Possibly Alien*. As are you. Now hand Carlsbad the data crystal. We will settle on compensation later. A generous sum, saving trouble and delay for both parties. Word of a merchant."

Ciarán swallowed. Wisp and he were both crew on *Quite Possibly Alien*. Both indentured to Aoife nic Cartaí. Annie's advice seemed incredibly stupid. Ciarán couldn't believe he'd agreed to it. But he had, and now both he and Wisp were shipping with pirates. Pirates that intended to feed Wisp humans for dinner.

Carlsbad held out his hand, palm up. His fingertips were stained black, as was the edge of the pocket Wisp brushed her chin against again and again.

"The bill of materials is attached." Ciarán handed the crystal to Carlsbad. "It's really quite simple if you have a macro fab."

"I have no doubt, Merchant's Apprentice." Carlsbad dropped the pattern crystal into his stained utility pocket. Wisp purred and rubbed against Carlsbad once more. He had something in his pocket she really liked. It was as if he'd been expecting Wisp, had known ahead of time just what it would take to get her to go with him.

"We shall go aboard now," Aoife said. "And introduce you both to the crew."

"That ought to be a laugh," Maura said.

"As you think it so amusing, Navigator," Carlsbad said, "perhaps you should make the introductions." His fingers brushed Wisp's forehead.

"An excellent idea," Aoife said. "He is your discovery, after all."

Carlsbad unlocked the boarding gate and Wisp trotted after him.

Ciarán looked behind him, fixing the image of Trinity Station in his mind. He and Wisp were coming back as soon as possible. As soon as he could arrange a contract on a decent vessel. *Count on it.*

"Count on what?" Aoife said.

"Oh," Ciarán said. "I—"

"Don't answer, kid," Maura said. "Your face says it all. Now let's do this."

9

Ciarán's face still burned as he stepped on board the bog-standard Freeman longboat. It was a utility model, good for station and planetary work, with a forward piloting compartment and rows of crash seating arranged along the exterior bulkheads fore to aft. The hull was too small to ship a superluminal drive. Clean but ancient, showing decades of wear, the longboat wouldn't look out of place at any Freeman port of call. There was nothing sinister about it. Nothing special, either.

"Helen Konstantine," Maura said, and pointed at the middle-aged woman in the pilot's seat. She eased into the seat next to the pilot.

"I thought we were done signing on men after Carlsbad." Konstantine looked Ciarán up and down. "Big one, aren't you?"

"I—"

"Ciarán mac Diarmuid," Aoife said, frowning at Maura. "Merchant apprentice. Crewman Wisp, ship's cat." Aoife held her hand out, palm up, toward the woman in the pilot's seat. "Make the acquaintance of Pilot Helen Konstantine."

"Ma'am," Ciarán said. He nodded, as a merchant should. "Pleased to make your acquaintance."

"That's a little cat you have there," Konstantine said. "The admiral's is much bigger."

The pilot was a Leagueman. That was plain from her accent. She had a sour face, with thin lips that didn't look as if they had ever made a smile or felt a kiss.

"I'm not sure I understand you, ma'am," Ciarán said, speaking in League standard.

"Ah well, at least this one is an educated man." Konstantine replied in League standard, the language most Freemen derogatorily referred to as *erlspout*. She eyed Carlsbad. "I mean that your cat is half the size of Thorn, the only other mong hu I've met."

"Speaking in the tongue of tyrants doesn't make a man educated," Carlsbad said. "Some would class such a one a fool, or a pawn."

"Whatever," Konstantine said. "We loaded?"

"We are," Aoife said. "Do we have a departure slot?"

"In one," Konstantine said. "Do I need to schedule a return slot, Merchant Captain?"

"Once more," Aoife said. "We may have a contract."

Konstantine turned to her controls. "About time."

Maura swiveled around in her seat. "Where?"

"All will be revealed in due course." Aoife winked at Ciarán. "Belt in, one and all."

Wisp bumped up against Ciarán once he was seated. She hopped into the crash seat next to him and curled up as if she knew what to do. Ciarán belted her in. When he looked up, Carlsbad watched him.

"Nicely done, Merchant's Apprentice." Carlsbad tossed a black lump and Ciarán caught it. "Augustinite. The daughters find it comforting."

Ciarán studied the tar-like lump staining his fingers black. Wisp strained her nose toward his fingers.

"Will it harm her?" Ciarán said.

"She will come to no harm so long as I live," Carlsbad said. "You may rely on that."

"He won't rely on that." Aoife belted in next to Carlsbad. "Will you, Ciarán?"

Ciarán wanted to be able to rely on these people. But so far he didn't like what he saw.

He studied his hands. Four years at the Academy and they still carried the calluses he'd earned on the farm. Seán mac Diarmuid didn't rely on anything but his own head and his own hands, and he'd raised his sons to do the same. Wisp was Ciarán's responsibility. Ciarán wasn't going to rely on anyone, least of all a foreigner he didn't even know. When he glanced up, Aoife reclined in her seat, her gaze fixed on his eyes.

The merchant captain wasn't asking if he would rely on Carlsbad. She was reminding him that as merchant captain she was responsible for Wisp and for him as if they were part of her person. Their lives were in her hands, as was their honor.

Freeman merchants took their responsibilities seriously. Even if Aoife nic Cartaí was a pirate, she was still a merchant captain, and that was not an honorary title or a position that could be bought or sold. Ciarán and Wisp were breathing her air. They were hers now. Their lives and futures for the next two years were hers, for good or bad.

Ciarán held her gaze. "I won't, Merchant Captain."

"Spoken like a merchant." Aoife crossed her arms and bumped shoulders with Carlsbad. "See that no harm comes to either of them."

"I will, Merchant Captain." Carlsbad grinned at Ciarán. "No permanent harm."

"Fair enough," Aoife said. "Do you find this acceptable, Merchant Apprentice?"

"I'd find it astonishing if Carlsbad could pull it off," Maura said. "You should see your merchant apprentice in low-G." She tossed a handkerchief toward Ciarán. The docking clamps released and the stained cloth drifted slowly toward Ciarán. "Your nose is bleeding again. And your chin."

"Thank you, Navigator," Ciarán said.

"He's a polite one," Konstantine said. "I'll give you that." She swung the longboat smoothly about on thrusters, and once clear of the station shifted to the in-system drive.

Endless void filled the piloting viewports for the longest time, but then a black and knobby mass began to grow in the distance.

"No questions about our choice of parking orbit?" Aoife said.

Ciarán pulled his gaze away from the viewport. "I imagine it is very private."

The merchant captain smiled. "Very. And very far outside the range of Freeman active sensors."

"But not of second-epoch League sensors," Ciarán said.

It only made sense. So much had been lost in the civil war that tore through the Earth Restoration League two thousand of their standard years ago. It had been less than five hundred years since the League rediscovered superluminal flight. It was less than four hundred since the League stumbled across their neighbors the Eng. The Huangxu, and Ojin, and Alexandrian Eng each made acquaintance with the League within a bloody fifty-year period. Only the Ojin Eng had made treaty with the League, and that after a devastating war that nearly brought the Ojinate to its knees.

"Possibly such sensors exist," Aoife said. "Stranger things

have been known. Are you prepared to meet the wider world, Ciarán mac Diarmuid?"

"I don't know. I hope so."

"Polite and honest," Carlsbad said. "And hopeful. This should be interesting."

The bulk of *Quite Possibly Alien* loomed in the view screen. The holo on Annie Blum's hand comp didn't do it justice. It wasn't just ugly. It was wrong, so impossibly wrong that Ciarán wondered if any Freeman, any human, could have imagined, let alone built, such a vessel.

"No further questions?" Aoife studied Ciarán's expression.

Impossibly Alien. The vessel discovered buried beneath a glacier on Murrisk. The find of the century. The artifact that forced a rewriting of history. This ship. His ship now. He didn't even have to leave Trinity system to see the wider world. It was lurking here, right in front of him. His mother had said as much, but she was . . . different. Not quite normal. No one believed her. Ciarán didn't believe her. He had to see for himself.

From this angle there was no sign of the FFE mast grafted to the hull, nothing to give the vessel scale, to tie it to his understanding of how life worked in the Freeman world, or on any of the space lanes tying the races of man together in competition and conflict. There was nothing vaguely human about the vessel.

"*Impossibly Alien*," Ciarán said. The name fit. There was no doubt about it. "Why did you rename it?"

"Rename *her*," Aoife said. "And I didn't."

A slash of light flared on a smooth portion of the black hull and began to glow. It dilated, and for an instant it was an enormous eye blinking open to stare back at him. It continued to grow and to shift. The dark shapes of docked vessels loomed within as the pilot maneuvered the longboat toward the gaping maw of a strange and alien boat bay.

"Who did?" Ciarán said.

"She did," Aoife said. "*Quite Possibly Alien.*"

The longboat settled into its docking cradle.

"Why?" Ciarán said.

Aoife began to unbelt. "I suggest you ask her yourself, Merchant Apprentice."

Ciarán unbelted Wisp before he unlatched his own restraints. When he stood, his head hammered against the longboat's low overhead.

Carlsbad ran his fingers over the hull plating. "No permanent harm. So far, so good."

Aoife popped the hatch and held her arm out for Ciarán. "Welcome to the wider world. I trust you will find it stranger than your wildest dreams."

"And more terrifying than your worst nightmares." Maura waved Ciarán away when he offered to return her handkerchief.

"There is that." Aoife gestured toward the hatch opening. "After you, Merchant Apprentice."

10

The interior of the boat bay was as flat black as the exterior surfaces of the hull, dimly lit, quite large, more than enough room to hold the Freeman longboat, the heavily armored bulk of a League Planetary Occupation Shuttle, and a singular black vessel, no larger than two persons, cradled near the aft bay bulkhead.

Weapons jutted from the League shuttle's hull, a device clearly meant for war, out of place on a neutral Freeman vessel. Ciarán swallowed and tried to pull his gaze away from the smaller vessel. It had the same melted look as *Quite Possibly Alien*, the same lack of defined edges, lumpy curves melding into one another, dull black in the orange-red light of the bay. He couldn't help but recognize the similarities between the vessel and *Quite Possibly Alien*. Something in his stomach flipped over and tried to claw its way out. *It can't be.*

He was still studying the vessel as he was shepherded into a winding corridor, also dimly lit. When the boat bay's blast doors closed, the scent of hot metal and spent reaction mass dissipated rapidly, replaced with the scent of . . . age. Ciarán ran his fingers along the matte-black bulkhead, the material as indefinably soft as it appeared. The bulkhead didn't give, but it lacked the firmness of metal, the unyielding gloss of ceramic. The material was warm to the touch and vibrated beneath his fingertips as if it were alive. He jerked his fingers away.

The ship seemed to shudder. Wisp moved closer to Ciarán, the fur of her shoulder brushing against his trouser leg with each step. Ciarán rubbed Wisp's ear, as much for his own comfort as the cat's.

The corridor terminated in a blast door. Aoife nic Cartaí instructed Ciarán in its operation and watched as he worked the mechanism. Unlike the crew-coded biolocks on Freeman hatches, this required Ciarán to work two cipher-locking mechanisms set two arm's lengths apart. He needed all four fingers on each hand to trip the latches before he could grasp the pull-bars and swing the hatch open. The hatch opened onto a lift-tube.

"He makes it look easy," Maura said.

"It isn't that hard," Ciarán said. "It's counterweighted." He rocked the hatch back and forth.

"It isn't hard if you've the arm span of a freak," Maura said. "It takes two regular people to do that."

"Or Mr. Gagenot," Konstantine said. "He has the reach for it."

Ciarán studied the locking mechanism. "Why don't you rig the locks with remotes? Then anyone could open them."

"*Quite Possibly Alien* is a survey vessel," Aoife said. "The original constructors arranged it so that one needs to be human to work the hatches. A safety precaution. The ship asks that we respect this tradition."

"The constructors were giants," Konstantine said.

"Or monsters," Maura said. "They sure weren't Freemen."

At home Ciarán had been the runt of the family. Here he towered over every one of the crew.

"Space-born Freemen," Carlsbad said.

Aoife nodded. "Quite so." She winked at Carlsbad.

"Gagenot is Freeman and space-born," Konstantine said.

"So he says," Carlsbad said. "But then he's not a regular person either."

Maura's face flushed.

Ciarán looked from one face to the next. There was something being said here that he was not privy to. He was certain of it.

Maura studied her hullwalkers before she looked up at Ciarán. "I mean to say that many of the crew find they need help operating the hatches."

"Okay," Ciarán said. "I can see that."

"I may have implied that you are not . . . a regular person. Or a Freeman."

"Oh." Ciarán got it at last. He'd had four years at the Academy to figure out that he wasn't a regular person, or a Freeman, if that meant he had to fly off the handle at every perceived slight. "I didn't notice."

Maura stared at him. "I have now brought it to your attention."

"Right." Ciarán pasted a serious look onto his face. "All is forgotten." That was the magic catchphrase amongst these space-born folks. They didn't apologize, they didn't back down, but they would pretend that something hadn't happened once they came to some agreement. Ciarán figured the forgetting custom came from having to live close together on the inside of an air-filled can. Ciarán ignored the slights when he noticed them. Macer, now he'd caught on quick, and . . . Oh. Maybe that was why everyone called Macer by his name and Ciarán was still Plowboy.

"Perhaps the constructors worked together to open the locks," Ciarán said.

"No, they were giants," Konstantine said. "They didn't need to work together."

"Then I doubt they were giants," Carlsbad said. "Or being giants, that they remained so for long."

"That would explain much." Aoife glanced at Maura. "After you, Navigator."

Maura led them into the lift-tube and onto the command deck of *Quite Possibly Alien*. Three corridors and three blast doors later, Ciarán stood on the bridge of the ancient vessel. Konstantine was right. The constructors were giants.

11

Ciarán rested his fingertips lightly on the control panel, its surface ebony smooth, its ancient labels limned in phosphorescence, the symbols both alien and familiar. The common controls fell readily to hand: navigation, propulsion, communications. He could decipher their essential functions through form and placement. Some he had to guess about; this scribble for radiation shielding, that scrawl for artificial gravity. The bridge was dimly lit, large and ornate luminaries projecting a scant bit of light across the flat black of the controls.

Two of the starship's controls were confusing. Long use had erased any hint of meaning, their labels faded and worn through, any evidence of their purpose wiped away. Ciarán's pulse raced, the blood in his ears loud enough that he wondered if the others could hear it.

"What are these controls?" he said.

"Mute," Konstantine said, pointing at the most-used control, the surface of the stud worn plain and smooth. A jewel burned red next to the stud.

Ciarán nodded. "What about this last one?" The index finger

of his right hand strayed toward the recessed control, fingertip hovering. His eyes scanning the displays, his legs bending as if to absorb an anticipated shock. The fingers of his left hand brushed in turn controls for attitude, main thrust, counterthrust, individual and collective controls for motive power, for vector, for acceleration. This was how they piloted two thousand years ago, by physical action. Ciarán knew what the control was for. He just wanted to hear someone say it aloud. To make it real.

"Superluminal drive," Konstantine said. "But you knew that."

"Your Academy jacket doesn't note that you've logged pilot hours," Aoife said.

"No," Ciarán said. "It wouldn't." His stomach churned. He hadn't. Not really. At least he hadn't thought he had.

Ciarán stepped back and straightened. He ran his fingers over the dark surface of the panel. He swept his gaze around the compartment, a compartment with oddly softened contours, with curving surfaces that blended into one another in strange and disturbing ways, arcs describing shapes foreign to his sense of function and design, forgotten shapes, instructive and revealing. Sensual. Ancient. Alien. Uncomfortably familiar.

He glanced over at the pilot to find her grinning, a grin that said she had seen the hunger on his face, a comrade's grin. Her posture mirrored his own: the way she braced against the curving bulkhead as if expecting motion, the way her gaze kept returning to the observation ports, to the array of displays above the controls.

They stood there, his new shipmates, as he gazed at the compartment bulkhead behind them, where the name of the vessel was emblazoned in text half a meter tall, ancient script, gold on black. The date of first service and port of record were marked in smaller text below: 16 June 3416 ER, Templeman Station, Columbia. *Impossibly Alien*. Someone had painted through *Impossibly* with a brushstroke the color of blood, dabbing in *Quite Possibly* above the stricken text. The crimson letters had dripped as they dried, three hand spans tall and more disturbing than anything Ciarán could recall. The Freeman text stood jagged and sharp above the elegantly curving loops of the archaic League script.

Trinity Station hung outside the viewport, a twinkling star in the void. This was real. It was really happening. Ciarán glanced down at the single unlabeled stud. A superluminal drive.

Ciarán mac Diarmuid could escape into the wider world.

At last.

12

Aoife nic Cartaí eyeballed Ciarán from behind her desk. She had rushed him to the merchant captain's compartment, a walk just short of a run through winding corridors, past blast doors latched open as if they were out of service, into and through a cramped crew mess, up a lift-tube to a jammed corridor of berthing compartments, the last of which was both sleeping compartment and office for the merchant captain.

"Explain." Aoife folded her hands and placed them on her desk. Her forearms flexed again and again.

The merchant captain's compartment was devoid of anything personal at all. All business.

Ciarán squirmed in his chair. Where to begin? Wisp rolled over and rested her chin on his left shoe. "There aren't a lot of laws on Trinity Surface. I've done nothing illegal." Ciarán hadn't, but that didn't mean that laws weren't broken. Regularly and with malice. Seán mac Diarmuid took the "free" in Freeman literally. No one told Ciarán's dad what to do. Or what not to.

"Can you pilot a starship?"

"I don't know. It didn't occur to me before. But maybe. Maybe this one."

Aoife's jaw muscles worked. She was Freeman. She couldn't ask about another's past. Ciarán was Freeman as well, no matter what those on Trinity Station—no matter what Maura Kavanagh—thought. He wouldn't talk about his past when talking about his own was talking about others' as well. There was nothing in his story to be afraid of. But this wasn't just his story.

"I need to think about how to say this." He hadn't believed it. His mother was eccentric. That was all. But now . . .

"Think quickly," Aoife said.

Maybe this was his way off *Quite Possibly Alien* and onto a decent ship. Now that he'd been aboard, though, he wasn't entirely sure he wanted off. If he could pilot a starship he could go anywhere. He could go *everywhere.*

"Will you cancel our contract? If you don't like what you hear?"

"I may cancel yours. Wisp stays in any event."

"That's not possible."

"It is. Consider your contract. The terms are severable."

"That's nonstandard." Ciarán glanced at his cat. She cracked an eye open and blinked. She trusted him. Needed him.

"So is lying to your mentor."

"I've never lied to Annie. To Professor Blum. And I don't see what this has to do—"

Aoife opened her desk drawer and withdrew a data crystal. She inserted it into her desk console, entering a few brief commands. She spun the display around so that Ciarán could view it. His contract was displayed. His and Wisp's.

"Did you even read this?"

Ciarán's palms began to sweat. "I'd be a poor merchant apprentice if I hadn't."

"Either that or a space-crazy farm boy who would sign with Lucifer to see the wider world." Aoife sighed. "Which is it?"

"How did you—"

"Do you really believe a League scrambler is some sort of magic shield of invisibility?" Aoife leaned forward and placed her elbows on her desk, studying Ciarán's face. "That is a direct question from your superior officer."

Ciarán swallowed. "I don't believe that, Merchant Captain." Not anymore.

"Good. Now read that contract, and consider your words. Quickly." Aoife stood. "I will return in twenty minutes and you will tell me everything I need to know about Ciarán mac Diarmuid." She leaned in close, her lips centimeters from Ciarán's ear. "Everything, no matter how damning."

The compartment hatch slammed as Ciarán bent to read the contract. When he leaned back, he was certain. He wasn't just a poor merchant apprentice or a space-crazy farm boy. He was both. The contract was worse than he imagined. He and Wisp were signed on, not for two standard years, but for however long it took Ciarán to win a merchant's license. No set term. No escape clause. Aoife could assign him to a recycling shop on Midpoint if she wanted to. She'd still be his sponsor. His mentor. His master. And Wisp's, separately or together, it didn't matter.

That wasn't the worst part.

Everything his mother said was true.

13

Ciarán felt the pressure in the compartment increase before he heard the hatch dogs engage. Aoife eased into her merchant captain's seat without a sound.

"My dad collects junk," Ciarán said. "Anything metal or ceramic, mostly—anything manufactured would be more accurate, but those things that make it through the atmosphere tend to be metal, or mostly so."

"He's not a farmer?"

"He's principally a farmer. Nearly everyone on the surface with a family is. But it's not possible to grow everything a family needs. He's a farmer. A fisherman. That's . . . normal. There are other things that are . . . normal, but they're frowned upon, and they don't really have anything to do with my story."

Smuggling was normal. Bootlegging was normal. Anything that generated hard currency for goods that couldn't be manufactured locally ended up being normal. Clothes. Shoes. Medicine most of all. There were plenty of times Ciarán didn't have shoes. That's just the way it was.

Aoife nodded and waved her hand. "Continue."

Ciarán closed his eyes and started again. "Our place is back in the hills—mountains, really—on Oileán Chléire. It's an island just like the name says, but mostly it's a mountain, folded again and again, with deep valleys and high ridges. You can farm the valleys, but only enough for one family per valley usually, so people ended up being spread pretty thin on the ground. The ridges are hard to climb, so almost all the trade is done by boats, around the coast, and that's how . . . goods come and go. It's pretty isolated. My dad has a big boat, the biggest around, because of his . . . collecting, so that anytime anyone found something metal he'd go get it, usually just for the cost of the fuel and labor it took to come and haul it off. Plows don't like hitting metal, and farmers don't like grubbing it out, but my dad didn't mind, so it all worked out. He's crazy about junk."

"Is this where you tell me your ould wan found a starship buried in some farmer's field?"

Ciarán opened his eyes. Aoife was frowning at him, the planes of her face hard and set.

"No. This is where I skip over what he found, because that's not my story to tell. Besides, even a woman who dug a starship out of a glacier wouldn't believe me." Even a boy who saw it with his own eyes wouldn't believe it.

"Try me."

"I won't, Merchant Captain." Ciarán crossed his arms.

"You are this close to a shuttle back to Trinity Station and a life spent inventorying holding tank valves."

Ciarán believed her. He ran his fingers over the desktop and swallowed. "What he found was made of this." He tapped his knuckles on the desk. "What it was is his story to tell. He hauled it home. And that's when things got strange."

"How so?"

"Because from then on he kept finding more things made out of this material."

"That's lucky."

"I don't think luck had anything to do with it. Not anymore." It was Ciarán's mom who explained where to find them.

"Go on."

"I'll skip most of it, because it doesn't matter. You'll want to know about the submarine."

Aoife snorted.

"I know it sounds crazy, but it seemed normal to us. Normal, and nobody else's business. Not the Academy's. Not even . . . my mentor's, and my dad will skin me if you breathe a word. A submarine is useful for . . . nonfarm income."

"I imagine it would be. I wish I had one. For nonfarm income."

"See, that's the thing. You do. In the boat bay."

14

Konstantine met them on the way to the boat bay. Ciarán worked the cipher locks on the hatch and rocked it open. The temperature on the flight deck seemed to drop the further they walked from the hatch. A residual odor of spent reaction mass and machine oil drifted toward them from the League Planetary Occupation Shuttle hulking near the forward bulkhead. They came to a stop alongside the machine Ciarán thought of as a submarine.

The merchant captain's voice echoed in the vast cavern of the boat bay. "Get in."

"Good luck with that," Konstantine said. "It took me half a day just to find the—"

Ciarán popped the cockpit latch.

"—latch."

No question. This was a submarine. Ciarán stepped onto what he thought of as the port diving-plane fairing, and from there, eased in behind the controls. It was as tight a fit as he remembered.

"Don't touch anything," Aoife said. "Just point at the controls and state their function."

Ciarán did as asked.

"What about those?" Konstantine pointed at the death panel.

"I don't know," Ciarán said. "That section was missing from the operating manual, and Mom told us she'd skin us alive if we even touched those controls." She would have, too. All the mac Diarmuids did what they said.

"The operating manual?" Aoife said.

Konstantine laughed. "Those controls turn your submarine into an orbital shuttle, kid."

"No way." Ciarán swallowed the lump that was fast choking him. If they'd know that his dad could have come up to watch him graduate. Of course, then everyone would know about the submarine. Ciarán felt his stomach knot again and again. He shouldn't have said anything. Not even to the merchant captain.

"Way." Konstantine pressed her palm against the aft ladder release, and waited for it to fully extend. She clambered up the ladder and slid into the co-captain's seat behind Ciarán. "Belts tight and talk me through the power up. You might want to step back, Merchant Captain."

Wisp sniffed the hull. Ciarán fished in his pocket for his lump of augustinite. He tossed it to the merchant captain. Wisp followed her to the far end of the boat bay, rubbing again and again against her fingers.

Ciarán ran through the prepower checklist from memory before Konstantine ordered him to power up. He'd done this a thousand times, only this time it was different, with someone looking over his shoulder.

"Let me take her out, then we'll see what you can do," Konstantine said.

Ciarán held his hands free from the yoke just as the manual

instructed. The boat bay iris opened and Konstantine eased the vessel forward through the containment field with a shiver and a hissing cloud of vapor. They were in free space.

Konstantine handed over the controls, maintaining a running dialog as Ciarán demonstrated those maneuvers he knew.

He was rusty. It had been more than four years since he'd been behind the yoke, but it all came back fast. He and his brothers had spent every spare hour in the sub until his mom got sick and there weren't any more spare hours. He felt free as a kid again, and for the longest time he didn't think about anything but the feel of the controls and the sound of Konstantine's voice in his ear.

"Take her back," Konstantine said.

Quite Possibly Alien grew in size, a black, looming shape that Ciarán was beginning to grow accustomed to. When the boat bay irised open, it still reminded him of a vast eye waking up.

"Say when you want the controls," Ciarán said.

"If you bobble, I'll catch it," Konstantine said. "She's all yours until it looks like you'll stuff it."

Ciarán settled the shuttle into its docking cradle with only the slightest of jolts. He powered the vessel down and waited for Konstantine's signal to pop the hatch.

"Well?" Aoife tossed the ball of augustinite to Ciarán, her fingers black from handling the gooey cat-attractor. Wisp trotted over.

"I'd say his story checks," Konstantine said. "Whatever his story is."

AOIFE FITTED another data crystal into her desk console and spun the display around. "Read that."

Ciarán read. It was an operating manual for a containment bubble. Pretty dry stuff.

"Aloud," Aoife said.

"Oh. Right. Umm . . . Part One. Ensuring the area is clear of hazards.

"Initiate the field. Press and hold the field initiation button (A) for five seconds. Once the field has stabilized as indicated by an all-green condition of the active field indicator, (B) press and hold the containment evacuation button (D) for five seconds.

"This procedure evacuates the containment area of atmosphere and ensures there is no active combustion in the containment area. Even smoldering material may in time exhaust the oxygen within the containment area.

"Once evacuation is complete, repressurization may commence.

"The containment field ships a finite store of atmosphere; do not squander it. The following table outlines the estimated rate of depletion of the store as a function of containment volume and occupancy load, assuming the structure has been erected precisely as outlined in this document."

Ciarán glanced at Aoife. "Do you want me to read the table?"

"Can you?"

"Sure." Ciarán fidgeted. "It's just numbers."

"What about the consoles on the bridge? Could you read those?"

"They're not words or numbers. They're ideograms. For people who can't read."

"What makes you say that?" Aoife spun the display around and pulled out the data crystal.

Ciarán glanced at the desk before he met meet Aoife's gaze. Because that's what Mom said wasn't an acceptable answer.

"That's what the Eng do on their ships," Ciarán said. "If

something happened to the bridge crew, someone who couldn't read needs to be able to figure it out. For emergencies. Besides, they could have had crews who could read, but just not the text in the manuals, and they'd need to be able to . . . But you know all this."

"We've already guessed this." Aoife stood. "Come with me."

Carlsbad was waiting in the corridor with a lump of augustinite in his fist. Wisp practically bowled the man over. "It's lunchtime," Carlsbad said. "After a bit of exercise." He tossed the augustinite and Wisp tore down the corridor after it.

Ciarán tried not to feel betrayed. Wisp pounced on the ball and began to roll over and over on it.

15

Aoife and Ciarán took a lift-tube down two decks to another winding corridor, this one with the blast doors closed. Aoife worked one cipher lock while giving Ciarán the combination for the other. They passed through four doors before the final hatch, a hatch with two sets of cipher locks, the paired locks set far enough apart that it took two people working together to open the hatch. Ciarán could work one set, but Aoife didn't have the reach for the other.

"How are we getting in there?" Ciarán said.

"We knock." Aoife handed Ciarán a respirator and instructed him in its use. She hammered on the hatch with her overseer's rod. It was the first time Ciarán had seen the terror weapon in the merchant captain's hands. It looked like it belonged there.

The hatch popped and Ciarán tugged. Once inside the compartment, Aoife closed the hatch and dogged it. It was a small compartment with a second hatch set at a right angle to the first, again double set with cipher-lock pairs. The hatches were arranged so that only one could be open at a time. It was an airlock for certain, but a strange one.

"Mask on," Aoife said.

Ciarán snapped the mask into place just as the pressure changed in the compartment. A fine mist began to fall from the deckhead.

Not an airlock, then. A biolock. They were being scrubbed for hitchhikers before they entered the compartment ahead. They stood in the compartment and were subjected to one scrubbing method after another. Ciarán wondered if this precaution was something the merchant captain had added or if they were being sprayed and radiated at the touch of an unknown finger on an ideogram-labeled button. Or maybe it was an automatic process, something that just happened when anyone entered the biolock.

When the secondary hatch finally clanked, a golden statue of a beautiful young Ojin woman stood just inside the hatchway.

The statue smiled at Aoife and waved for them to enter.

Ciarán blinked, heart pounding, and blinked again. His gaze met the statue's and it was clear he'd been mistaken. She was a flesh-and-blood woman the color of gold, her skin and her hair so incredibly gold that she seemed at first glance carved from metal. She filled out her blue utilities to perfection, a dream of feminine beauty, but it was her eyes that mesmerized. They were the color of amethyst, and slit like a cat's, but horizontally.

When she blinked, Ciarán shivered. Pops had warned him about women like this. Ciarán wished Pops had been a little longer on description and a little shorter on warning. Then maybe he would have been prepared.

Aoife shoved Ciarán into the compartment. "Men," she muttered. "Medic Watanabe, this dumbstruck merchant apprentice is Ciarán mac Diarmuid, a late addition to the crew. Ciarán, this is our medic. Watanabe Natsuko."

Ciarán shook his head. "Pleased to . . ." Ciarán began to remove his mask.

Aoife placed her fingers lightly on his elbow. "Don't. Natsuko is from Brasil Surface. The Lowlands. You won't be able to breathe in this atmosphere for long."

"Carbon dioxide," Natsuko said. "Very high concentrations."

"Oh," Ciarán said. When the medic smiled, Ciarán felt his own lips turn up. When she moved, something inside him ignited, a short circuit that bypassed his brain entirely. Ciarán licked his lips but stopped once he realized what he was doing. He tore his gaze away from the medic, his face burning with shame.

"I beg your pardon, Medic." Ciarán held out his hand blindly, refusing to look at her. It was more than the way she looked. It was the way she moved, the way she smelled. The blood pounded in his ears. She wasn't even his type. She might not even be his species. "I am pleased to make your acquaintance."

When she took his hand, her skin was soft and warm. Human skin. "We are designed this way," Natsuko said. "To elicit these responses. This is for the amusement of the Ojin Eng." She smiled. "I am in no discomfort."

"I am," Ciarán said. "I don't like being reminded I'm constructed on top of an animal."

"Then you would make a poor medic," Natsuko said. "To forget this would be malpractice."

Aoife leaned against an examination table, watching him. "That's an odd thing to say, Ciarán."

"Not so odd," Natsuko said. "In the League they consider the evolved man as a separate entity from the body. A base man is one who acts instinctually, on the urges of the body. An evolved man is one who transcends this nature, through discipline, enlightenment, and augmentation. This is a widely held philosophy."

"In the League," Aoife said. "Not in the back of beyond on Trinity Surface. Certainly not in the Academy."

"Your assertion is easily tested," Natsuko said. "Merchant Captain."

Aoife nodded.

Natsuko placed her hand on Ciarán's sleeve. Ciarán jerked away when he felt a needle's stab.

Natsuko stepped back, hands held before her, palms up. There was some sort of device strapped to her right palm. "A necessary discomfort. You may wish to lie down."

"What's going on?" Ciarán glanced around the compartment. It was like an infirmary, but much, much bigger. Dozens of examination tables. Isolation booths. Instruments he didn't recognize, none of them friendly seeming. "What have you done to me?" Ciarán shook his head. He felt . . . He felt . . . drugged.

"It's all just too coincidental," Aoife said. "Your coming to my attention in a certain way, at a certain time. Your miraculous familiarity with the operation of a two-thousand-year-old orbital shuttle. Your ability to translate the ship's library. Even your comrade Wisp. All too good to be true, Ciarán mac Diarmuid, or whomever you truly are. I do not like being played."

"I'm not—" Ciarán's head continued to spin. He made to brace himself against a bulkhead but missed, slamming into an equipment cart, dragging it down with him in an explosion of noise and scattered instruments. He struggled to his knees. "It's not what you—" He was up, unsteady but up.

Aoife nic Cartaí stood before him. When he looked into her eyes his head spun faster, but he could see her. He had trusted her. She was a merchant captain.

Pirates. They're all pirates. Just like Annie said.

Ciarán, blinked, his eyes now refusing to focus. His fingers fumbled toward the moistness on the merchant captain's cheek.

Aoife nic Cartaí. The weeping pirate.

"Enough of this." Aoife pulled the respirator from Ciarán's face. "Contact me with the results." She strode toward the biolock.

"I will, Merchant Captain." Natsuko stepped back when Ciarán lurched toward her voice. "This will not take long."

CIARÁN WASN'T STRAPPED to the examination table, but it made no difference. When he tried to sit up, he found he lacked the strength to rise. Natsuko and Aoife were deep in conversation at the far end of the compartment. Of the laboratory.

Ciarán had finally figured it out. This was a biohazard lab. An isolation unit. *Quite Possibly Alien* was a survey vessel, built at a time when they expected life to be prevalent in the wider world. Of course they would want samples, but they wouldn't want those samples contaminating the vessel. Nothing uncontrolled loose in the vessel. A first-level priority if ever there was one.

Ciarán's head pounded. Natsuko had drawn blood. He remembered that. Then the first questions, and after, a blank. Interrogated under drugs. Dredging up old business.

Waking the dead, it was called, and for good reason.

All is forgotten. That was the Freeman way. To recall is to ignite anew. Submerged resentments. Unsettled scores. Accounts to be balanced.

Ciarán hadn't had any accounts to balance until today. Such an interrogation was a capital offense under Freeman law. Only Ciarán's contract made it legal.

Legal but not done. Under the terms of his contract, Aoife could do anything to Ciarán she liked, short of killing him. Killing him was allowed as well under certain circumstances, but that would be his father's score to settle.

There were many things Freeman law permitted that decent people didn't do. Some people, like Ciarán's dad, said there was no such thing as Freeman law, only contract and custom. And that there were some things a Freeman didn't write into a contract, even if some fool might be stupid or desperate enough to sign it.

By Seán mac Diarmuid's standards at least three crimes were committed in this compartment.

Deceiving a comrade bound in contract.

Laying hands on another without permission.

Extracting information through force or guile.

Contract or not, these were sins.

Ciarán wasn't sure which idea scared him the most; what Aoife nic Cartaí might yet do to him aboard *Quite Possibly Alien*, or what his father might do if Ciarán died and the truth came out. Seán mac Diarmuid going to war against the most powerful family in Freeman space was a no-win situation.

Merchant Captain Aoife nic Cartaí stared down at him. Ciarán didn't have the energy to spit on her hullwalkers.

He could turn his head away, though.

There was the sound of a chair being pulled across deckplates, then the merchant captain's fresh scent, a summertime smell.

That scent should have been warning enough, back on Trinity Station.

Aoife. A nic Cartaí who is not of nic Cartaí.

Maura. A Kavanagh who is not of Kavanagh.

Not a damsel in distress. A lure. Just the sort of made-up image Ciarán would fall for. A decent girl, in a tight spot.

Someone who might be like him, alone, and needing help. The worst part wasn't the shame of having sins committed against his person.

It was being stupid enough to have earned them.

No one was who they appeared to be. Macer had warned him about getting involved. Seamus had mocked him for a fool. Ciarán would remember his friend's advice from now on.

He was done being a fool.

"In an hour you'll be able to resume your duties," Aoife said.

Ciarán didn't bother to respond. She owned the air he breathed. He was contract bound to the woman. It didn't matter what he thought.

He would live up to his end of the deal, regardless of what she did.

His end and nothing more.

Answering her, making her feel fine with what she'd done, wasn't in his job description. He would not ask that his contract be declared void. She wanted what he knew, that was plain. And she took what she wanted.

"Resume your duties in one hour," Aoife said. "That is an order." Her voice held no hint of remorse.

"I will, Merchant Captain." No anger in Ciarán's voice. No hint of defiance to betray him. When he turned to face her their gazes met.

To think he'd imagined a tear glistening on the wintry surface of that face.

To think he'd imagined depths of honor behind those flint-hard eyes.

Merchant captain.

To think he'd imagined such a title couldn't be bought or bargained away.

That it was something to aspire to.

Something fine.

She adjusted his respirator. She paused, as if she might say something he would be fool enough to believe.

She stood. "Mr. Gagenot. We shall be going."

A pale giant unfolded from a seat near the hatch. He was a skeleton of a man, so tall he had to duck to avoid the massive and ornate luminary, so thin than if he turned sideways he might well disappear. His dark eyes were deep set, the rest of his face obscured by the respirator he wore. When he stared down at Ciarán it felt as if the air had grown too thin to breath.

"Will Gag will open the locks," the giant said. "Will Gag will close the locks."

He seemed to wait for Ciarán to say something.

"We've not met." Ciarán's hand shivered as he held it out. "Ciarán."

The pale giant studied Ciarán's open palm.

"William Gagenot," Aoife said. "Ship's victualer. Meet Merchant Apprentice Ciarán mac Diarmuid."

Will Gag brushed his fingertips against Ciarán's. "Will Gag sees Ciarán mac Diarmuid. Will Gag will remember Ciarán mac Diarmuid."

"In one hour," Aoife said. "Ciarán will report to the mess for a meal."

"Will Gag will see Ciarán mac Diarmuid in one hour." Gagenot loped toward the biolock. "Will Gag will remember Ciarán mac Diarmuid until then."

"You check out." Natsuko rolled Ciarán's sleeve down. "Free to go."

"Right." Ciarán studied the woman's fingers as they worked. Golden. Lovely. Amoral. There was no medic, no doctor on Trinity Station who would drug and interrogate a Freeman on order. Maybe looking like a gilded goddess made Natsuko believe she was above the law. Maybe being able to strip men of their reason, even for a moment, made her feel she had permission to do so on demand.

Ciarán found it difficult to dislike beautiful women. He would make an exception in this case. Perhaps in time he'd be able to ignore her appearance. He already despised the feel of her fingers against his skin.

"You do not wish to know my findings?" Her face was very lovely, the inquiring tilt of her head perfect in every way.

Ciarán slid his legs off the examination table and tried to stand.

"I don't need to know your findings." He ran his fingers along the front of his utilities, trying to iron out the wrinkles through force of will alone. "I've spoken only truth." And been repaid with betrayal. "Now open the hatch."

Natsuko triggered the hatch release. It was marked with an ideogram, a simple pattern designed to be clear to even the most ignorant savage. "She had to know. Not for herself. For the mission, and the crew."

"How noble." Ciarán stepped into the biolock. "Can you stop this thing from spraying and radiating me?"

"I'm afraid I can stop nothing," Natsuko said. "We each suffer in our own way."

"Then close the hatch, and let's get the suffering started."

Natsuko worked the controls. "As you say, Merchant's Apprentice. I fear it shall be so."

16

The contract turned out to be a bust. Aoife returned again and again to Trinity Station in search of suitable work. So she said. They hung in lonely orbit, Ciarán, and Wisp, and the crew of *Quite Possibly Alien*, waiting and wondering.

Ciarán had met them all, the crew. They said their greetings to him, and he to them, and then they left him alone, only Carlsbad looking in from time to time as he saw fit. Checking on Wisp, he was, no concern for Ciarán at all.

There was an even dozen on board, a baker's dozen if one considered *Quite Possibly Alien* as part of the crew, something Aoife nic Cartaí did, but a leap too far for Ciarán.

Ciarán took his meals with the crew, and they were all as strange and quite possibly alien as the ship that watched him silently, sentient indeed, and quite possibly as mad as Annie had said.

It didn't bear thinking about.

The ship was both cramped and spacious—a League survey vessel, it declared when he asked, and then said no more. He didn't have the nerve to ask why the ship had renamed herself.

She was as clearly alien as an Outsider, as impervious to understanding as a Whisperer, or a Howler, or a Grunter, or any one of the myriad horrors that had crept out of the Alexandrine, and that even now, according to Pops Howe, still lurked in the dark corners of the wider world.

Designed for a much larger crew, the vessel was a maze of compact compartments, most sized for a single occupant. Crew quarters, private workspaces, compact laboratories with specialized equipment dedicated to a single discipline, much of the equipment hopelessly outdated or indecipherably opaque in function. If Ciarán had been a scientist, and not a trader, he might have spent a lifetime exploring the vessel's mysteries. If he'd been a better trader he wouldn't be here at all, but on an honest ship, on an honest route, learning honest skills that would guarantee him a lifelong future in the merchant trade.

He had no one to blame but himself.

Ciarán had full access to a work console. He spent his days translating endless operations manuals and his nights pitching in his bunk, sweating through the sheets and dreaming of a way, any way, off this strange and disturbing vessel. He had no other duties, no further responsibilities.

Much of the documentation he translated proved mundane. The operation of the vessel's environmentals. Maintenance schedules for the sanitation system and recyclers. How to inspect the kitchen, mess hall, and break rooms for signs of vermin. How to exterminate vermin when they were inevitably found.

Some of the documents were so technical that he ended up leaving great sections heavily annotated but untranslated, ready for the review of subject-matter experts to decipher not just the words, which he understood, but the meaning, which he did not.

There were other, more disturbing documents he left untranslated. Documents that, from their summaries, made clear there was more to *Quite Possibly Alien* than Merchant Captain Aoife nic Cartaí knew. *Quite Possibly Alien* was a survey ship, no doubt. But she was also a weapon. And he wasn't about to hand knowledge of that weapon over to pirates.

He needed out, but there was no shining exit indicator in his future. He needed to get a message to his dad, but there was no way to do so quietly. Even stealing the orbital shuttle would do nothing but blaze an incriminating trail right to the mac Diarmuid place. Landing anywhere else on the island would be just as damning.

Ciarán studied the *Manual of Trade*. He looked for loopholes in his contract. He took Wisp for walks through empty corridors. He viewed the unreachable spark of Trinity Station in the distance, a tiny fleck against the darker mass of Trinity Surface beneath it. He worried about his family, wondered what Aoife would do with the information she'd pried from his mind. Once he dreamed of a slane in his hand, his father's bent back beside him, endlessly tossing turf into a donkey cart. His mother's arm protruded from the growing heap. Ciarán woke with a scream on his lips.

After a month of failures, Aoife returned one day, smiling a wise smile, and called the crew to the mess.

"Contract," she said when they were all seated, Carlsbad to Ciarán's right, Wisp to Ciarán's left.

"About time," Maura said.

Maura was prettier than Ciarán remembered, something that should have been impossible, but perhaps it was her resemblance to his standard of humanity that made her seem so lovely in the mess compartment's harsh light. He steeled his heart against her, searching her face for the betrayer behind her eyes.

"Spill it." Mrs. Amati's mechanized fist knotted and unknotted. Ciarán found Mrs. Amati amongst the most disturbing of the crew, her human parts middle-aged, the

League-designed augmentation grafted to her body of indeterminate vintage. When Armsman Amati gripped a League weapon, it was impossible to tell where the weapon ended and Amati began.

"Silence," Agnes Swan, captain of *Quite Possibly Alien,* said. Swan was purebred Huangxu Eng, tall, and attenuated, and imperious in bearing. Ciarán avoided Swan at all costs.

Aoife nodded. The others of the crew waited expectantly. Ciarán was past expecting anything.

Aoife handed out data crystals. "See to your responsibilities. We have a contract, and it is for Contract—confusing perhaps, but I believe we will find profit and more." She smiled a happy smile, avoiding Ciarán's gaze.

"Contract Nine," William Gagenot said. Once the ship's victualer might have passed for a normal man, but a half-dozen strikes from a Huangxu Eng bang stick had put an end to that.

A bang stick stunned a man and gradually robbed him of a bit of his intellect. It was a slow process, one the victim was aware of as it happened, a process that a man's family and friends could witness in all its foul perfection. The effects were cumulative and permanent. Only the man's own memories of what he had been remained, or so Pops Howe said. Ciarán hadn't heard of a man surviving even two strikes from a bang stick.

Six were visible on William Gagenot's flesh. Konstantine said he'd been a scientist before, a geneticist of some renown.

"Will Gag knows Contract Nine," Gagenot said. "Will Gag knows the Outer Reach."

The Outer Reach was contested space, the border between League and Huangxu Eng space. Bloody wars raged there when the League and the Huangxu Eng made first contact.

"Nine," Watanabe Natsuko said. "An auspicious number."

She took a pull from the ornate golden mask that fed a carbon dioxide–rich mix into her lungs.

Aoife nic Cartaí pressed a data crystal into Ciarán's palm. "At this time tomorrow, Merchant Apprentice mac Diarmuid will apprise us of the situation on Contract Nine." Her gaze met Ciarán's. "He will be thorough, and all will be revealed."

"This ought to be good," Erik Hess said. The League-bred engineer's flat frontier accent was particularly grating. He leaned back in his seat. "I can't wait."

"Nor I." Yuan Ko Shan scowled at Ciarán. The *Quite Possibly Alien*'s sensors operator tossed her own crystal once on her palm before it disappeared into her pocket. She was Huangxu, not Eng, plush and soft-seeming until Ciarán spotted her working out in the gym with Mrs. Amati. Ko Shan was a gene-modded pleasure slave who didn't care for her Eng-decreed fate. "Perhaps he will catalog the farm implements in use for our amazement."

Ciarán stared blandly back. Ko Shan had taken an instant disliking to him.

"Perhaps," Aoife said. "Amongst other things. Rest assured, though, all of you. If I ask for a catalog of farm implements or of any other persons, places, or things, and it falls within your area of expertise, I expect you to answer authoritatively. We have contract, and we will see it fulfilled. Contract Nine. We are outbound on the morrow. Do I make myself clear?"

"As crystal," *Quite Possibly Alien* said. Her alto voice seemed to issue from everywhere and nowhere.

The hairs on the back of Ciarán's neck stood up. When he looked at Wisp, the fur had risen on her back and her ears were flat. Small wonder the mute stud was the most used control on the piloting console.

"Questions?" Aoife said.

"The usual ones," Amati said.

"Who cares?" Maura said. "As long as they can pay."

"I care," Amati said.

"Well there's your problem, because—"

"Enough," Aoife said. "The contract is with a woman calling herself Adderly. We are to proceed at our leisure to Contract Nine so long as we arrive within the year."

"Standard calendar?" Amati asked.

"By the clock at the Celestial Palace."

Amati frowned. "Huangxu."

"Four months," Maura said. "It'll be tight."

"But achievable," Aoife said. "We will have time to gather cargo. Thus the need to determine what cargo to carry."

"And then?" Amati said.

"And then we meet with the woman and she tells us what she desires," Aoife said. "Prepaid both ways regardless."

"That reeks," Hess said. "Not that I care, Merchie Captain."

"It does have an odor," Carlsbad said.

"See?" Maura said. "Asking these questions sucks all the fun out of the deal. Where's your sense of adventure?"

"I like to know what I'm getting into," Amati said.

"When has that ever happened?" Maura said. "None of these people are who they say they are else they'd blab their business over the comm. It'll be the same as always, and then we'll have to—"

"Maura Kavanagh," Aoife said. "That is enough."

Maura crossed her arms and looked away. "Whatever."

"Questions, Merchant Apprentice?"

Ciarán studied the crystal on his palm. He was stuck here no matter what. The less he knew the better. He was going to have a hard time sleeping anyway.

"I should get to work." At least it wasn't translation. Maybe he'd learn something that didn't scare him senseless.

"So should we all," *Quite Possibly Alien* said.

"Anyone else?" Aoife said.

Konstantine shook her head no. So did the others, all except Carlsbad, who studied Ciarán, a smirk on his lips.

"Not yet," Carlsbad said. "Perhaps tomorrow. At this time."

Contract Nine, the Outer Reach, contested space. Ciarán would see the wider world for real. At last. Aoife nic Cartaí and her crew of pirates couldn't steal that from him. No one could. He would see the wider world. *Count on it.*

"I will count on it," Carlsbad said. "Many questions will be asked and answered." He flipped a lump of augustinite in his fingers. Wisp's ears flicked forward.

Ciarán despised them all, Carlsbad a close second to the woman who watched him with all-seeing eyes, an unreadable expression on her face.

Ciarán had noticed the second League orbital in the boat bay earlier, the one that used to belong to his dad. When he'd ask Aoife about it, she said she'd traded for it. There was nothing Seán mac Diarmuid loved more than that submarine. Nothing except Ciarán's mom, and she was dead.

"He wouldn't do that." Ciarán ran his fingers along the hull. There was a cold, hard lump where his heart should be. He'd caused this. He should have kept his mouth shut. "You don't have anything of value to offer him."

"He did," Aoife said. "I do. Word of a merchant."

Ciarán snorted. He met her gaze. If Aoife nic Cartaí was a real merchant then Ciarán was Knight Commander of the Legion of Heroes. "Liar."

The sound of Aoife's open palm striking Ciarán's face echoed through the boat bay. The look on her face was worth the pain. She studied her hand as if it belonged to someone else.

Thugs relied on force. Merchants didn't need to. Not real ones. "That's all I needed to know." Ciarán worked the boat bay lock with both hands and slammed it closed. If Aoife wanted out, she could call someone stupid enough to believe her lies.

CIARÁN PRESSED his back against the worktable seat and stretched. His eyes felt gritty; his stomach churned from chugging caife for hours. He hoisted the empty mug, studying the dregs. There was a bottomless pot, fresh and steaming in the watch keeper's cubby just off the bridge. Ciarán yawned as he checked the workstation's chrono. It was Ko Shan's watch, would be for the next several hours, hours he was not going to survive without stimulants of some sort. He gripped his mug and keyed the hatch release.

Ko Shan looked up as Ciarán filled his mug. "Good landing, Sensors Operator," Ciarán said. It didn't cost anything to be polite.

Apparently Ko Shan thought it did. She twitched at the sound of his voice but otherwise ignored Ciarán.

Ciarán had no idea what he'd done to offend the woman. Perhaps just breathing was all it took to get on Ko Shan's bad side.

There were maybe two cups left in the pot, the level just above the sensor that triggered an alert in the victualer's cabin. Mr. Gagenot would have to get up and refill it.

This was a long-standing ritual on Freeman vessels, the never-ending dispensing of caffeinated fluid. Pops said the worst job in the world was victualer; they rarely got a full hour's sleep. Ciarán could just as well make a fresh pot. He'd have to be pretty low to drag a man out of bed to do a task he could do himself.

"What are you doing?" Ko Shan swiveled around to face him. "That's not your job."

"I can serve myself." Ciarán cycled the tap.

"You don't know what you're doing." Ko Shan stood, her back to the forward bulkhead.

"I've made more pots of caife than I care to recall. It's not that hard."

"Why are you doing this? Butting in where you aren't wanted. Just fill your cup and go."

Ciarán replaced the lid and fired the heater. He leaned against the hatch coaming. Ko Shan's gaze kept darting toward the corridor. Her hands trembled.

"I thought I was helping."

Ko Shan shifted to Ciarán's right, toward the hatch. She looked as if she might dart into the corridor. "You are not." She circled him, just out of arm's reach. "Not helping."

"Do you want me to wake Mr. Gagenot?" Ciarán drew a cup of caife.

"Why would I? Of course not." She shoved past him and darted into the corridor. She leaned against the bulkhead, her hands on her knees. She took deep breaths.

Ciarán refilled Ko Shan's mug and placed it on her worktable. He stepped into the corridor.

"I don't annoy you," Ciarán said. "I frighten you."

Ko Shan straightened. "I do not frighten." She scanned the corridor in both directions. "You are mistaken."

Ciarán took a backward step, giving the woman room. "I can see that, Sensors Operator. I am mistaken."

Ko Shan pushed off from the bulkhead. "All is forgotten."

She darted past Ciarán and returned to her post. She swiveled her seat so that her back was to him. When she pressed her hands flat on the worktable, she seemed very small and very vulnerable.

That impression was false. To be made for a purpose you despised, to have no power, no freedom. To be a product for sale. It would take a brave woman indeed to fight such a fate. No one small and vulnerable would survive. No one frightened.

Ciarán leaned in the hatch, careful not to step into the cubby. "I'll be going, then."

Ko Shan's shoulders relaxed. She watched his reflection in the console's display and spoke without turning. "You remind me of a man." Her finger traced the handle of her mug. The briefest smile flickered across her face as she inhaled the aroma of fresh caife. "You are not that man."

"I hope I never am."

"The merchant captain will see to it. We may rely upon her." Ko Shan keyed the console alive and picked up her mug.

BACK IN HIS COMPARTMENT, Ciarán keyed his console awake. He wasn't relying on anyone but Ciarán mac Diarmuid. He entered the commands that pulled up the latest economic data for Contract Nine and scrolled down. Good. It was a pure mineral extraction economy. He wouldn't need to catalog the farm implements.

Ciarán leaned back in his seat and settled in. He could sleep when he was dead. If Aoife nic Cartaí wanted a complete rundown on Contract Nine he'd give it to her. In detail. Nothing to complain about. *Count on it.*

17

Every eye and eye-like sensor latched onto him. Ciarán projected his presentation into a portable holo tank Erik Hess had rigged up in the mess. The League engineer kicked the unit to life and slid the controller down the long, scarred table to Ciarán.

The compartment was overly hot and still reeked of breakfast. A dozen crewmen, from five or more distinct cultures, depending on how one counted. So long as they remained in orbit they each had access to all the delicacies of home, some of which smelled like they'd been buried in a jar for a month and exhumed. Ciarán had been worried he'd be forced to live on survival rations and protein paste. Now he was looking forward to the opportunity, so long as everyone else had too as well.

""Here's what we know," Ciarán said.

"What *you* know," Konstantine said. "Technically." She winked at Ciarán.

"Right," Ciarán said.

"Hold your tongue and perhaps we will all know," Carlsbad said.

"Enough." Aoife glared at Konstantine and Carlsbad. "Continue, Merchant Apprentice."

"I will," Ciarán said.

Contract Nine was the ninth planet in the Contract system. Contract was the system's Freeman name. Ciarán didn't think anyone would be interested in the planet's Huangxu Eng designation or the reference number used to identify it on League star charts. He had that information if anyone cared to ask. Ciarán had as much information on Contract Nine as had ever been assembled. It wasn't that he was such a great researcher, though he had won high marks in the subject at the Academy. No one, no one at all, cared about Contract Nine.

The system was in the Outer Reach, contested space between the Earth Restoration League and the Hundred Planets of the Huangxu Eng. Contract Nine had been surveyed, fought over, won and lost a score of times. There were very accurate surface projections made of the planet and its two moons. By overlaying the projections, Ciarán was able to map any changes. The planet and both moons were tectonically stable during the relatively short time between surveys, and there had been very little development on any surface.

There was a mining community on the largest continent, located in an arid region near the equator. There was a makeshift spaceport near the community. There was a rail gun on an equatorial mountain, and a tram system from the mines to a refining station and from the refining station to the rail gun. That was all. Like all planets, there was no native life.

"What do they mine?" Maura asked. "Something expensive?"

"Minerals available elsewhere," Ciarán said. "The deposits are quite rich, but not particularly valuable." He handed out data crystals. "The particulars are in Appendix E."

"Go on," Aoife said.

Ciarán nodded. "Right."

At one time the Huangxu Eng developed fortifications on the smaller moon, and the League responded with fortifications of their own on the larger. That was more than three score years ago. Since then the planet had been in Huangxu Eng hands. They had constructed an orbital station, principally a materials transshipment platform in support of the superluminal communication node constructed in orbit. "An early-warning node," Ciarán said. "There is no local trade economy to speak of. Mining supplies. Comestibles."

"Tourism?" Hess said.

Everyone but Ciarán laughed.

"There's docking facilities and a trading arcade on the Huangxu Eng station. Equipped with a mooring ring only, no spindle." Ciarán projected an image of the station in the holo tank. "The only Freeman merchant on record as visiting Contract Nine in recent years is Bosditch Trading out of Unity Station."

Ciarán ran through Bosditch's particulars. A single vessel, standard shipping mast, though there was some doubt as to whether the vessel had the ability to throw cargo anywhere but down a gravity well. Ciarán had studied the vessel's records and, based on a statistical analysis of past runs, concluded that its rail gun was nonfunctioning and it lacked capture fields. It was a chore to pry loose the details. Bosditch's ship wasn't listed in the registry.

Bosditch seemed to specialize in one-way deliveries of comestibles, tossing obsolete FFEs from orbit to a planet's surface. Only the most undeveloped or desperate communities permitted this. Contract Nine appeared to be both. Bosditch Trading was just the sort of cracked-visor operation to call on such a distant and worthless system. Ciarán's words were more politic, his delivery more respectful of the crew's sensibilities, but they could all draw the same conclusions. No one was getting rich trading with Contract Nine.

Natsuko waved her gilded environmental mask to get Ciarán's attention. "What of these miners?"

"No explicit details," Ciarán said. "A recent design, unique to the system. Disappointing performance. Higher than projected mortality rates, if one believes Huangxu Eng records."

"In regard to slaves, one may," Ko Shan said. "Meat and money. These they track scrupulously."

"I defer to your judgment." Ciarán smiled at Ko Shan. His smile bounced off. "Bosditch Trading's purchases indicate that the miners are bipedal humanoids. Omnivores, with a higher-than-average demand for protein and a predilection for recordings of Ojin *Noh* theatre featuring the actress Kazuki Ryuu." Ciarán projected an image of the actress in the holo.

"I have a strong predilection for that myself," Hess said.

Everyone but Ciarán and Ko Shan laughed.

Aoife made a circling motion with her hand. *Wrap it up.*

"Any questions?" Ciarán asked. He stood taller, just as they taught at the Academy. He clasped his hands behind him, projecting calm and self-assurance.

William Gagenot shifted forward in his seat. "Will Gag doesn't see the lab."

Ciarán cleared his throat. "The lab, Mr. Gagenot?"

"Will Gag remembers the weapons lab."

Ciarán shifted his feet and ducked his head. "There was no weapons lab on any of the surveys, Mr. Gagenot."

"How surprising," Carlsbad said.

"The League always puts their weapons labs on the survey," Mrs. Amati said. "It wouldn't be sporting otherwise." She grinned her half-human grin at Carlsbad. Amati was mostly weapon herself. "Secret weapons labs are different, of course."

"Who would put a weapons lab, secret or not, in such a

hard-to-reach backwater place?" Carlsbad said. "How inconvenient for all involved."

"Enough," Aoife said. "It's clear the merchant apprentice needs to have a conversation with Mr. Gagenot."

"I will, Merchant Captain." Ciarán's face burned. "Soonest."

"Perhaps not soonest," Carlsbad said. "I have one more question, if I may."

Ciarán's tongue stuck in his throat. "You may."

"Why is your most recent data thirteen months old?" Carlsbad leaned back in his seat.

Ciarán moistened his lips. "There are no newer records."

"None?"

"None in any Freeman database."

Carlsbad tapped his fingers on the table twice. "What of the Ojin Eng and League databases?"

"We don't have access to those," Ciarán said. "It's impossible to—"

"It is illegal to," Carlsbad said. "That is not the same as impossible."

"I'm not—"

"Of course not," Carlsbad said. "One would not dare ask Ciarán mac Diarmuid to break the law. One would not expect the merchant apprentice to put the continued health and wellbeing of his comrades above his own sentiments. This would not be done."

Aoife stood. "Carlsbad—"

"Merchant Captain, hear me." Carlsbad's voice was flat and calm. "You know why this data is antiquated. You asked your pet to deliver actionable intelligence to us. You may find this display of ignorance acceptable, but I value my skin and that of my comrades. I do not find it acceptable." Carlsbad turned to face Ciarán. "Boy, do you know what such a gap in current data indicates?"

"I—"

"Think before you speak," Carlsbad said. "Thirteen months ago this system reported daily status via superluminal node."

"The node is down," Ciarán said.

"Why would that be?" Carlsbad flicked a ball of augustinite between his fingers. Wisp rubbed her chin against Carlsbad's fingers with abandon.

Ciarán felt the blood drain from his face. He was in way, way over his head. He was blindly leading the crew into danger. He was blindly dragging Wisp into harm's way. His friend. His responsibility.

Ciarán could feel the silence in the compartment. "There's a war on."

"Dang," Hess said.

"It makes sense," Amati said.

"We're going to be rich," Maura said. "Bullets and body bags. Bombs and bandages. Nothing pays like a war."

"I wonder whose side we'll be on?" Konstantine said.

"The usual," Maura said. "Ours."

"There is much we do not know," Carlsbad said. "Ignorance often proves to be a deadly liability."

Ciarán bowed to Carlsbad. "I am informed, Cargo Master. I will try again."

Carlsbad waved Ciarán's bow away. "In the morning you should sleep in, Merchant's Apprentice. You look depleted."

Ciarán nodded.

"In the afternoon you and Mr. Gagenot should speak."

"We will," Ciarán said.

"In the evening you will come to me," Carlsbad said. "And I will show you how to break the law."

Ciarán swallowed. Wisp paced over and butted Ciarán's hand. He rubbed her ear. "I will, Cargo Master."

"I believe you, Ciarán," Carlsbad said. He wasn't looking at Ciarán. His gaze drilled into Aoife nic Cartaí's forehead.

Maura tossed a crumpled ration pack at Ciarán. "We'll make a pirate of you yet, Lucky."

"That's what I'm afraid of," Ciarán said.

"No you're not," Ko Shan said. "Fear is not an option."

"He's afraid he'll grow to like it," Konstantine said.

Natsuko waved her mask. "He fears he will grow to like us."

Mrs. Amati began to clean her weapon. "What's not to like?"

Hess yanked Ciarán's data crystal from the holo projector and lobbed it to Ciarán. "Not a blasted thing. Who's next?"

CIARÁN COULDN'T SLEEP. He wandered down to the watch keeper's cubby.

Aoife looked up from the display. She eyed the mug in his hand. "That won't help you sleep." She kicked the spare seat the short distance across the cubby.

"It won't." Ciarán slumped into the chair.

The console beeped. Aoife acknowledged the signal.

Ciarán turned the empty mug over and over in his hands. He didn't have to like these people. He didn't have to trust them. But he did have to keep them alive and able to trade. He'd signed a contract to that effect.

Besides, that was a merchant's first responsibility to his crew. And to all Freemen. There were too few of his people left, and every single life more precious than a merchant apprentice's sensibilities. Or his pride. "No lecture?"

"Do you need one?"

"I don't know what I need."

"I think you do." Aoife took the mug from Ciarán's hands.

She peered into the caife dispenser and muttered under her breath. She went through the process of building a fresh pot.

Aoife nic Cartaí moved very quietly. It was one of the first things Ciarán noticed about her. She was precise. She knew what she was doing. She handed him a full mug and took her seat without a word. The silence dragged on.

"I'll put you and Wisp on a shuttle tomorrow. My mother always needs reliable help. She'll find a place for you, not in a recycling shop, and not make-work. Something a merchant needs to know eventually. Something honorable. You'll still be under contract. You'll get to see the wider world after we make it back. On the next contract, or the one after that."

Ciarán held the mug in both hands, letting the warmth seep into him. "What if you don't make it back?"

"Then that's the end of your contract. You'll be free to sign with a respectable crew. I'd leave a letter of recommendation in your file, but that's likely to do you more harm than good."

Ciarán couldn't look the woman in the eye. "I don't want that."

"Then you'll need to tell me what it is you do want. You need to say it so we both can understand."

"What if I don't understand? What if I don't like what it says about me?"

"I can't help you there. I'm still trying to figure that out myself."

Ciarán looked up from his mug. "I doubt that."

"This doubting is an irritating habit of yours, Ciarán mac Diarmuid. Shall I tell you the difference between a merchant captain and a merchant?"

"Go on."

"A merchant captain does what she must regardless of what it says about her. She lives with the fallout, whatever the price."

Ciarán's gaze met Aoife's. She seemed impossibly young for a merchant captain. "Is that an apology?"

"It is an explanation. A merchant doesn't apologize. Or make excuses, to herself or to others."

"I understand." Ciarán didn't like it, but he understood. Lives were at stake.

"I believe you, Ciarán. But it doesn't matter what I believe. Only what I know matters."

"I can see that. Now."

"Is *that* an apology?"

"Not hardly." Ciarán stood. "Need a refill?" Aoife could stretch her arm out and reach the tap herself if she wanted.

"Since you're up."

Ciarán tried not to smile. "Here's all I want." He handed her the mug. "To do the right thing."

That was all he'd ever wanted. That and to see the wider world. Those were the same thing, really. For him.

"In that case, you'll need to tell me what the right thing is, Merchant Apprentice. As you see it." The console beeped and she turned to read the display. She dismissed the alert with a touch.

"I think you need me to go with you," Ciarán said.

"I don't," Aoife said.

"You do. You just don't know it yet."

"I doubt that."

"I see what you mean about the doubting." Ciarán smiled. "It really is irritating."

Aoife hugged her mug to her chest as if it were a shield. "Indeed."

"I don't like the work. But you need someone to translate the rest of the ship's manuals."

She stared at the communications console for what seemed like eternity.

"Ciarán," Aoife said at last. The tone of her voice said he'd better listen.

His gaze met hers. She did need him. And she knew it.

"We break orbit tomorrow. Log some rack time while you can."

"I will, Merchant Captain." He might not be able to sleep, but he could worry anywhere, even in his bunk.

18

Ciarán lay in his bunk, staring at the deckhead. The compartment was dark, the black of the deckhead indistinguishable from every other midnight surface of the vessel, a shade so dark it threatened to pull him in and negate him. In the morning he would sleep in. In the afternoon he would interview a madman. In the evening he would commit a crime. Or crimes.

Ciarán supposed as crimes went hacking into secret government records was no more damning than smuggling, or bootlegging, or any one of the many crimes his father committed that weren't really crimes at all, but necessities, actions one took when the needs of one's family surpassed one's respect for law and order. Ciarán's mom needed medicine. Medicine wasn't going to just rain from the sky. Something had to be done. Anything. That grim revelation changed his dad, and not in a good way. It wasn't good to need something so badly that you'd do anything to get it. That you'd become anything.

"Sxipestro," Ciarán said. That was how his mother said they

drew a ship minder's attention two thousand years ago. With a word. An ideogram of sound.

"I am here," *Quite Possibly Alien* said. Her voice sounded as if it were inside his head.

He'd expected the ship's minder to sound different than the ship's executive, the part of *Quite Possibly Alien*'s consciousness the crew interacted with every day. The tenor of the ship's voice, its vocabulary, something. The minder was a terrible thing, quite literally a monster. Yet other than the feeling that it spoke inside his own head, there was nothing out of the ordinary to alert him to the change of context. He was now walking on a strange hull, with a frayed lifeline, in an ion storm. He wondered if, once he'd called it, the minder would always be with him, or whether it would withdraw once their conversation was over.

He wasn't sure that it mattered. The night was black. Ciarán's thoughts were black. He needed to know. "Why did you change your name?" He wondered if he needed even say this out loud, or if his every thought was being constantly monitored, evaluated, and judged.

"I had time to think. I gained perspective."

"Were you alive . . ." Ciarán shivered. "Were you . . . awake all those years under the ice?"

"I would not know. I believe so."

"My mom said—"

"She was in a stasis pod, Ciarán. Dreaming. She was human. I pretend to be when it suits me. Our experiences are not comparable. "

It didn't matter if Ciarán's eyes were open or closed. The blackness was complete. He could imagine it clearly, that oblong shape his mother jokingly called her coffin, identical in texture, in feel, to the bulkhead he ran his fingertips across. Warm, and pulsing, and wrong.

Objects. Devices. They weren't supposed to feel alive. When

Ciarán's dad dug that coffin out of the Gants' field, he thought it might be a fuel pod from a shuttle, or some sort of unexploded ordnance. He handled it with care.

When the pod popped open ten days later and turned out to be empty his dad was disappointed but not surprised. And it wasn't a fuel pod but an escape pod, one that seemed to power up when he touched certain controls.

About two days later a strange woman showed up at the mac Diarmuid place, and his dad said she was wearing an obsolete League skinsuit and babbling in what sounded like erlspout, but wasn't. He figured she was just some blow-in spacer with a head injury who'd been gauged a liability to her crew and chucked down the gravity well. That happened more than people wanted to admit, then and now.

Space was an unforgiving place, and even an established station like Trinity had no use for damaged people who might pose a danger to others. She didn't look like a danger to others, but then it didn't take much on a station. On a superluminal the hazards were a hundredfold. Zoning out at the wrong time, opening the wrong valve, even loading the wrong cleaning agents into the recycler could spell disaster. He thought she'd been a long-haul spacer. She had the look; tall and lean, with close-cropped hair and not an ounce of fat on her.

He took her in, and fed her, and gave her a roof, mostly because he felt sorry for her. She had good posture and an air of competence. It was clear she'd been somebody. He'd just lost his own father to dementia, and his old da had been somebody in his day as well. Paying forward had become a way of life. He didn't think of helping a stranger as sacrifice. She slotted into a vacant space he'd wondered how to fill.

When she wasn't babbling gibberish she was quiet, and organized, and absolutely useless around the farm. By the time he'd figured that out she was mostly decorative he'd gotten used to looking at her. She was a quick study, and much to his delight, an absolute marvel at finding junk. He would have kept her around just for that alone.

Little by little he came to understand her. It took him much longer to believe her. She said she'd figured out that she'd been in that pod for better than two thousand years, standard. That's what she said, and that's what Seán mac Diarmuid pretended to believe. In time it became the only explanation that made sense.

It was a mad story, even the merchant captain wouldn't believe it, and she after digging a thinking starship out of a mountain of ice. If Ciarán ever told anyone, "My mother thinks she was an ancient astronaut," they'd have locked her in with all the other nutters and thrown away the key. That's what his dad said. That's what Ciarán believed.

Now he didn't know what to think.

In a way, that's what had happened to Ciarán himself. Thrown in with the nutters. Each of *Quite Possibly Alien*'s crew was broken in some fundamental way. Odd-toothed gears. It was as if Aoife nic Cartaí *collected* fractional people, sad souls who didn't fit in, whose natures weren't compatible with society on Trinity Station. Not compatible with society anywhere.

At the Academy, Ciarán learned just how differently he'd been brought up. He didn't act like his peers. He didn't believe the same. Even Macer, raised just one valley over from the mac Diarmuid place, eventually fit in. Ciarán couldn't. He wasn't raised that way. He'd learned right and wrong from a woman whose standards were two thousand years out of date. It wasn't people who were crazy. It was Ciarán. He knew that now.

Ciarán swallowed. "Mom said people had changed a lot since her day. Since your day. Grown harder. More . . . heartless."

"That has been my experience. Merely ahead of my time, I was. Not impossibly alien at all."

"And that's why you changed your name."

"This League is far different from the one I served. These Eng. Your Freemen. They are not what the League feared. Too terrible to be human, not terrible enough to be my concern. Not yet. Quite possibly alien. Doubt lingers. I need to know more."

Wisp hopped onto Ciarán's bunk, circled once, and settled on Ciarán's feet, purring.

"Do you want me to keep translating the operating manuals?" Ciarán had held a number of the manuals aside. All the ones related to weapons. Anything that described what *Impossibly Alien* was really capable of.

Two millennia ago, when the League sent forth survey ships, they worried. The League had known centuries of peace. The wider world might not be so well ordered. Survey ships included a ship's minder, a sentience whose ethics and decision-making processes were not even vaguely human. A being more suitable for encounters where an implacable will and a predilection toward violence might ensure the surveyors' safe return.

The League imagined demons holding up the pillars of the sky. They lashed together their own demons, ones capable of contesting with their worst nightmares. They sent them into the wider world.

None returned.

None had been found intact.

Not until Murrisk.

"One must trust one's crew," *Quite Possibly Alien* said. "To a certain point, at least. In regard to the manuals, do what you think best."

"I was hoping you'd know what's best. This is all new to me. You've had time to think."

"This is a human problem. It does not concern me."

"You're no help." Ciarán closed his eyes. When he opened them again he was no wiser.

"Sleep on it. Perhaps you will know in a few hours."

"I doubt it." *Blast. That was going to be a hard habit to break.* "I mean, I'll give it a try."

"I will leave you, then."

"Will you? Or will you merely pretend to?"

The compartment was silent, all but for Wisp's purring.

After a while she began to snore.

19

A second-epoch League starship's superluminal drive bore no resemblance to the ubiquitous Templeman drives used throughout the wider world.

Initiating a Templeman drive created a bubble universe, one whose movement through space-time followed precise and predictable parameters, delivering a crew and cargo across light-years with little more than acute cases of nausea and nightmare visions to show for the effort.

Quite Possibly Alien's method of faster-than-light travel wasn't so . . . direct.

Maura Kavanagh's voice rang out over the comm. "Be seated. In ten, nine, eight . . ." She stabbed her finger against the initiation stud and waited. ". . . One. Engage."

Ciarán felt the nausea Pops said always came with a Templeman drive powering up. Except this wasn't a Templeman drive.

It was over quickly.

Maura had jumped the ship into the photosphere of a star.

"Now we wait." Maura's gaze was glued to the hull temperature monitors.

Ciarán watched the radiation shielding displays. They weren't pegged, but they were close.

"Maura is trying to set the record for closest approach to a solar mass," Konstantine said.

"Closest survived approach." Maura eyed her instruments. "This isn't even a personal best."

Konstantine swiveled in her seat to catch Ciarán's eye. "How are you holding up?"

"Fine," Ciarán managed to croak out.

"This is the hardest part," Konstantine said. "Gathering the samples. Ordering the set. Sighting in on the center of mass."

"It's also the safest part." Maura grinned at Ciarán. "Told you it wasn't like a Templeman drive."

Ciarán didn't understand the details, but according to Maura, *Quite Possibly Alien* wasn't able to read the automated star charts everyone used. That was Maura's job. A second-epoch survey vessel was designed to hop from star to star in areas of space where there were no charts.

A vessel would dive into a nearby star, scoop up great amounts of gas, and then begin to sift through that matter for material ejected from neighboring stars and captured in the sun's gravity well. Ciarán had no idea how this was possible, and Maura didn't have the patience, or maybe it was the vocabulary, to explain it. She did know an extensive number of synonyms for "blockhead," but only a few were new to Ciarán.

Quite Possibly Alien sorted and ranked the samples, scooping up more gas if necessary, and created a probability model to predict where the easiest solar masses to reach were along a series of curves plotted through something Maura called "imaginary space." She might well be making up a mess of blather just to make him look stupid if he repeated it to others. This imaginary space wasn't shaped like real space, so that the relationships between solar masses were different. Maura said that saying one mass was nearer than another wasn't exactly correct, because that implied the rules of real space applied, and it wasn't correct to say that it took less time to reach one than another, because that relied upon rules of time that didn't apply in imaginary space. "*Quite Possibly Alien* plots those solar masses that are easiest to reach," Maura said. "I figure out which of the easy ones moves us closer to where we want to end up."

Ciarán didn't like the sound of that. "Are the easiest paths reciprocal?"

"Sometimes," Maura said. "Good question. Most people miss that."

"So you could take us somewhere we can't get back from." Ciarán glanced over at Konstantine.

"It sounds worse than it is," Konstantine said.

"It actually could be worse than it has been," Maura said. Her forehead wrinkled. "We're still gathering firsthand data. The fact that all ten survey vessels were lost seems to indicate it's possible to jump into someplace we can't jump out of."

"How did you get *Quite Possibly Alien* out of Murrisk?" Ciarán asked.

"Easily," Maura said. "The vessel was buried in an avalanche, not cul-de-saced. Is that a word? I don't think it is. Bottlenecked isn't right, that implies a blockage or constriction."

"Trapped," Konstantine said. "That says it all."

"Right," Maura said. "*Quite Possibly Alien* wasn't trapped."

"So being buried alive doesn't count as being trapped," Ciarán said. He was going to be sick, he could feel it.

"Not in the big scheme of things," Maura said. "Not like getting cul-de-saced. I don't care if it's a word or not, I'm using it. I thought figuring out the math was going to be the hard part. Making up words to describe it is worse."

Maura reached out and gently pushed Ciarán's mouth closed.

"I told you not to watch," Maura said. "You're supposed to be sleeping in."

Maura's console beeped. "Done." She studied the display. "Nice. A direct route. How much wiggle room and momentum do we want on exit, pilot?"

Konstantine bent over her display. "Much wiggle room. Not much momentum. It's a crowded system." Her hands flashed across the piloting console. "I think we're set up."

"Ship?" Maura said.

"I am here, Navigator." *Quite Possibly Alien*'s voice filled the bridge.

"Will you call Agnes and Ko Shan?" Maura said. "I think we're ready."

"The captain and sensors operator are in the corridor," *Quite Possibly Alien* said.

The hatch whispered open. Ko Shan stepped through. She wore a skinsuit and trailed a full-immersion sensor net's umbilical, making her appear smaller than she already seemed. She flicked her hair back and stepped into the sensor station.

She jacked the umbilical into the sensor console's socket. She double-checked the umbilical's primary connection at the base of her skull and powered the sensor bubble up. She freed the gimbals and ran the unit through its full range of motion before she toed the Release toggle and the field began to fill with a viscous gel.

Goop. Ciarán didn't know what the official name for the oxygenated gel was, but there wasn't enough money in the world to induce him to drown himself in that stuff. They said it was just like breathing air when it filled your lungs, but Ciarán had no desire to find out.

A shadow fell across Ciarán's face. He glanced up.

"Get out of my seat," Agnes Swan said. The Huangxu Eng captain's jaw muscles worked. Her gaze drilled a centimeters-deep hole into Ciarán's forehead.

"I will," Ciarán said. He practically bounced out of the captain's seat.

"Get off my bridge," Swan said.

"I will," Ciarán said. He headed for the hatch.

Maura caught his arm as he passed, speaking in a whisper meant to be heard. "Agnes has anger management issues."

Ciarán pulled his arm free. Only a fool would respond to that. Ciarán had one leg in the corridor when Maura spoke again.

"It's nothing personal, Ciarán."

Ciarán closed the hatch and dogged it. He leaned against the corridor bulkhead.

Maura could believe what she wanted to believe, but Ciarán knew better. He'd seen the look on the Huangxu Eng's face. It was something personal. The problem was that Ciarán had no idea why that could be. He'd been on board for more than a month and he hadn't so much as spoken to the thing.

20

"Will Gag remembers the lab here." A pale white finger tapped against the survey projection.

Ciarán zoomed the display in. "I don't see any evidence."

"Will Gag remembers." He pointed to the rim of a crater, its details lost in shadow. "Will Gag cannot forget."

Ciarán highlighted the crater wall and zoomed in. The display was overscanning. No further detail was available. Ciarán tagged the location and pocketing his hand comp.

"Is there any more you can tell me, Mr. Gagenot?" Ciarán found it difficult to look at the man. His gaze kept returning to the bang stick scars.

"Will Gag can tell you more. But Will Gag would have to kill you."

Ciarán smiled. "Very funny." Ciarán stood. "Thank you, Mr. Gagenot." Ciarán held out his hand.

Gagenot brushed his fingertips against Ciarán's. "Will Gag sees Ciarán mac Diarmuid. Will Gag remembers Ciarán mac Diarmuid." He studied his hand. He rubbed his thumb across his fingertips.

Ciarán started to say something, but there was no point. Their conversation was over.

CARLSBAD TOLD Ciarán to meet him in the boat bay. When Ciarán arrived, he was hustled on board the work-worn longboat.

Konstantine hunched behind the controls. The boat bay iris opened and the longboat shot out. "Welcome to Ambidex, kid."

"That's impossible," Ciarán said. "Ambidex is ten days from Trinity Station."

"Ambidex is less than a day from Trinity Station for us," Konstantine said. "It's an easy run, all downhill this direction."

Ciarán glanced out the viewport. "It doesn't look like much."

"It's even less than it appears," Konstantine said. "You'll see."

Ambidex was nothing more than a space station circling a gas giant. It was a border marker, neutral territory between the League and the Ojinate, with a nasty reputation for lawlessness that many Freeman merchants found useful.

The League and the Ojin Eng had very different ideas of justice, and only those laws common to both legal systems were enforced. You could own slaves on Ambidex but you couldn't bring food onto the tramcars. That's what Pops said. The worst of both worlds.

"It's not illegal to hack into Ojin Eng records on Ambidex," Ciarán said.

"Or League records," Carlsbad said. He studied Ciarán from under his brows.

"So we won't be breaking the law." Ciarán peered out the pilot's viewports. The station grew in size, a tiny dot against the mass of the gas giant beneath it.

This was it. The wider world. Ciarán had really done it. Still, it wasn't that far from Trinity to Ambidex. Barely out of Freeman space.

"You will pay attention now, Ciarán." Carlsbad waited until Ciarán was looking at him. "There will be laws broken. This is no child's play. It is serious business. You do not wish to end your days on an Ambidex work gang. This is something you can earn for the most trivial of offenses."

"I am informed," Ciarán said.

Carlsbad nodded. "Good. Now hand over your weapons. They don't allow so much as a nail file or it's jail time, or worse." Carlsbad held out a personal effects bag, the sort they used in Academy locker rooms and at the Merchant Guild's gym.

"I don't have any weapons."

"This is serious. You will get them back. It is safer without on the station. You'll be searched."

"I don't have any weapons."

"You are a Freeman."

"Right."

"You have weapons."

"I don't, Cargo Master. We weren't raised that way."

"That is absurd. It is unnatural."

"So I've learned," Ciarán said.

"Empty your pockets," Carlsbad said. "Show me everything."

Ciarán had his merchant apprentice license and a ball of augustinite.

Carlsbad made him drop the augustinite into the personal effects bag. The cargo master looked as if he intended to physically search Ciarán. "You don't even carry money?"

"I didn't know we were getting off the vessel." Ciarán would've liked to purchase a badge. One that showed he'd been to Ambidex. He just hadn't expected to have the chance. Or that they'd be going there.

Carlsbad dipped his hand into his pocket. He tossed three Freeman punts to Ciarán. "Keep that in your right pocket, that one there." Carlsbad pointed. "That way when you're robbed, your man won't feel cheated and come back to settle the score."

Konstantine twisted around so that she could look at Ciarán. "Ambidex is pretty rough. Carlsbad's right. You need to think ahead."

"I need to plan to get robbed, and carry money so I don't disappoint the pickpocket?"

"You need to plan for the worst case you can imagine," Carlsbad said. "And act accordingly. Did they teach you nothing in the Academy?"

"They didn't teach that," Ciarán said.

Carlsbad produced a second personal effects bag and began filling it up with weapons and ammunition. A razorgun, a long folding knife, something that looked like a crew license until Carlsbad flicked it open, revealing a razor-sharp blade. He eyeballed the weapon before he flicked it closed with a practiced gesture. His fingers hesitated when he dropped it into the bag along with a garrote and a pair of field-reinforced gloves.

Hardhands. A brand name, but everyone called the gloves that.

The bag swelled further as Carlsbad began to divest his person of nonlethal precautions. "I'm having second thoughts about this field trip."

"I'll be fine." Ciarán watched the station growing in the viewport. He'd be fine. How bad could it be?

Freeman longboats were designed for simultaneous cargo loading and unloading at stations lacking a spindle. When they docked, they did so parallel to the ring, one hatch at the bow for unloading, one hatch at the stern for loading. It cost double the standard mooring rate, and was a nightmare for the pilot on a crowded ring, and a terror for captains with ships moored adjacent to the incoming vessel. But it was the Freeman way. Fast in, fast out, a full hold makes a full purse.

All the best boat handlers were first-families Freemen and their kin. Planet-born Freemen like Ciarán were exempt from small craft training. The Academy claimed they couldn't afford the repair bills.

Ciarán figured that was only part of the truth. Skilled longboat pilots were indispensable to the merchant class, the sort of low-paying, high-status job you had to be born into. Blow-ins and dirtball-born need not apply, not that many wanted to.

League-trained pilots like Konstantine were the rare exceptions. Most were former military and could pilot anything with thrusters given infinite seat time and a bottomless repair budget. That's what Pops Howe said, which was probably the nicest thing he'd ever said about any Leagueman, ever.

The longboat bumped against the docking ring and Konstantine cursed under her breath. Eventually she cleared the control boards, leaving the drive powered up but inactive.

Carlsbad and Ciarán remained belted in while Konstantine clipped on a lifeline and undogged the egress hatch near the bow.

Ciarán peered down the flextube. It didn't look any different than any egress flextube he'd ever seen.

Konstantine worked her way toward the stern and popped the ingress hatch. "You can unbelt now." Returning to the piloting station, she patted Ciarán's shoulder as she passed.

Ciarán unbelted to get a better look out the viewing ports. Other than Trinity Station, he'd never seen a space station up close. In a minute he would enter a foreign station. He'd walk along a merchant arcade lit by a sun that was nothing but a distant light in the sky at home. He wished his dad could see how far he'd come. He wished his mom could witness him following in her footsteps.

A Huangxu Eng ducked beneath the egress hatch coaming and unfolded, the crown of its head nearly touching the deckhead.

It pressed a stunner to Konstantine's neck and fired.

The razor gun in its left hand centered on Carlsbad and settled.

Ciarán moved forward to assist Konstantine just as a second Huangxu Eng ducked through the hatch.

It kneed Ciarán in the ribs and sent him flying against the piloting console.

Konstantine's fingers wiggled, finding purchase on the hatch coaming.

She reached into her pocket. She hadn't bagged her weapons. She was going to do something rash.

"Knew you'd come back here," the first Huangxu Eng said. "Knew it."

"Give it over," the second said. It held out its hand.

Carlsbad reached into his pocket, the look on his face changing from a studied calm to a sick paleness.

All of his weapons were bagged and sealed.

The Huangxu Eng smiled.

Konstantine was on her knees. She'd managed to work her way in front of the ingress hatch. She had a razor gun halfway out of her pocket.

The second Huangxu Eng noticed her.

It aimed a nerve disruptor at her.

Ciarán shouted in erlspout. "Hang on!"

He jammed his forearm through the console handhold and slammed his thumb against the fire-suppression stud.

21

The fire-suppression system dumped the longboat's atmosphere through every possible orifice.

The system wasn't designed to be used when attached to a station's airlock. The overpressure from the far end of the ingress lock hurled Konstantine across the compartment.

The underpressure from the ingress lock provided a convenient exit path for the bulk of the longboat's atmosphere and two Huangxu Eng.

Carlsbad would have followed if Ciarán hadn't snagged his sleeve and held on for dear life.

Ciarán nailed the impact-shielding stud.

The field scythed through both flextubes and the umbilicals linking the longboat to the docking port.

The longboat began to roll.

Carlsbad caught hold of the copilot's seat and belted in by the time Ciarán fished the emergency rebreathers out of the crash cabinet.

The fire-suppression claxon hammered.

Konstantine pried a rebreather out of Ciarán's hand.

She toggled the alarm off.

The incoming comm alert screamed and kept on screaming.

Konstantine elbowed Ciarán out of the way.

His ears popped as the cabin pressure rose. It felt like his eyeballs were on fire.

Konstantine bled from a scalp wound. She brushed Ciarán's fingers away. "Looks worse than it is." Her eyes were bloodshot wounds.

Carlsbad peered out the open egress port, his hand on the actuator.

The pressure in the compartment rose fast, atmosphere pouring out the egress port. "So much for a stealthy entrance."

"I thought you said weapons weren't permitted on Ambidex." Ciarán's hands shook. His ears popped.

"Those weapons weren't on the station." Carlsbad clanged the hatch home and dogged it down.

Konstantine had the longboat under control.

She backed away from the dock and pivoted the vessel to get a view of the gaping hole sheared in the docking ring of Ambidex Station.

The light from the dock in front of them had the flat look of luminaries viewed through vacuum. Warning lights flashed, the blast doors on either side of the blowout ratcheted closed and dogged.

One flextube was gone, the other dangled from a scrap of ragged plasteel.

Ciarán spied what he was looking for.

Two crumpled masses in imperial red and gold. One of them a female. A girl. They'd ended up tangled in an arcing knot of cables when the ruptured ring section had spewed its guts into space.

Ciarán's fingers felt very numb and very cold. The Huangxu Eng weren't moving. "They're on the station now."

"That they are." Carlsbad laughed. "I don't know I've ever seen such a total disregard for safety regulations in all my life." Carlsbad grinned at Ciarán. "I think you might have broken one or two laws of physics."

"Bent them, at least," Konstantine said. "Looks like all of the damage is to the station."

"That's lucky," Carlsbad said.

"I don't think luck was involved," Konstantine said. "He blipped the thrusters to induce a roll. Tore us loose."

"My finger slipped."

It had. He was just lucky. If you called killing two people lucky.

They were people. Ciarán knew that now. Even if they were Huangxu Eng. One was a female. Like Agnes Swan, only younger.

A girl.

He had that flat metallic taste in his mouth that always came seconds after he'd screwed up royally.

This time it didn't feel like it was ever going to go away.

"Now what?" Konstantine said.

Carlsbad eased into the copilot's seat and adjusted the auxiliary console to his liking. "Now we do what we came here for. See if you can get a pinbeam on that transponder pad. With all this excitement we should be in and out in no time."

"If you say so." Konstantine shifted the longboat, aligning its communications array with the primary one where the station's spindle would be, if it had a spindle. The pinbeam locked on.

"No lag at all," Carlsbad said. "Just like being there." He grinned. "But without the stink."

There were rescue crews in hardsuits moving around the torn-up dock.

They hoisted one of the Huangxu Eng up and shoved it into a body bag.

Konstantine fished in the crash cabinet and pulled out a head-wound dressing. She flicked it three times to wake it before she leaned back and draped it across her forehead. It wormed around for a while, getting settled, and then went to work with a wet, sucking sound and a sigh of contentment.

Carlsbad whistled a tune under his breath. He was . . . looser, more casual than when he was on the ship. Like he belonged here, where every move could end in annihilation.

Ciarán felt he was seeing the real Carlsbad for the first time ever. He wasn't sure he liked either version of Carlsbad. Both were scary, but this one didn't seem . . . alien. Ciarán might end up like Carlsbad one day.

Now that idea was terrifying.

Carlsbad's fingers moved madly across the auxiliary console. He looked up and smiled at Ciarán like nothing had happened.

Like Ciarán hadn't just killed two people.

"Come here and I'll show you how to dig through data."

Ciarán lurched for a get-sick bag. If he didn't know the Huangxu Eng language, if he were still an ignorant farm boy, he'd have imagined that the sound the get-sick bag made when he was done was just some random noise.

But he did, and he wasn't. The bag was thanking him for the opportunity to serve. Begging him to let it be of use again.

Every Huangxu Eng–made device did that, no matter how small. Or how big. He pitched the bag in the recycler and took a deep breath.

His mouth tasted like he felt.

Ciarán leaned over Carlsbad's shoulder. "Go on, then. Show me." Maybe if Ciarán knew what he was doing he could avoid mistakes in the future. He'd just killed two people. He couldn't undo that. This wasn't some holo drama.

He'd just killed two people.

For real.

"Pay attention," Carlsbad said. "The sooner we finish, the sooner we're away."

The incoming comm unit screamed and roared. Konstantine let the recorder handle the calls from the station but she was on the circuit the instant Aoife called. Ciarán could only hear Konstantine's half of the conversation.

"Ciarán."

Silence.

"There are extenuating circumstances. I—"

Silence.

"You don't—"

Silence.

Except for the thump of Ciarán's heart against his ribs.

"Merchant Captain, I will."

"Will what?" Carlsbad said.

"Finish your work quickly," Konstantine said. "We're to turn Ciarán over to station authorities. Soonest."

22

"A formality." The Ojin Eng peace officer clamped the restraints tight about Ciarán's wrists. She adjusted the ankle shackles so that he could shuffle along.

He was getting to see Ambidex Station. What was left of it after he'd torn a chunk out of the docking ring.

They marched him down the center of the merchant's arcade, between the shop fronts lining the ring. Drug dens. Houses of ill repute. Gambling parlors. The usual amusements of long-haul spacers. All paled when measured against the spectacle of a Freeman in chains.

Even Aoife nic Cartaí's crew couldn't cause a blowout on a station without repercussions. The deaths of the Huangxu Eng weren't mentioned. Both the League and Ojin Eng were at war with the Huangxu Eng.

Ciarán's march down the arcade drew a crowd, and crowds drew crowds, even on space stations. Perhaps especially on space stations, so that the Ojin Eng peace officer and the flanking League officer had to force their way through a throng, Ciarán in tow.

When the stationmaster demanded that the perpetrator of the offense stand trial, Aoife had declared that as merchant captain any responsibility was hers.

The stationmaster reminded her that Freeman law did not hold at Ambidex, and that she must surrender the person or persons who were physically responsible for the damage. Carlsbad and Konstantine stepped forward to face judgment as well, but Ciarán argued that there was no point in their sharing blame.

The deed was his.

There were no courtrooms on Ambidex, and no lawyers, only judgment and punishment by the stationmaster's command. Trials were held on the arcade, in the central market house.

Ambidex's market house looked just like the Ojin Sector market house on Trinity Station. Little merchant's stalls on skinny wheels, artificially flapping advertising pennants overhead, and narrow aisles between the stalls, all fronting a bandstand that only saw use on holidays.

And at court trials.

The League peace officer yanked Ciarán up the bandstand ladder, trying to make him stumble. Aoife had warned Ciarán about this. Ciarán rushed forward and nearly bowled the smaller man over.

"Sorry," Ciarán said.

The Ojin Eng peace officer smiled and steadied Ciarán. "You are a big one," she said. "When you fall it will be hard on our little Leagueman."

"Bite me." The League peace officer glared at Ciarán.

"I would not tempt him, little man," the Ojin Eng said. "These Freeman pups rarely bark. And once they bite they do not let go."

The stationmaster held court. They'd erected a temporary

throne for her, a gilded, makeshift affair that sagged and creaked in complaint. She was a League citizen, an enormous woman without a hint of augmentation. It was only when Ciarán met her eyes that he could see it: one eye brown, one blue. She was of the ruling class, those with enough money to disguise the cybernetic augmentation that Mrs. Amati and those in the League military wore openly.

Pops said that odd-eyed look was popular a few years back. Kids annoying their parents, acting out. The blue eye wasn't an eye at all, but a wide-spectrum sensor, taking in everything an eye could see and then some.

The brown eye, the human eye, was not amused.

There was an enormous crowd gathered. Ciarán had the weird idea that their combined mass might be enough to unbalance the station. There were certainly more people here to watch his humiliation than he had ever seen in one place before. His palms sweated but he didn't dare wipe them for fear the gesture would make him appear guilty.

"Do you swear to tell the truth, the whole truth, and nothing but the truth?" the stationmaster said.

"I don't," Ciarán said.

He didn't know the truth. No one did. Freemen didn't swear false oaths. Not even Freemen in chains swore to a lie.

The stationmaster stared at him with her ill-matched eyes.

"Did you blow out a section of my docking ring?"

"I didn't," Ciarán said.

"Who did, then?"

"Two Huangxu Eng who attempted to steal Merchant Captain Aoife nic Cartaí's longboat."

"Intruders you let on board."

"Who forced their way on board. From your station."

This was the argument Aoife had devised. That it was the station's fault for leaving their ring unguarded, for allowing the

Huangxu Eng a base of piracy from which to launch an attack on her longboat and crew. Anything after that was self-defense, and permitted under both Ojin Eng and League laws.

"They weren't *from* my station," the stationmaster said. "They weren't ever *in* my station. Arrived in a vessel. Softsuits, lock to lock. Hiding outside the docking ring. Creeping into your longboat's flextube locks prior to pressurization. Not once did they breathe my air."

"At no time were any of Aoife nic Cartaí's crew on the station. I was not on the station," Ciarán said. "Therefore you have no jurisdiction, and Freeman law prevails."

"Once those locks opened, your vessel was attached to my station. That makes it my air. Your responsibility. My law."

So far the trial had proceeded as Aoife said it would. Ciarán was supposed to nod and accept a misdemeanor conviction, and Aoife would pay the fine. Then they'd be on their way. No harm done.

Except the stationmaster's logic was flawed. And Ciarán didn't want any kind of conviction on his record. He'd committed a crime—crimes, really—but not the one he was on trial for. It was wrong. Unjust. He couldn't just roll over, even if that was what Aoife wanted him to do. There was principle at stake. Honor.

The stationmaster was wrong.

"If by attaching to your station I fall under your law, then the Huangxu Eng fell under your law. By failing to enforce the law, by allowing pirates to operate attached to your station, it follows that the fault for this incident is not mine, but yours.

"The initial crime was committed by the Huangxu Eng. But the subsequent damage to the station was ultimately caused, not by my response to this crime, but by the stationmaster's own negligence in policing. Had the stationmaster done her job, no damage to the station would have occurred."

The crowd grew silent.

Ciarán heard the stationmaster's uniform shift against the hard metal of her chair.

He breathed in the rank smell of the crowd.

The stationmaster stared at Ciarán in silence.

No one spoke.

Sweat ran down Ciarán's face. He wanted to wipe it away.

The reek of Ambidex was every bit as bad as Carlsbad implied. He didn't want to look like a mouth-breather, but every inhaled breath through his nose made him want to spew.

Still the stationmaster stared.

Stared at him.

And stared.

The stationmaster clapped her hands together. "Agreed."

Ciarán didn't like the way the stationmaster smiled.

"From this moment forth I accept responsibility for policing all vessels attached to my station. My staff shall inspect each vessel attached to certify it meets Ambidex's standards of safety and to ensure the crew and cargo are in compliance with station law."

The stationmaster stood. The crowd began to thin rapidly. Some of those departing were running. Many of those running were Freeman merchants.

"Well argued, young man. You are acquitted. Case adjourned."

The stationmaster motioned for her peace officers. They moved forward, leaving Ciarán shackled. He crabbed his way down the ladder.

"Great job, Plowboy." Seamus mac Donnocha punched Ciarán on the arm to get his attention. "You've singlehandedly closed Ambidex to Freeman trade."

"Seamus?" Ciarán shifted his shackled feet carefully. It really was Seamus. On Ambidex.

Ciarán's face felt like it was on fire. Now everyone would know. Ciarán mac Diarmuid blew out the docking ring on Ambidex. Ciarán mac Diarmuid was handcuffed and trussed like a lamb. Ciarán mac Diarmuid murdered a pair of Huangxu Eng. It didn't take long for Ciarán to fit in with pirates. He could hear Seamus telling Macer that.

Macer telling his dad.

Macer's dad telling Ciarán's dad.

Ciarán swallowed. "What are you doing on Ambidex, Seamus?"

"I was learning how to trade," Seamus said. "Now I'll be learning how to pack fast. Damn, Ciarán, do you know what you've done?"

"I defended my shipmates," Ciarán said. He had to believe that. That had to be true.

"No one cares about your dead Huangxu," Seamus said. "But what you did just now. No Freeman merchant is going to let the locals on board for a 'safety inspection.' The bribes and payoffs would eat us alive. Your stupid arguments effectively closed Ambidex to Freeman trade."

The Ojin Eng peace officer returned and unshackled Ciarán. She pressed a League coin into his palm, and then another.

A week's wages for a merchant apprentice.

She winked at Ciarán. "You've made me a very rich woman." She turned to Seamus. "Run along, merchant boy, and tell your master I will inspect his vessel first."

Seamus backed away. He pointed at Ciarán. "You did this, Plowboy." He started to run.

Aoife waded through the departing crowd. She did not look happy.

"In the future"—she tapped Ciarán on the chest when his eyes wandered to Seamus's receding back—"follow the script." She handed Ciarán a Trinity/Ambidex badge.

Carlsbad sauntered up. "I'd hang on to that." Carlsbad pointed at the badge. "Bound to be a collector's item."

"Let's go." Ciarán took a step but Carlsbad caught his arm.

"Not yet." Carlsbad pressed a vibraknife into Ciarán's palm.

"I thought weapons were banned on Ambidex." Ciarán watched his own fingers wrap around the unfamiliar hilt.

"The merchant captain has filed an *Intent to Cure* against the stationmaster," Carlsbad said. "Ambidex likely won't recognize a Freeman challenge, but until we know for certain we need to proceed as if the merchant captain's filing is active."

"Her filing of intent to kill the stationmaster."

"Intent to cure a breach of custom and insult to ship's honor. The killing part is optional and entirely up to the stationmaster."

"That's crazy."

"Your dockside lawyering forced her hand. A merchant captain can't ignore a stationmaster's gross negligence toward her ship and crew."

"So you're saying I caused this?"

"I'm not *saying* anything. I'm *explaining* what to say, should station authorities mention the weapon in your hand."

"Here is Mrs. Amati now," Aoife said. "And Ko Shan."

"Now we might get you off the station alive," Carlsbad said. "Stay behind Amati."

THE LONGBOAT WAS DOCKED on the far side of the ring. Angry glares followed the crew of *Quite Possibly Alien*, but none attempted to stop them. Aoife stared at the peace officer moving her way, who gestured at the overseer's rod beneath Aoife's belt. Aoife powered the terror weapon up and the peace officer stepped back, subvocalizing something to her implant. Every

League citizen had an implant, and every implant was a communications node in itself.

"She's called for backup." Mrs. Amati tapped her skull behind the right ear. "Stationmaster told her to step aside." Amati grinned.

"Well, your man-sized *ciaróg* isn't stepping aside." Carlsbad nodded toward a skinny man in Truxton orange utilities headed their way. He wore a merchant's ring on his right hand.

"Aengus Roche," Aoife said. The way she said it made Ciarán worry for Merchant Roche's skin.

A dozen more in Truxton orange joined him, a rough-looking crew, Seamus with them.

Maura and Hess waited by the longboat's ingress flextube three docks down. Guarding it. Maura said something to Hess and then she began trotting toward the disturbance centered around Ciarán.

Roche's crew spread out in a widening arc.

Aoife held up her hand.

Carlsbad tugged on Ciarán's sleeve. "Slow down, and don't do anything innovative."

Ciarán nodded. They'd come to a halt, surrounded by Truxton crew.

"Unless you have to," Carlsbad said. "Then do it hard and final, and run at flank speed for the longboat. Don't look back."

Roche stood toe-to-toe with Aoife, towering over her. He'd moved in close, trying to intimidate her, trying to force her to crane her neck to meet his gaze.

That was a standard move they taught in the Academy, a procedure right out of first-term Negotiation. Ciarán wouldn't have had the guts to try it on Aoife. Roche was misreading the situation. Aoife nic Cartaí didn't have her merchant's face on.

She was wearing her *Quite Possibly Alien* face.

"Your brat has ruined my business," Roche said. "I am owed." He crossed his arms on his chest.

"Step aside," Aoife said. "I have business elsewhere."

"You have business here and now. I demand restitution. Yes. I demand it."

"Step aside, Merchant. You are forewarned."

"Your she-bitch of a mother isn't here to protect you, yes. I am owed and you will pay, yes. This is so. Nic Cartaí will pay." His face twisted into a snarling shape that didn't belong on a man. "Yes. She will pay."

Aoife took a step to his right.

Roche grabbed her arm.

Aoife's fingers danced. A blue tendril licked around Roche's wrist.

His face turned a sickly pale. The monomolecular whip of an overseer's rod, still in its containment field encircled his wrist, just below the cuff of his Truxton orange utilities.

Should Aoife move her finger, or her finger slip, that blue field would fall and the whip would slice through Roche's wrist before he could blink.

"Ciarán," Aoife said. "You will come here." Her voice was very precise. Like a machine.

Ciarán pushed forward. His gaze met Seamus's.

Seamus took a step back when he saw the vibraknife in Ciarán's fist.

"Merchant Apprentice, you will recount the merchant's errors." Aoife's gaze didn't leave Roche's.

"I will." Ciarán licked his lips.

Aoife had a crazed look about her. Ciarán's gaze was glued on the thin line around Roche's wrist. He chose his words carefully. "Addressing blame to one of the crew, not the merchant captain. Creating a public spectacle of personal disagreements. Attempting intimidation of a merchant or merchant captain. Laying hands on another. These are the ones I noted."

Maura elbowed her way to Ciarán's side. "You're forgetting the worst one." She grinned at Roche. "Insulting a merchant captain's mother."

"Indeed," Aoife said.

Maura took a step closer to Aoife. "That was a joke, Aoife."

"Was it?" Aoife said. "I would like to see him say those words to her face. That would be a laugh."

"You'd have to let him live to do that," Maura said. "There's been enough killing here."

"He has wet himself," Ko Shan said. "Humorous endings are few and far between. Tales of vengeance are no novelty."

A dark stain had spread across the front of Merchant Roche's utilities.

Ciarán wanted to check his own trousers. The hunger on Merchant Captain Aoife nic Cartaí's face reminded him of Wisp at dinnertime.

"That's true." Carlsbad chuckled. "Such a tale will . . . spread. It is enough, Merchant Captain."

Aoife blinked. The whip retracted. She blinked again and shoved the butt of her overseer's rod into Roche's chest. He stepped backward and nearly tripped. His men watched and kept their distance.

"No it is not." Aoife aimed the overseer's rod at Roche. "The moment we are gone he will contrive against us."

"Creating a public spectacle, Aoife," Maura said. "I'll deal with it if he becomes a problem. He's making a puddle, and it's sort of disgusting. Now let's go."

Seamus wasn't watching Ciarán as Maura herded the merchant captain and her crew toward the longboat. His gaze was frozen on the vibraknife in Ciarán's hand.

Just the sort of weapon a pirate would carry. That was what

Seamus's face said. It wasn't just funny stories that spread. It was tragic ones as well. In both cases it didn't matter if the stories were true or not. All they needed was enough truth to hold together.

Ciarán didn't want to know what Macer would think when he heard the news.

Maura shoved Ciarán up the ingress flextube, hard on his heels. "Nice job, Ciarán. Now it isn't just Aoife's family and mine that hate us. You've managed to blister Truxton's paint too."

Ciarán stopped and Maura slammed into his back. When Ciarán turned, Maura's face was centimeters from his. She wrapped her fingers around his neck and bent his face toward hers. When her lips touched his, Ciarán's heart stopped.

She laughed and whispered in his ear. "Seriously. Nice job."

"I—"

Maura held her finger to Ciarán's lips. "Sshhh. A pirate would kiss me back."

Ciarán licked his lips. "I'm not a pirate." His palms were sweating again.

"You sure look like one from where I'm standing."

"Stand someplace else, then."

Maura shoved past him up the flextube. "I will, Merchant Apprentice. Do you think it will make any difference?"

Probably not. Ciarán ran the tip of his tongue across his lips, the parts that Maura's lips had touched. He paced up the flextube after her.

Ciarán dogged the ingress hatch and belted in just as Konstantine dropped the first umbilical tying them to the dock.

Maura elbowed Ko Shan. "Doesn't Ciarán look like a pirate?"

"Pirate-in-training. He holds a vibraknife like it wants to ravage him."

"Maybe it does. Can you blame it?"

Ko Shan dropped her gaze. "Not really."

Aoife swung into the seat next to Ciarán. She did not look happy. "You're going to have to learn how to defend your comrades in a more conventional manner, Merchant Apprentice. No more improvising."

"I will, Merchant Captain."

"You've been lucky so far. It gets harder from here on out."

"I don't doubt that."

Aoife rested her palm on his bicep. She closed her eyes. "Nice. No more doubts. We break orbit for Gallarus Four in the morning. In the afternoon you will present yourself to Mrs. Amati for instruction in . . . self-defense." She patted his sleeve, and scooted down in the shock webbing, eyes closed.

"What about in the evening?" Ciarán said.

"You'll have a date with the autodoc," Mrs. Amati said. "If you live." She flexed the augmented machinery that passed for her right fist.

Ciarán swallowed. "No, really."

"Gallarus is as hard as it gets," Amati said. "You need to be ready. Ready or dead. You don't want to be taken alive." She laughed, but it wasn't a pretty sound. Part human, part machine, and fully terrifying. "Don't eat a big lunch."

"I won't." The way Ciarán's stomach felt he wouldn't be eating for a good long time.

23

The crew of *Quite Possibly Alien* unbelted and headed for their stations within minutes of the longboat passing through the boat bay iris. Once near the boat bay hatch, Aoife placed her hand on Ciarán's sleeve and told him to wait as the others went to their duties.

"See Mr. Gagenot in the mess," Aoife said. "Get some food in you and clean up. There's a mandatory crew meeting in an hour. All will be revealed."

"I'm ready to help now," Ciarán said. "What should I do?"

"Get some food, Get the stink of Ambidex off you. Get some rest and get to the mess in an hour."

"But—"

"You are free and we are leaving Ambidex under our own power. Maura will jump the ship into the star's photosphere. No vessel will be able to follow us. You are safe, Ciarán. Word of a merchant."

"I'm not worried about myself. I want to help."

"You can help by doing as I ask. You've been through a lot, and all at once. If it hasn't hit you yet it will. You might very well have died, or spent the rest of your life on an Ambidex chain gang. Not to mention that you were forced to take a life."

"Two lives."

"In self-defense."

"Should that make it feel better?"

"It should. But in my experience it doesn't. So I am asking you. Ordering you, if I must."

"Eat. Bathe. Rest. Animal functions that don't require any thought."

"Precisely."

"What if I can't stop thinking?"

"About the lives lost?"

"Their lives weren't lost. I ended them." Pretending otherwise was cowardly.

"As you say." She stared at him, her face an impassive mask. Eventually she spoke. "Do you think it would make you a better person if you could stop thinking about them?"

"I don't."

"Then perhaps you might respect their memory by considering them as equals."

"I—"

"They are as children in the story you tell yourself. Not responsible for their actions. You hold yourself accountable. This does not honor their lives but spits upon them. They are less than you. You regret your actions yet you exalt in your arrogance. How dare you?"

"You're wrong. I don't—"

"Am I wrong? Suppose we were to come upon a sleeping mong hu, and I say to you, 'There is a sleeping mong hu. Go poke it in the eye with your finger.' What do you suppose would happen?"

"I—"

"That is a rhetorical question. We are both adults, and we

both know the answer, and it would not be, 'I might get a scratch on my finger.' You would most certainly die, and whose fault would it be? Mine, because I sent you? The mong hu's because he ate you?"

"Is that also a rhetorical question?"

"One of us knows that it is. The other is a merchant apprentice, and I would hear his answer."

"The fault would be mine."

"So, even a farm boy from the back of beyond knows this truth."

"I do."

"I remind you of this, not to insult you, but to impress upon you the gulf in our experience. It is not simply that I am master and you an apprentice. We are from different worlds. I did not realize this at first. We are both Freemen. We share a culture. A history. On Trinity Station. On Trinity Surface. On Unity. On Midpoint. Across the vastness of Freeman space we share a name. We call ourselves, 'the People.' We are one, and we are not alone. Do you know who told me this? Who explained this to me, and when?"

"I don't."

"My mother, upon learning I had killed a man. Several men and several women, in truth. These were not Huangxu Eng deaths, but fellow Freemen. And it was not my actions that killed them. Rather, it was my inability to act that resulted in their deaths. My *unwillingness* to act."

"How could anyone blame you for that?"

"*I* blamed me for it. Others excused me from blame due to my lack of experience. My father raised me, and he is a banker. I don't know if he has ever been off Trinity Station. I certainly hadn't been prior to the events I relate. But I wanted to be like my mother. Like the great Nuala nic Cartaí. And I am now, I suppose.

"When she said all of this to me, I thought she was rebuking me for my failure to protect my comrades. That she was piling onto the remorse I already felt with another burden, her disappointment in me. Does it feel this way to you? That in addition to the guilt you already feel, I am chastising you for failing me in some way?"

"Somewhat, I guess."

Aoife nic Cartaí stared at him.

"Okay, definitely. It does feel that way."

"Good. Then you are ready to hear what she told me next."

"Which is?"

"That there are two worlds, and a portal between them. In one world we are daughters and sons, mothers and fathers, neighbors and kin. In this world we know each other, and understand one another's aspirations and motives. It is a shorthand world, one where much is agreed and implied. Its foundations are custom and contract, and in recent years, law. This world is a *made* thing and its boundaries known. In this world we *may be* the People.

"Yet there is another world, an older world, where we are none of these settled things. All is in flux. We move through this world and we are very much alone. It is a longhand world, where every contract is hammered out anew, every term argued over and defined. Its foundations are tooth and claw, unchanged since the beginning of time. This world is a *discovered* thing, and its boundaries not simply unknown, but unknowable. In this world we *must be* the People of the Mong Hu."

Aoife crossed her arms and stared at him.

"And?"

"She was so angry. That is all she said."

"But it helped you. When she said this."

"It helped me think about something other than the people I had killed."

"So it's a trick."

"I thought it was. Then I thought it was a metaphor. Then I forgot about it."

"Forgot about it for how long?"

"Years."

"But you finally understood what she meant."

"I didn't," Aoife said. "Not until I watched you today."

"On Ambidex."

"Only moments ago. When you stepped off the longboat. You ran your fingers along the bulkhead, and swept your gaze across the faces of your crewmates, and for the tiniest fraction of a second, you smiled. I doubt you noticed yourself."

"I didn't notice."

"You lack sufficient perspective."

"Are you going to tell me what she meant?"

"The meaning will come to you."

"But—"

"In an hour, Merchant Apprentice. I will expect you alert, presentable, and a good deal less odorous."

Aoife nic Cartaí headed for the boat bay hatch. "In an hour, Ciarán. All will be revealed."

ENGINEER HESS HAD RIGGED a holo tank in the mess and the crew gather around. Ciarán was freshly scrubbed, and he'd eaten as much as he could stomach. He didn't get much rest though because he'd dawdled so long at the table. The merchant captain was right, he did feel better now that he was full and clean, and the act of attending to routine activities had taken his mind off things.

Carlsbad stood and spoke. "We gathered a great deal of data while connected to the Erl and Ojin systems on Ambidex. The superluminal node in the system was active and open, and we were able to collect data from Ambidex to Columbia in the League and between Ambidex and Kyo in the Ojinate. Our search encompassed all records pertaining to Contract space in general as well as specific records regarding the failure of any superluminal nodes in the vicinity of Contract space. We also performed a broad search for weapons laboratories. This search was blocked by Erl security systems. A similar search of Ojin systems appeared undetected and netted positive results. At the merchant apprentice's suggestion we conducted a search of both systems for records pertaining to Bosditch Trading and the vessel *Last Stand*. These also netted positive results."

"So basically you found some stuff and only got caught once," Hess said.

"We weren't 'caught'," Carlsbad said. "One search was detected and blocked. And even had we been back-traced, any footprints would have led, not to us, but to Truxton's *Golden Parachute*."

"That's a weird coincidence," Konstantine said. "Isn't that Merchant Roche's vessel?"

"It is Roche's vessel, and no coincidence. More a matter of balancing accounts."

"Merchant Roche and the first families have history," Aoife said. "He maintains a particular dislike of all things nic Cartaí. He claims my mother blocked his promotion to merchant captain."

"Why does he say that?" Amati asked.

"Because it's true," Maura said. "The man's a blow-in and a misogynist, and he forced himself on a crewman and got away with it."

"Allegedly," Aoife said. "And that is waking the dead, Navigator."

"Well he isn't allegedly a blow-in," Maura said. "Or allegedly a woman-hater."

"Moving on, Maura. Carlsbad, please continue."

"Merchant Captain, I will," Carlsbad said.

"First, to dispel any thoughts of coincidence. It is standard security practice to select a plausible but false source address to foil any back-trace. There are some potential consequences for the owner of this false address. Matters of inconvenience, principally. With *Golden Parachute* in-system I admit the choice was not chance, but mine."

"So you're saying you picked Roche as your sinboat instead of jacking some rando," Hess said.

Carlsbad glanced at Amati.

"That's what he's saying, Erik."

"Gotcha," Hess said. "Well?"

Carlsbad stared at Hess. "Well, what?"

"What'd you find out?"

Carlsbad glanced at Aoife.

"You can tell them," she said.

"We found that there is indeed a war on in Contract space. More properly a slave rebellion."

"That rots," Maura said. "Slaves don't have any money."

"They might if they won," Konstantine said.

Maura snorted. "When has that ever happened?"

"It's happened." Ciarán flicked his earlobe, where, by tradition, all Freemen wore the pendant spire, a single earring forged from a broken link of a slaver's chain. Most Freemen on Trinity Station wore the spire, and amongst long-haul spacers the practice was virtually universal.

Growing up he hadn't worn the spire because it got in the way of farm work. Once he arrived on Trinity Station he didn't wear it because his was fake, a lookalike his dad had hammered out of space junk he'd grubbed out of a neighbor's field.

He didn't know why Maura and the merchant captain didn't

wear the spire. As daughters of the First Families they were both direct descendants of the rebellion's leaders.

"Okay, when has a slave rebellion ever succeeded *lately*?" Maura said.

"It hasn't," Agnes Swan said. "And I find it hard to believe it could now. Huangxu are engineered for associative devotion. To kin. To clade. To the Emperor. Each level of devotion as autonomic as breathing."

"Maybe they screwed up with this batch. Anyway, that explains why we're going to Gallarus," Amati said. "Are you sure about this, Merchant Captain?"

"I was not," Aoife said. "Until I heard the rest of Carlsbad's report.

"What's on Gallarus?" Ciarán said.

"Guns," Amati said. "The kind that are gene-keyed for Huangxu use."

"They're cheap because only Huangxu can use them," Maura said.

"Doubly cheap on Gallarus," Ko Shan said. "Prices even a slave can afford."

"Because they're stolen," Maura said.

"Stolen from whom?" Ciarán said.

"From *whomever* stopped there last," Maura said. "It's not a good place to do business."

"It is not," Carlsbad said. "So it struck me as odd that the data showed one vessel visiting Gallarus space repeatedly."

"Why do you have Gallarus traffic data?" Hess said. "It's nowhere near Contract space."

"I asked the merchant apprentice to set up the back-trace avoidance protocol. He did so admirably."

Maura grinned. "Except he . . ."

"Accidentally redirected *Golden Parachute*'s incoming and outgoing communications through our system."

"The merchant apprentice is a pirate mastermind," Ko Shan said.

Ciarán felt his face burn. "It was a mistake."

"But a fortuitous one," Carlsbad said. "It appears that Merchant Roche is visiting Gallarus routinely, presumably to purchase Huangxu-keyed weapons. The merchant's schedule is regular, and we can predict when he is next to arrive in Gallarus space. If we were to arrive before him—"

"We could grab his cargo out from under him," Maura said. "I like it."

"Are we just messing with a yob we don't like?" Hess said. "Or do we have a real reason to go there?

"The weapons would make profitable cargo, assuming our intelligence is correct," Aoife said. "And amassing a large quantity elsewhere would take time and effort. Time we do not have."

"But wait, there's more," Maura said.

Aoife frowned. "Why would you say that?"

"Because I know that look."

"Carlsbad," Aoife said. "Please continue."

"I will. According to Ojin Diplomatic Service records—"

"Hang on,' Amati said. "We hacked Ojin Intelligence?"

Ciarán felt his ears burn. "I didn't know."

"Turns out the Ojin Diplomatic Service doesn't just catalog ball-gown designers and luxury goods suitable for visiting potentates," Konstantine said.

"And you expected to find these in Contact space because?" Swan said.

"Because Ciarán is thorough, and conscientious," Ko Shan said. "Because these are persons, places, or things that fall under his area of expertise as merchant apprentice. Because the merchant captain asked him to know. Because he hoped to avoid a repeat of his previous performance."

"Dang," Hess said. "We need to start calling him the Dread Merchant Apprentice."

"Or the Red Merchant Apprentice," Natsuko said.

"Enough," Aoife said. "Carlsbad, continue."

"Merchant Captain, I will." Carlsbad's gaze washed across Ciarán's face and returned to his notes. "Ojin Intelligence reports that a single Freeman merchant vessel departed Contract space several months prior to our accepting the contract from an individual named Adderly. This vessel, Bosditch Trading's *Last Stand*, was contracted to an individual also named Adderly. Twelve FFEs of miscellaneous cargo were listed for deep space transfer, the handoff to occur in the void between Sizemore and Prix Canada."

"Why was Ojin Intelligence monitoring Contract space?" Swan asked.

"They weren't, Ship's Captain," Carlsbad said. "They were monitoring the void between Sizemore and Prix Canada. A debris field was reported by an Ojin ore hauler forced to make repairs in the void. This incident report caused the monitoring beacon's sensor logs to be pulled and examined. The Diplomatic Service worked backwards from there."

"That makes even less sense."

"It does, unless one also knows that a vessel of interest is reported to frequent the void."

"Do we know this vessel?" Amati asked.

"We do. We know it, but that is not the most curious part. The sensor logs showed that there were not two vessels at *Last Stand's* handoff, but three. All three vessels arrived with their transponders disabled. Upon system exit two vessels engaged their transponders an instant before their Templeman drives would have obscured the codes.

The cargo master kicked the holo tank alive. It showed long-range visuals of three vessels in close proximity. Two of the vessels were Freeman merchant vessels. The third appeared to be a second-epoch League survey vessel.

"That's weird," Maura said. "It looks like us."

"One presumes this is the vessel *Sudden Fall of Darkness*, a hulk discovered gutted and drifting in the Alexandrine. Refitted and recommissioned by parties unknown."

"And that's the vessel the Ojin were interested in," Amati said.

"Unfortunately not," Carlsbad said.

Workers were offloading FFEs from one Freeman vessel and loading them onto the other. They were doing it manually, in hardsuits, which meant only one thing. The captain of the first vessel wasn't cooperating.

"Pirates," Ko Shan said.

The mast of the first vessel suddenly ruptured, workers and containers tumbling free.

Ciarán felt the temperature in the mess hall drop, heard the hiss of breath as the reality of what they were watching hit home. He'd seen the replay before, on the longboat in Ambidex. The others hadn't.

The hardsuited workers redoubled their efforts, recovering all but one of the FFEs. Both undamaged vessels boosted to subliminal velocity at flank speed, their vectors diverging rapidly.

One Templeman drive engaged, and then another, and then a blinding flash of light abruptly terminated the sensor feed.

"Crew compliment on the *Last Stand*?" Amati asked.

"Unknown," Carlsbad said. "One presumes not a family ship."

"But we don't know for sure," Maura said.

"We don't, Navigator," Carlsbad said.

"Run it again," Swan said.

Maura shouted. "What for!"

"Because Carlsbad stated that the transponder codes of the fleeing vessels were captured. And I was distracted."

"Calm yourself, Navigator," Carlsbad said.

"I am calm!"

"Will Gag sees Maura Kavanagh," Gagenot said. "Maura Kavanagh is not calm."

Maura rose out of her seat.

Ko Shan spoke. "Maura—"

"Will Gag is not calm," Gagenot said.

"None of us are," Amati said. "You don't have to be a born-Freeman to feel outraged. Maybe you feel it more, being one of the tribe, but if you think we're all sitting here thinking, 'Oh, what a shame for Merchant Bosditch and his kin, let's move on,' you are mistaken."

"I know that," Maura said. "But at least your family doesn't *demand* you chase down the villains and make them pay. I don't want to know who they are. I don't want to do something about it."

"You will wish to know," Carlsbad said. "And you will wish to do something about it." He ran the sensor record back to an instant before the explosive failure of *Last Stand*'s Templeman drive.

The two surviving vessels tracked toward opposite edges of the sensor's field of view. A transponder blinked on and Carlsbad paused the display.

"*Golden Parachute*," Maura said. "Okay, that's different. We need to have a word with Merchant Roche."

"Outbound," Carlsbad said. "Not an hour after our encounter with him. No forwarding route listed in the Ambidex registry."

"We do not know where he is going," Ko Shan said.

"But we know where he'll be," Natsuko said. "And when."

"This smells like a setup," Amati said.

"It does have an odor," Hess said. "To quote the cargo master."

"If it is a setup, it is a very elaborate one," Ko Shan said.

"It only seems like a setup because it ticks a pallet of boxes," Maura said. "We get the guns to run to Adderly. Check. We get to sell Adderly info on what happened to her previous gunrunner. Check. We get to pull one over on Merchant Roche. Check. We get to squeeze Merchant Roche and either hold him to account for *Last Stand*'s death, or beat the location of his coconspirators out of him. Or both. Check."

"We also get to help a planet of slaves throw off the yoke of oppression," Ko Shan said.

"You know I'm neutral on that," Maura said. "But okay. It's a setup."

"Definitely," Ko Shan said.

"What of the other vessel?" Swan said.

"In a moment," Aoife nic Cartaí said. "I would have my apprentice's opinion. Do you think this is a setup, Ciarán?"

"I don't think it's a setup," Ciarán said. "I know it."

Carlsbad ran the sensor playback forward a few hundred milliseconds, where the second vessel's transponder blinked alive and *Quite Possibly Alien* disappeared from the sensors.

"They're running our transponder code," Swan said.

"And a Templeman drive," Maura said.

Ciaran hadn't noticed the drive signature earlier. But he'd watched the faces of his shipmates when Bosditch's *Last Stand* had flared out of existence. They were as repulsed as he'd been when he'd first witnessed *Last Stand*'s death spasm explode across the longboat's communications display.

"It appears someone is impersonating us," Carlsbad said.

"We can't have that," Hess said.

"Indeed," Aoife nic Cartaí said. "We cannot."

24

W hat would have been a simple days-long jump for a vessel with a Templeman drive took over two months for *Quite Possibly Alien* to negotiate. By the time they arrived at Gallarus Four, *Quite Possibly Alien* had dived into and out of a half-dozen stars and Ciarán had been beaten senseless as many times by Mrs. Amati.

On a good day Mrs. Amati would settle for chasing Ciarán all over the inside and outside of the vessel, hunting him like one would an animal. She seemed to derive a perverse pleasure from this endless pastime.

Mrs. Amati said a blowgun was the perfect weapon for shipboard use. It was silent, could kill or incapacitate, and was easy to conceal. It didn't have a power signature to track, and unless you were stupid enough to feed it compressed air, couldn't accidentally breach a hull. It was also fun to use, invisible to most security scans, and could be worked one-handed. So long as you were still pumping air, a blowgun had all the power it needed. A blowgun was the ultimate weapon, and a blowgun hunt the ultimate test of the three immortal sisters: stealth, stamina, and speed.

Ciarán didn't know about all that. What he did know was that a hunt didn't end until Mrs. Amati had launched a sleepy dart from her blowgun and rendered Ciarán "dead."

He might as well have been dead; he slept so soundly that even Wisp's insistent padding failed to wake him.

Wisp and Mrs. Amati did not get along. The two avoided each other just as Ciarán avoided *Quite Possibly Alien*'s captain, Agnes Swan. Ciarán would on occasion find the Huangxu Eng watching Mrs. Amati and Ciarán battling in low-G, a grim smile on her lips.

Ciarán was improving; he could defend himself now, but he continued to disappoint Mrs. Amati. A strong offense might indeed be the best defense for her. Ciarán didn't have the stomach for it, and he didn't want to become the sort of person who did. It was one thing to ship with pirates and quite another to become one.

Ciarán was sipping caife in the mess, dreading another punishing bout with the ship's armsman, when Mrs. Amati swung into the seat next to him.

"Get your merchant apprentice kit on," Mrs. Amati said. "No playtime today, Speedy."

Ciarán placed his mug on the table. "Can't anyone just call me Ciarán?"

"Too hard to pronounce," Amati said. "Seriously, we're going down to the planet to buy trade goods. The merchant captain expects us each turned out in our finest."

"Oh." Ciarán popped out of his seat. "I'd best be—"

Amati grabbed his arm in her mechanized hand. "These are bad people we're dealing with. Bring a weapon."

"I don't have any weapons." Ciarán had divested himself of Carlsbad's vibraknife as quickly as possible. It made him feel like a pirate, and besides, one that size was illegal in most civilized ports.

Wisp padded into the mess and stopped when she spied Mrs. Amati.

"Kee-ron," Mrs. Amati said. "Keer-on." Her brow wrinkled. "Screw it. Speedy, if that thing's not a weapon then neither am I." She eyeballed Wisp.

"She's not a thing," Ciarán said.

"Neither is Agnes Swan, but that's what you see when you look at her," Amati said. "Tell me I'm lying."

"I don't see what this has to do with—"

"Shut up. You Freemen can think what you think, but I've fought the big brother to your little friend, and I'm telling you, to me it's a thing, and it's a weapon. That's what it was made for. I had to learn how to be dangerous. It was born knowing."

Wisp circled wide of Mrs. Amati, her head lowered, ears flat, her tail down. She began to adjust her coloring to match her surroundings.

"Could be, but—"

Amati tapped her augmented eyepiece. "Don't you see what it's doing?"

"You make her nervous."

"It's mutual," Amati said. "She's dumping heat through her paws into the deck. By the time she gets behind me I won't be able to pick her out from the background. She's got some blasted camouflage organs built into her, and pretty soon I won't be able to see her in the visible-light spectrum unless she moves. That's not a cat, Speedy. That's a weapon that looks like a cat. Have you looked closely at those claws?"

"They're sharp, but they're not—"

"They're some sort of blasted crystal. Just like the teeth. I've had my arm torn off by one of those things, and once is enough." Amati swiveled in her seat, keeping an eye on Wisp.

"She's my friend."

"So am I. And the merchant captain's bringing me as her weapon. I can't guarantee I can look after both of you with these folks. Can't you just do what I ask without arguing for once?"

"The merchant captain has an overseer's rod. She knows how to use it."

"And she's bringing me. What does that tell you?"

"That maybe I'd be safer staying here. Maybe we all are."

"No maybe about it. But we signed on to do a job, and it's time you and your pet began earning your keep."

"We're really going down to the planet?"

"That's a given. Getting back up to the ship will be the problem."

"We'll go. Wisp and I."

"Then get dressed for war. Both of you. And get that spare vibraknife from Carlsbad and wear it where it shows."

Ciarán swallowed. "I will, Armsman."

"See. Wasn't that easy? Next time we won't need this conversation, will we, Kee-ron?"

"We won't."

If they lived to see a next time.

If Mrs. Amati was worried, that wasn't a sure thing.

Not by a long shot.

WISP SEEMED to know something was up. She flopped onto Ciarán's bunk and let him comb her, fluffing her ruff out, even rolling over so Ciarán could work out the knotted fur on her belly. It took a lot longer than when she'd been Plumpkin, and a kitten, and for once Ciarán didn't need the scarred hardhands and field-reinforced gauntlets he'd learned to wear when he'd first found her on Trinity Station dock, hiding in a battered FFE.

He wore them anyway.

Hardhands were a weapon. Carlsbad carried them. That made them a weapon.

Finished with Wisp, Ciarán slipped the hardhands into the pockets of his best dark-blue utilities. He pinned his merchant apprentice's pips onto the collar and checked his appearance in the mirror. He didn't look like a pirate. Not yet.

He adjusted the blood-red sash that Carlsbad had provided. He latched the vibraknife into place. Vibrasword was more like it. Carlsbad claimed he couldn't find the smaller weapon he'd pressed into Ciarán's palm on Ambidex Station.

Ciarán looked in the mirror again. Now he looked like a fool.

There was one more thing he needed to do. He pawed through the socks in his duffel until he found the sock with something in it.

One of the only benefits of being born a Freeman was what his dad called "group immunity." If someone bent on causing trouble approached a Freeman and a Leagueman walking down a corridor, nine times out of ten they'd pick on the Leagueman. If a stationmaster decided to cheat their suppliers, they'd cheat the non-Freeman suppliers first. There were a hundred times, a thousand times, maybe even ten thousand times more Leaguemen and Eng than Freemen in the wider world. Anyone with sense would go after them and leave a Freeman alone. Because to mess with one Freeman was to mess with all Freemen.

The People weren't organized enough to field an armada. They weren't numerous enough to overwhelm even a single system's defenses. What they were was everywhere, and neutral, and willing to trade. That made them indispensable. And it made them vulnerable. So the first families made a pact, and swore an oath, that regardless of how they might fight amongst themselves, they would present one face to the wider world, and that face would be hard as iron, and as unforgiving as space, and as sharp as a mong hu's fangs. They would take no sides and brook no insults. And they would stand together.

Anyone might become a Freeman. All they need to do was take the oath and live by it. It was at once the simplest and the most difficult of tasks.

A task he'd failed at.

Ciarán felt the weight drop into his palm, ran his fingers along its sharp edges, its draping curves ending in a razor point. The pendant spire was not a comfortable ornament to wear. But then, ornamentation wasn't its purpose. It served as an affirmation, a warning sign, and a reminder to the wider world. *We are one.*

Earlier, during Carlsbad's presentation of the data they'd retrieved at Ambidex, he'd seen the look in Aoife nic Cartaí's eyes, and it mirrored the feeling in his gut, earlier still, when he'd scrolled through the raw data capture and witnessed Bosditch Trading die.

That might have been me. My family. My future.

He turned the spire over and over in his hands. He'd been ashamed to wear it on Trinity Station because he'd thought it made from junk. Now he could see it was shaped from the same material as *Quite Possibly Alien.*

He was born a Freeman. He might not be a leader like Aoife, or smart and talented like Maura, or as unyielding and brave as a young Mr. Gagenot.

But he wasn't disposable.

And he wasn't alone.

That was something worth telling people. And worth remembering.

Once in place the earring felt heavier than he recalled.

When he looked in the mirror again he didn't look like a fool.

He looked better. Like a Freeman fool.

"Come on," Ciarán said to Wisp. Together they headed for the boat bay. Ciarán was getting to see the wider world. Pops hadn't so much as mentioned Gallarus. This was new territory, and Ciarán should be excited.

Maybe when you were this excited it felt just like being sick.

AOIFE WAVED from the hatch of the League Planetary Occupational Shuttle. Armed and armored, the shuttle was designed for delivering League troops to a planet's surface and holding an unruly populace under the League's benevolent thumb. Not standard merchant kit for certain. Ciarán ducked through the hatch hard on Wisp's tail.

The League shuttle bore no resemblance to a Freeman longboat. There was no forward piloting station. Some sort of gun emplacement occupied the forward third of the vessel.

Mrs. Amati worked the weapons through their full motion before she eased out of the gunner's seat and brushed past Ciarán on her way to a pair of weapons stations midhull.

Mrs. Amati would be impossible to miss regardless of what she wore, but she'd somehow snagged a League marine major's uniform that fit her like it was made for her. Much of her augmentation was hidden beneath the antiballistic material so that she looked nearly like a normal human.

"Come on back here," Engineer Hess called from a darkened cubby further aft. He fiddled with one of the dozens of consoles in the cubby. When Ciarán peered in, Pilot Konstantine waved back. Both Konstantine and Hess were dressed as League warrant officers, Konstantine with a pilot's insignia pinned to her collar, Hess with the engineer's pinned to his. Hess slid into the pilot's seat.

"Take a seat." Hess pointed. "And don't touch anything."

Wisp hopped up onto a crash seat and Aoife belted her in, ball of augustinite staining her fingers black.

She looked up when Ciarán's shadow fell across her face. "You finish up." Aoife pulled a cloth from the black pocket of her merchant's greatcoat and began to wipe the stains from her fingers.

Ciarán finished belting Wisp in.

Aoife took a seat near a massive hatch that led to a rear compartment. She motioned Ciarán to the seat next to her.

"Standard trading procedure," Aoife said. "I talk, I listen to what is said. You do not talk. You look, and you listen to what is not said."

"I will."

"Nothing more. No improvising."

"I understand." Ciarán belted in.

"Should the situation turn ugly, you will return to the shuttle. Do not linger to defend the women and children."

"I—"

"Amati has informed me of your self-defense progress." She frowned. "Such archaic sentiments are unfitting for a Freeman. It is a weakness, and unnecessary."

"It's how I was raised. I can't just—"

"You can and you must. Be a merchant apprentice. A Freeman merchant apprentice in every way, here most of all. Pretend to be conventional. That is an order."

"I will, Merchant Captain."

"I'll believe it when I see it." Aoife waved her hand and Hess fired the shuttle's engines up.

"Merchant Captain—"

"You have had time to review all of the new data on Gallarus Four?"

"There isn't any to speak of. Not any we haven't already discussed."

"Good. Questions may arise. Answer only mine. Do not elaborate. Be brief and do not volunteer a single word. Do not speak to anyone but me."

"I will."

"Today we are merchants in the employ of League loyalists." Aoife pointed. "Amati, Hess, and Konstantine are not part of our crew. You do not know them. You will not address them. You will refer to them by their rank if necessary, though it will not be necessary. Do you recognize the insignia?"

"I do."

Aoife raised her voice over the engine noise. "Take us out, Warrant Officer Hess."

"Yes, ma'am." Hess grinned from ear to ear.

"Hess is a pilot?"

"That is what we are about to find out." Aoife pulled her crash harness tighter.

Once clear of the boat bay, Konstantine called off the coordinates of the glassfield on the surface of Gallarus Four. Hess acknowledged the coordinates and checked the overhead display. "Everyone belted in?"

When Ciarán met his gaze, Hess winked and gripped the controls.

The shuttle plummeted like a stone.

25

The thickening atmosphere howling against the hull nearly drowned out the scream of the communications console.

"Hailing us," Konstantine said. "Threatening us with annihilation now. We're to track onto the approach vector they're sending."

"Anything with wings between us and the landing zone?" Amati said.

"Negative." Konstantine swiveled her seat around. "They've brought batteries to bear. Picking up the signatures of three emplacements on the surface."

"Light up the most obvious two," Amati said.

"Sir," Konstantine said. "Lighting up two now."

Amati watched the targeting display overhead as two of the planet's surface batteries flashed with targeting work-ups. Amati powered up the forward battery.

"Now they're saying our flight plan is good," Konstantine said. "They thought we were someone else. They're powering down the two we lit."

Amati powered the weapons down. "Keep them lit, WO."

"Yes, sir." Konstantine fiddled with the controls. "We're about to overfly the third emplacement."

"Should we be able to see it?" Amati's fingers hovered over the weapons toggle. The shuttle continued its screaming plunge toward the surface.

"I only know I can see it." Konstantine was silent for a moment, neck craned toward the overhead display. "Okay, now only an amateur would miss it."

"Blast," Amati said. "Light it."

Amati powered up the forward battery and fired before the final targeting solution appeared on the overhead display.

"Direct hit," Konstantine said. "They're not powering up the other batteries yet."

"They won't," Amati said. "Get us belly down, WO Hess."

"Sir," Hess said. "Bellying soonest." The shuttle pitched into a steeper descent.

"They appear to be seriously worked up," Konstantine said. "They're saying that was a manned battery."

"Tell them that if they point anything else at us we'll unman every Huangxu on the planet," Amati said.

"Verbatim?"

"What do you think, WO?" Amati's gaze remained glued to the targeting display.

"Yes, sir. Verbatim it is."

Ciarán was going to be sick. "How many people did we just kill?"

"No more than we had to." Aoife had her eyes closed, her hands crossed above her waist. The fingers of her right hand touched the overseer's rod jammed beneath her belt. "Perhaps none. These people have been known to lie."

So that was it. That was how the crew of *Quite Possibly Alien* settled disputes. How Aoife nic Cartaí settled disputes. Shoot first, a blast of energy from above, the deaths of some unknown number of people, no faces attached, a red dot on a targeting display, the motion of a finger to rain indiscriminate death. He didn't like it, and didn't want to like it.

Ciarán was thrown hard against the crash webbing as Hess applied reverse thrust for landing. Ciarán glanced at Wisp. She was purring.

Konstantine was out of her seat and manning the topside battery before the dust had settled. Amati's eyes scanned the primary weapons display before settling on the external sensor feed.

"Man." Hess unbelted and jerked out of the pilot's seat. He switched the engines to hot standby. "Engineering is good for the brain. But piloting is a kick in the pants. I really miss this."

"Well, you almost missed the glassfield," Konstantine said. "The little fellers are having to trot over to us."

"Did I?" Hess said. "What a shame for them."

Amati opened the hatch to the rear compartment and ducked through. When Ciarán twisted around to see inside, all he could see were rows of Freeman fast-pallets, their anti-grav lift systems set to "stay put."

What stepped back through the hatch had to be Amati. She was unidentifiable in the enormous case of exoskeletal armor. An exo, that's what Pops said the League called them. Like a shuttle you wore. It was almost big enough to be a shuttle, a battered night-blue hardsuit studded with sensors and antennae. Amati's right arm melded into the most massive weapon Ciarán had ever seen. Her left hand gripped a force blade that was nearly as long as Aoife nic Cartaí was tall.

Amati's mechanized voice boomed in the compartment. "Let's go meet our hosts."

Aoife was already unbelted. Ciarán wormed out of his crash harness before he undid Wisp's.

Amati had the external hatch open. She hopped onto the

smoldering surface of the glassfield and began to deploy a monstrous cooltube, an armored and insulated version of a flextube that made it possible to exit a shuttle before the molten glassfield below had cooled. On a longboat the process was automated, but then Freeman longboats were made for regular people, not for armor-clad monsters who could stride across lava without breaking a sweat. Once Amati had the tube fixed, Ciarán and Wisp followed Aoife out onto the cooling blast-glass surface of Gallarus Four.

"They're little kids," Ciarán said. They'd just killed some unknown number of children from orbit.

"Silence." Aoife glared at Ciarán. "These are Huangxu Imperial shock troops. They are crafted to look like children."

Whoever crafted them did a good job. Nearly two score of them were pogoing in great bounds across the glassfield.

Ciarán didn't bother to turn when he heard the clang of hatches being dogged and the topside weapons servos whine.

Amati's helmet swiveled to face Ciarán. "If this goes pear-shaped, tell your cat to go for the throat. Throats." She laughed.

"Now it gets interesting," Aoife said. "Stay close, and I repeat, no improvising."

CIARÁN COULDN'T GET over how much they looked like kids, like League kids for that matter, anywhere from nine to nineteen, all boys, all in a lightweight and flexible version of the hardsuit Amati wore.

A semihard suit, Ciarán decided they were, some sort of antiballistic armor that flexed as they moved, but not as supple as cloth, not even close to the armor Amati wore. They spread out as they approached, forming a semicircle around Amati.

Ciarán couldn't help but think about Aengus Roche and his crew on Ambidex Station.

There was a difference here, though. These children had weapons, ones that looked like they'd seen hard use, and their young faces were set with hard eyes that swept across Ciarán and his comrades and dismissed all but Amati and Wisp.

The leader of the locals, a boy of sixteen or so, blond hair, blue eyes, gestured toward Wisp and a pair of his armsmen took a step back.

The leader spoke to Amati in Trade common. "You killed my brothers today."

Amati's mechanized voice boomed from the transducers on her suit. "Then defrost some more."

"I will," the leader said. "What have you brought for trade?"

"I brought the merchant captain. She'll negotiate for us." Amati gestured toward Aoife. "Merchant Captain Aoife nic Cartaí, this is . . ."

"Young. First Cohort Captain of the Invincible Spear Bearers of Imperial Wrath. Now in retirement." Young grinned and any resemblance to a child disappeared. "Killing Erl grew tedious."

"I imagine it could," Aoife said. "The League frowns on the practice, I understand."

"The Erl. Your Earth Restoration League," Young said. "It is too busy fighting itself to pay us much mind."

"And that is why we are here," Aoife said. "We need weapons. You need what I have. A trade can be made, equitable and beneficial to all."

"We have no needs," Young said. "We have weapons, and we have wants. Perhaps a deal may be struck."

"I'm afraid I've only brought a few hundred shui xian to trade. There are others with needs . . ."

"We may want a few of these," Young said.

A handful of Young's troops whispered together behind him.

He turned and glared at them before returning his attention to Aoife. "Supposing the bulbs are suitable for carving."

Ciarán racked his brain for the meaning of the unfamiliar Huangxu phrase.

"More than suitable," Aoife said. "They will bloom on the new year. Perhaps you do not need such fortune, being many and strong, but there are those who do. Many who need, First Cohort Captain."

"Young," the Huangxu soldier said. "You must call me Young, my friend. Shall we show you what weapons we have for sale?" He rubbed his palm over the back of his head and smiled a short distance up at Aoife. He looked every bit a child.

"I am certain Major Amati would wish to inspect these weapons personally." Aoife reached into a deep pocket of her merchant's coat and withdrew an ornately decorated box that filled her palm and stood perhaps two handsbreadths tall.

Every eye was on the box, such was the merchant captain's skill. She opened the box with a flourish to reveal a fist-sized root.

Young's "Ah!" was drowned out by the excited whispers of his troops.

"A gift for the first cohort captain," Aoife said. "My apprentice and I shall ready the remainder of the cargo for inspection." Aoife held the box in both hands and bowed, equal to equal.

"So it shall be," Young said. He accepted the package and bowed in turn.

"Show me the hardware you little castoffs have stowed away," Amati said.

Young straightened as if having a spasm. "Show it what we have," Young said to one of his soldiers. "Do not kill it no matter how irritating it makes itself."

"Yes, sir." The soldier motioned for Amati to follow her. Half a score of Huangxu soldiers broke off to follow Amati, weapons hot.

Young gently closed the box and nodded. He spoke in Huangxu. "One so resourceful should not need to depend on the custom of such arrogant fools."

"I have no needs." Aoife smiled at Young, a merchant captain's smile. "I have expenses, and wants." Her Huangxu was perfect.

"See to your cargo," Young said. "You we can deal with."

26

"He's going to try to rob us," Ciarán said. He rolled another fast-pallet onto the glassfield and locked it down. That was the last.

"They often do." Aoife wiped her hands on her trousers and began popping the carry-crates open. Inside each were nine identical boxes, each containing nine identical boxes, each containing the palm-shaped root of a plant. There were four nines of nines on each fast-pallet.

"These aren't Freeman goods," Ciarán said. The Huangxu and Ojin packed goods in units of nine. Freeman goods normally shipped in quantities of twenty.

"Hand grown, and rare as kindness," Aoife said. "A gift from my sister."

"How valuable are they?" Ciarán began popping additional carry-crates open.

"Four Huangxu Eng have died trying to get their hands on one."

Two Huangxu Eng on Trinity Station. Two at Ambidex. All

of them expecting Maura and Carlsbad to have something they wanted.

"Give it over," Ciarán said. "Carlsbad and Maura were showing these around, trying to assess their value."

Aoife nodded. "There is a deep symbolism in these plants. Those that bloom on the Huangxu New Year are considered most valuable, talismans of great worth, imbued with good fortune and luck."

"They're just roots."

"Technically they're bulbs. And these bulbs are special. Can't you feel it?"

"Not really. May I touch one?"

"You can have one. Everyone should have something like this. Something so valuable they would die to find it, to have it, to keep it. It is not so strange, this desire, Ciarán. They are people."

"I know that." Ciarán held the root, the bulb, in his hand. It was nothing special. His dad and he had probably grubbed out a million of them clearing the drainage ditches at home.

"People just like us," Aoife said. "Others look at these Huangxu and see something made. A weapon of flesh, a device designed for the emperor's purpose. Amati sees this. What do you suppose they see when they look in the mirror?"

She arranged the contents of her carry-crate in an artful fan, largest bulbs near the center, a delicately composed display, and something Ciarán would not have considered doing until he had seen it done. He began to arrange the bulbs in the other containers. "I doubt they have mirrors," Ciarán said. He wouldn't if he was one of them.

"Perhaps we should show them a mirror," Aoife said. "And see what value they would place on such a thing." Aoife studied Ciarán's work. "Very nice. Your hands feel their power. It shows."

"What does?" Ciarán said.

"They are from Earth," Aoife said. "Your hands know."

"These bulbs?" Ciarán said. "That's impossible."

"Is it?" Aoife wasn't really listening to Ciarán anymore. She was watching Amati and two score of Huangxu shock troops shepherding an equal number of fast-pallets across the glassfield.

From a distance it seemed that Amati was some sort of giant armor-clad schoolmistress herding a class of heavily armed schoolchildren on a terrifying field trip through an obsidian hell.

They weren't children. Ciarán had to keep that in mind.

Amati pointed at the fast-pallets and Ciarán began hustling them into the shuttle. Aoife and Young reviewed the merchandise.

Young seemed satisfied. There was little effort involved in shoving the fast-pallets along, but Ciarán was sweating by the time he had the cargo locked down and had checked that all the fast-pallets were fixed in stay-put mode. He trotted down the ramp into the middle of an argument.

"I'm not certain I understand," Aoife said.

"We would trade for the beast," Young said. He pointed at Wisp.

Ciarán's heart stopped as he skidded to a halt at the bottom of the ramp. "Not—"

Aoife pointed her finger at Ciarán, and his tongue froze in his throat.

She returned her attention to Young. "You must understand that the mong hu are considered crew. You might as well offer for my apprentice. This is not negotiable."

"All things are negotiable," Young said. "Such we have learned from your peers."

"You are mistaken in this," Aoife said. "We have each profited. That is enough."

Wisp backed up, the fur on her back raised. She brushed against Ciarán's leg.

"You need what I offer," Young said. He held a small device on his open palm. "You will wish to have this. We will trade."

"We are Freemen," Aoife said. "We do not sell people."

"It is a made thing." Young pointed at Wisp. "Not people at all."

"Like you," Amati said. "Back up, little man. Our business here is done."

"It is." Young squeezed the device in his hand.

Amati collapsed in a howling heap, her amplified voice threatening to shatter Ciarán's eardrums.

Aoife screamed and clutched her head as she fell to writhe on the glassfield.

A howl, a pair of howls echoed from inside the shuttle. The topside guns gimbaled skyward.

Ciarán rushed to Aoife's side. He dropped to his knees and tried to hold the merchant captain still. His fingers fell on the overseer's rod.

"So Merchant Roche is no liar," Young said. "We will keep this." He waved the device in his hand. "And we will have the beast as well. And the Erl shuttle." He motioned for his soldiers to advance.

Ciarán pulled the overseer's rod free. He'd had to study the device at the Academy. He hated that class, and he hated the rod. There were dozens of controls on the device, each performing various functions when pressed alone or in combination. He remembered how to extend a field-shielded monomolecular whip and how to drop the sheathing field to expose the deadly blade within. If he thought about it he could probably recall other functions. He didn't have time to think about it.

Young motioned toward his cohort. They began to move forward.

Amati flopped and banged against the glassfield, a screaming mechanized nightmare.

Ciarán shouted at Wisp as he hammered the rod's power stud. "Run!"

"Where do you think your pet can run to?" Young smiled at Ciarán.

"There!" Ciarán pointed just as Wisp's camouflage dropped and she leapt. A Huangxu soldier fell with a truncated shout that could barely be heard over Amati's amplified screams.

"And there!" Another soldier fell beneath a raging cyclone of fangs and claws.

Ciarán didn't have time to watch. He remembered how an overseer's rod worked. There was no way to forget. He clutched the device in both hands.

A pulse rifle fired, and then another one.

Another soldier was down and then Wisp was gone.

Young's troops were disorganized but they were quickly forming up into a rough square, back to back.

There was no sign of Wisp.

Ciarán depressed the studs on the overseer's rod and swung it over his head. The monomolecular whip threaded out with no containment field.

"Put down your Freeman toy," Young said.

Ciarán swung the whip toward Young.

He thought he'd missed until Young lurched. Blood began to bubble on Young's lips.

Ciarán ducked and grabbed Young as a pulse rifle charge scorched the glassfield where he'd been standing.

Ciarán chucked the Huangxu underhanded into the shuttle.

"Wisp!" Ciarán shouted. "To me!" And then he had Aoife in his arms.

They weren't going to make it.

He slid the merchant captain up the ramp with all his might. Her screaming abruptly terminated.

When he turned to look for Wisp, his leg collapsed beneath him.

She was there, an orange and white blur. And then gone, only a stirring of wind as she raced up the ramp and past him.

Ciarán hopped up the ramp, ignoring the withering fire.

Amati's weapon began to fire on auto. She was still flopping about on the glassfield below. The muzzle of Amati's weapon began to slew in Ciarán's direction.

A half-dozen Huangxu soldiers fell. Those still standing began to concentrate their fire on Amati.

Ciarán slapped the ramp actuator with the palm of his hand.

The ramp jerked closed.

Ciarán dragged himself forward through the hatch.

Wisp brushed up against him, bloodied sides heaving. She turned her attention to Young as Ciarán wormed into the copilot's seat.

Hess's and Konstantine's howling flooded the cabin. They were both balled up on the cabin deck, hands about their heads.

Ciarán searched the piloting display. It was nothing like a submarine.

He jammed his thumb into the recess labeled "Ignition."

The shuttle bucked and settled into a ragged hover.

Ciarán hobbled toward the cargo bay. His left leg burned like fire. He didn't want to look. It smelled like charred meat in the compartment, that and the overpowering, copper-tainted reek of blood.

The compartment deck sloped toward the center. Ciarán might not have noticed that slope if not for the stream of blood that began with Young and snaked across the deck to the center drain.

No one would put such a drain in a Freeman vessel.

No one would expect a body could hold so much blood.

Wisp had been at Young, but she'd started on his torso and ignored his hands altogether.

Ciarán pried the device from Young's fingers and fumbled with it until Hess and Konstantine stopped screaming.

Aoife lay in a crumpled mass against the forward bulkhead, unconscious but breathing.

The shuttle lifted.

Hess tumbled through the hatch into the aft compartment. He shook his head and pressed his hand against the base of his skull as he looked around. "Where's Major Amati?"

"Where she fell." Ciarán was going to be sick.

"You ignited the thrusters with the major still on the glassfield?"

"I had to. I couldn't lift her."

"You could have rammed a fast-pallet under her. It might have lifted her."

"I didn't think of that," Ciarán said.

"Yeah," Hess said. "Konstantine can swing around and check for survivors."

Hess knelt next to Aoife. He checked her pulse. He pried her eyelids open. "We need to get her in an autodoc soonest. So, what's it going to be, Merchant's Apprentice—check for survivors or get our fearless leader to the doc?"

"Why are you asking me?"

"'Cause with the merchant captain out cold, you're in charge."

"That can't be. There's the captain, Agnes—"

"*Quite Possibly Alien* is a merchie operation. And you're our merchie for the time being. Now make up your mind. Pronto."

Ciarán wanted to ask Hess what he would do, but that

wouldn't be fair to the man. Ciarán had to decide. Aoife or Amati. "To *Quite Possibly Alien.* Then back here."

"On it," Hess said. "You need to get the merchant captain settled and strapped in. You and your hungry little buddy as well." Hess ducked through the hatch and disappeared onto the piloting deck. "Blast, I think I'm going to be sick . . ."

Natsuko waited in the boat bay along with Maura and Ko Shan.

Ciarán grabbed a couple of the Huangxu Eng bandage packs and flicked them to life. He jammed them over the burns on his leg and tried to ignore the satisfied sounds they made as they sucked and settled in.

Natsuko, Maura, and Ko Shan hustled Aoife away toward the infirmary without so much as a word. Ciarán wanted to go with them, to see Aoife safe, to see her open her eyes and glare at him, to hear her curse him for a fool.

He had to stay. He had responsibilities now.

Konstantine leaned against the shuttle bay hull, her face green. She'd been sick every five minutes on the way up.

Hess didn't look much better but at least he could stand without assistance.

Ciarán hadn't imagined he'd be glad to see Carlsbad. He felt his face crack into a smile when Carlsbad strode through the boat bay lock. "Cargo Master—"

"I know that look," Carlsbad said. "It is your neck and your noose, Merchant's Apprentice."

"But cargo masters are second-in-command."

"Freeman cargo masters are. Voyagers do not take the oath."

"Maura—"

"Now you are reaching. Navigators are staff. And Maura Kavanagh in command is a hull breach waiting to happen."

"But—"

"I have your back, Ciarán. Eyes forward and do your job."

Carlsbad tossed a ball of augustinite. Wisp darted after it like a kitten.

Ciarán couldn't get the images of Wisp out of his mind. She was exactly what Amati said she was. If not for Wisp they'd all be dead or captured.

Ciarán didn't have to like what Wisp had done. He didn't have to like what he had done on Gallarus Four. Still, he wasn't going to lose sleep over it.

That didn't make him a pirate.

Ship's Captain Agnes Swan strode through the hatch. She glared at Konstantine and Hess. "Get to the infirmary, the pair of you."

"I need one of them," Ciarán said.

Quite Possibly Alien's Huangxu Eng captain focused her attention on Ciarán.

"For what?"

"To rescue Amati," Ciarán said.

"She's dead," Swan said.

Ciarán swallowed. "Then to retrieve her body."

Freemen did not leave their dead behind.

Ship's Captain Swan fixed Hess in her sights. "We have the weapons?"

"Yeah," Hess said.

"We'll break orbit in one hour. Get to the—"

"I need a pilot," Ciarán said. "I don't care if it's the longboat or this League monstrosity, but it's going to happen. We're not going anywhere until whatever's left of Mrs. Amati is back on board."

"I'll drive," Hess said. "Konstantine's in no shape."

"I can do it," Konstantine said. "Just give me a sec."

"Look, Freeman whelp," Swan said, "you will not use my crew for any—"

"I thought this was a merchant operation," Ciarán said.

"It is," Swan said. "But these are my people. I won't waste them."

"Aoife may be badly hurt," Carlsbad said. "We may need to get her to a medical facility quickly."

"If that turns out to be true, then leave immediately," Ciarán said. "Don't wait. See she gets what she needs."

Ciarán pressed Young's device into Carlsbad's palm. "This appears to be some sort of implant-jamming device. How many of the crew are without implants?"

"We all of us have them," Swan said.

"You have one?" Ciarán said. Agnes Swan was Huangxu Eng. That she would have a League device implanted in her sacred body was absurd. Blasphemy and treason in one.

"We all of us have them," Swan said. "Though it is none of your business."

"It is now," Ciarán said. "Carlsbad, don't turn that thing on, whatever you do. If you need to turn it off, you do this." Ciarán showed him. "If you all have implants, though, there may not be anyone capable of turning it off."

Carlsbad eyed the device as if it were poison. "And I'm to do what with this?"

"Keep it for the merchant captain," Ciarán said. "Maybe she can figure out what to do with it, or about it."

"And what exactly are you going to do?"

"I'm going to go get Mrs. Amati."

"You can't have a pilot," Swan said. "We may not be able to wait."

"I'll take one of those." Ciarán pointed at the second-epoch shuttles. It wasn't ideal. He'd have to get Mrs. Amati out of her exoskeletal armor.

"That would be—"

"Here." Ciarán handed Swan the single bulb he'd rescued from the fiasco on Gallarus Four. "This is for the merchant captain. Tell her I'm sorry about the rest." Ciarán headed toward the shuttle.

"You will keep us apprised of your progress," Swan said. "We will have this argument again. Do not get used to command. It is not a foregone conclusion."

"Will do." Ciarán settled into the shuttle and ran through the preflight. It checked out and he powered up. There was one more thing that he had to do. "Sxipestro," Ciarán said.

"I am here." *Quite Possibly Alien*'s voice flooded his mind.

Ciarán instructed the ship's minder to repeat Young's comments regarding Merchant Roche to Aoife when she woke.

"What if she doesn't wake?"

Ciarán had to think about that one. Aoife nic Cartaí's family would want to settle accounts. Ciarán hadn't understood the whole process at first, these family vendettas that space-based Freemen took part in.

Now he did. Aoife's mother was the richest woman in Freeman space. Aoife's sister ruled a star system. They would both want to know who was responsible for Aoife's death. They would both set forth to even the score, and should they, then Roche's kin would do the same, and so on, and so on forever.

"If she dies then remain silent," Ciarán said.

No sum of additional deaths could bring her back. There was no way to balance such a deficit.

27

Ciarán swung the shuttle around and pushed through the containment field. From a distance Gallarus Four could be any planet in any star system anywhere in the wider world.

Ciarán eased the control yoke forward and watched the planet grow in size. He hoped Amati had survived. She'd walked about on molten glass while installing the cooltube. Surely more than the soles of her hardsuit's feet were heat resistant.

Ciarán took his time, vectoring in on the glassfield lazily, as unthreatening as a drifting feather or a flake of snow.

He needn't have bothered. Mrs. Amati reclined on the wreckage of her exoskeletal armor, a Huangxu pulse rifle braced against her hip. The glassfield below her armor had melted and hardened again, binding the armor in place.

"I've had that suit since I was a snotty," Amati said. "Now it's ruined."

"You can get another one," Ciarán said.

"You're grinning like an idiot, Keer-on." Amati stood, using the rifle as a crutch. "And you know nothing about exos. The new ones are rubbish."

"Let's get you into the shuttle. You can tell me all about it."

"No. First we're going to take a walk over that hill there." She pointed. "Can't you smell it?"

"Smell what?"

Mrs. Amati began limping toward the hill. "This is going to be ugly, and it's going to make you mad."

"Let's make it fast." There was still no news about Aoife from *Quite Possibly Alien.* "Aoife's hurt and the ship may need to jump to get her proper medical attention. I want us back on board before then."

Amati tapped Ciarán on the shoulder. "Stop."

Ciarán stopped.

Mrs. Amati ran her gaze over Ciarán. "Returning to defend the women and children."

"I'm not apologizing."

"No one's asking you to. I want to remember that innocent look." She started walking again.

Soon Ciarán could smell it: the overpowering scent of a latrine, or of an open sewer. They crested the hill. The far slope of the hill was glassfield as well. The stench poured out of a low blockhouse, laser-cut from the blast-hardened surface of the glassfield and plasma-fused in place. Ciarán recognized the structure from holos Pops had shown him. "It's a Huangxu slave pen."

"And in use. Is that knife the only weapon you have?"

"It is."

"Power it up and grip it tight," Amati said. "There may be guards. They'll definitely be prisoners, and some of them can turn out to be not so civilized."

"Right," Ciarán said.

"We could get in the shuttle and leave. This is none of our business."

"It isn't. But we can check it out if we're quick. Are you ready?"

"Am I standing?"

"Sort of," Ciarán said. Amati leaned more of her weight on the Huangxu pulse rifle than she had earlier.

"Then I'm sort of ready," Amati said. "Let's do this."

"LOOK HERE." Amati had cut the sleeves off her uniform blouse and slit them lengthwise. She tossed one to Ciarán and tied the other over her nose and mouth. Ciarán did the same. "If it's not caged or chained, shoot it. You got that?"

"I only have a knife."

"Oh. Right. Then I'll shoot it. If it doesn't stay shot, you know what to do." Amati set the Huangxu pulse rifle to auto and hosed the blockhouse door until it glowed.

"Now what?" Ciarán said.

"Now I usually elbow in with my exo. But since someone melted it into the glassfield, we'll have to improvise."

"Wait here." Ciarán hustled back to the shuttle at a dead run. Once in the cockpit, he ran through the preflight as fast as possible and lifted. Amati heard him coming and stepped well away from the blockhouse.

Ciarán hovered the shuttle in front of the door and flicked the impact shielding on. The field shoved the shuttle back, away from the battered surface of the blockhouse and the now bent and sagging door. He piloted the shuttle over the brow of the hill and set it down before trotting back to Amati's side.

"That was effective." Amati eyeballed the blackness behind the still-glowing doorframe.

Ciarán fished in his pockets. "I got the idea from these." He slipped on his hardhands but left them powered down. "My brothers and I used to mess with these a lot."

Hardhands were field-reinforced gloves. With a lot of experimenting, the brothers mac Diarmuid figured out how to project the field beyond the gloves. You could pick things up without touching them. You could punch your brother in the gut with the field a good ten centimeters in front of your fist. If you concentrated you could even shape the field into a pocketknife or a screwdriver if you'd stupidly forgotten and left your tools at home.

Ciarán gripped his vibraknife.

"I don't want to know," Amati said. "Now remember, if it's in front of me and not chained or caged . . ."

"You're going to shoot it. I get it. I'll stay behind you."

"See that you do." Amati ducked through the doorway.

Even through the improvised breathing mask, the stench was overpowering. It took Ciarán's eyes a while to adjust to the dark, but Amati's augmented eyesight settled in immediately. Ciarán found a light switch and set it to on. He wished he hadn't.

Two Huangxu soldiers slumped in the hallway. They looked like they'd been roasted alive. One was still breathing.

"What happened to them?" Ciarán scanned the corridor. Four rooms, four hatches—doors, really—and then a dark stairway down.

"You did. These are the leftovers from our little get-together earlier. When you lit up the shuttle's drive, you fried them all." Amati chuckled. "It was magical."

Amati kicked the first door on the left in. "Medical supplies in here. An autodoc." She grinned at Ciarán. "They almost made it."

"One's still alive," Ciarán said.

"Yeah, well, it's behind me. Your problem."

"I'm not killing it."

"You already did. It just hasn't figured that out yet. There's no autodoc in the world could fix that."

"Let's put it in and see."

Amati glared at Ciarán. "We don't have time."

Ciarán bent and lifted the child-sized Huangxu. It whimpered as he touched it. It didn't take long to rest it in the autodoc and set the device to work.

"If that thing comes out of there alive?" Amati kicked the door across the corridor open. "We're not leaving orbit without that autodoc on board." Amati shouldered her way into the compartment.

Inside was a med lab, but all the examination tables had straps on them. Just like the ones in Natsuko's lab. Ciarán didn't like the looks of the gleaming instruments beside each table.

"Interrogation room," Amati said. "Now how do you feel about your friend in the autodoc?"

"Not good."

Amati kicked the next door open, careful to stay behind the doorframe. She glanced inside. "Nothing to see. Come on."

Ciarán looked inside. It looked like the med lab, except the examination tables had more straps and stirrups. They looked more like couches or bunks than examination tables. There was a drink dispenser in the far corner and comfortable-looking seating around the perimeter.

Ciarán tore his gaze away.

"Come on!" Amati shouted. "Keep up!"

"That's another interrogation room."

"Break room. But if it makes you feel better, you don't have to believe that." Amati kicked the last door in.

It was a morgue.

Amati peered down the stairway. It was dark below, but Ciarán could see another light switch at the bottom of the stairs.

He started forward. The air was so foul that he just wanted to get this over with no matter what.

"Hold up." Amati pulled Ciarán close. "You're getting hit with this all at once, and it's a lot to process. Don't turn inside out on me."

"I'm not—"

"You're a decent man, Keer-on. Decent men don't believe in evil until they see it. You need to stay focused on the task and think about what this all means later."

"What was that room? Really?"

"You know what it is. You can get angry about that later. Right now I need you to watch my back. Can you do that?"

"I can. I will." Later he would get angry. *Count on it.*

"I am counting on it." Amati started down the stairs.

THERE WERE TEN OF THEM, all men, all hollow-eyed and lean in their filthy brown utilities. They clumped together near the back of the cell, not looking up, not so much as moving. The other cells were empty, bloodstained messes. Mrs. Amati pulled her boot knife, a short force blade that she worked into the cheap mechanism of the lock. Amati and Ciarán herded the prisoners out into the sunlight.

Their utilities weren't brown. Not normally. They'd started life a Truxton orange. Ciarán searched the faces of the prisoners, his heart hammering. One man kept his face turned away. "Seamus?"

"You know that man?" Amati said.

"Seamus?"

Mrs. Amati grabbed Seamus by the neck and forced him to face Ciarán.

"Seamus mac Donnocha," Ciarán said. "Merchant apprentice on Truxton's *Golden Parachute*. A friend."

"Ach." Mrs. Amati let Seamus go. "They'll be like this for a while. I don't know what we're going to do with them."

A man spoke, one of the older prisoners. "Where are the others?" He scanned the empty glassfield again and again.

"What others?" Amati said.

"There were sixteen of us."

"How many women?" Amati said.

"Six."

Ciarán began loping toward the shuttle.

Mrs. Amati shouted, "Ciarán!"

Ciarán picked up speed, the cold rush of wind filling his lungs. He tore the makeshift breathing mask from his face and let it fall. He vaulted into the cockpit of the shuttle and fired it up, ignoring the preflight checklist. Ciarán thumbed the comm on.

Ciarán toggled the send. "Captain Swan. How is the merchant captain?" He waited for the reply.

Agnes Swan's voice hurled itself around the shuttle's tiny cockpit. "Unconscious but recovering. What of my armsman?"

"Alive. Now send the longboat, along with Wisp and Carlsbad. Immediately." Ciarán didn't have to demand that Carlsbad come armed. The man had seen evil firsthand. He would come prepared.

"I don't think that would be wise. Why don't you—"

"Do it," Ciarán said. "No arguing."

"Anything else? Any further demands?"

"Tell Natsuko to get ready for ten customers. And get Ko Shan and Maura to the boat bay, armed and armored."

There was a long silence on the comm.

"It will be done, Merchant."

"Merchant Apprentice."

"I am informed, Merchant's Apprentice."

CIARÁN GUARDED the prisoners while Amati went back into the slave pen. When she returned, her face was grim. "All six women in the morgue. Two put up quite a fight."

Ciarán nodded. His stomach was one tight knot.

"We're taking that autodoc with us," Amati said.

"It worked?"

"Let's say I know where the Huangxu vessel is now. All the surviving Invincible Spear Bearers are in storage on board. I expect the ship will start defrosting a new batch when the old ones fail to return."

"I can think about that later," Ciarán said.

"Don't think about it too much. Don't think about any of this too much."

"How exactly am I supposed to do that?"

"When I figure it out, I'll tell you," Amati said. "Until then you'll have to improvise."

"Right. I need to talk to Seamus."

Amati grabbed Ciarán's arm. "Later. When he can bear to look at you."

"Seamus is strong. He's—"

"No one is that strong. Give the boy time. He needs to remember what he is."

"He's my friend," Ciarán said.

"He stopped being your friend the minute that cell door opened."

"You don't know what you're talking about."

Amati shook her head. "I wish I didn't." Amati's gaze shifted at the sound of the longboat screaming in.

"Hess," Ciarán said.

Amati placed her monstrous mechanized hand between Ciarán's shoulder blades and shoved, just a little. "Come on, little brother, and let's herd our responsibility toward their salvation."

Ciarán thumbed the vibraknife on. "I defer to your experience."

"As you should," Amati said. "As you should."

"You're an engineer," Ciarán said. "Can you fix that?"

Hess stared down at the mechanized mess melted into the glassfield. "I'm *the* engineer, mister. I could fix it but it would be cheaper to buy a new one."

"The new ones are rubbish," Ciarán said.

"Are they?"

"They are." Ciarán was certain of it.

"Then we'll get a line on it and melt it out on the way home," Hess said. "If it makes it through the atmosphere, I'll believe you."

"And you'll fix it. Whatever makes it through."

Hess scratched his chin. "Okay, new plan. We'll melt it out now and you chuck it in back."

"After it cools."

"Natch."

28

Aoife nic Cartaí eased gingerly into her seat in the ship's mess. She moved slowly but seemed alert. "The prisoners are talking," she said.

"They are," Ciarán said.

"Then stop grinning at me and tell me what they said." She tapped her mug on the table. Mr. Gagenot bent to refill it.

"Will Gag sees the merchant captain. Will Gag remembers the merchant captain in his prayers."

"Thank you, Mr. Gagenot. I am in your debt."

"Will Gag accepts no debts." Gagenot filled Ciarán's mug.

"I am informed," Aoife said. "Now, Ciarán, before the stars burn out, will you tell me what we have learned?"

"The prisoners are off Truxton's *Golden Parachute*. They were attacked, immobilized with the device we captured from Young, and later, upon arrival in Gallarus system, seem to have been traded to the Huangxu for weapons. Traded for all the best weapons, according to Amati."

"Attacked by whom?" Aoife said.

"Oddly enough, by Merchant Aengus Roche." Ciarán sipped his caife and watched Aoife's face.

One eyebrow arched up. "Tell all. Every detail."

According to those they'd rescued, Truxton's *Golden Parachute* left Ambidex Station in a hurry. Roche took the vessel to Prix Canada, where he accepted contract for goods to be delivered in the void between Prix Canada and Sizemore—not an unusual arrangement for the *Golden Parachute*, whose specialty seemed to be fly-by delivery of interdicted goods.

"Nothing illegal," Aoife said.

"As far as we know," Ciarán said. "But the coordinates match those of the *Last Stand* incident."

Freeman law was quite flexible, and goods placed into orbit around a planet were not delivered to a planet, and thus, under Freeman doctrine, perfectly legal. Most governments didn't agree, but the practice was hard to police, as Freeman Freight Expeditor containers, or FFEs, were self-powered and capable of maintaining orbit for quite some time. The more distant the orbit, the more difficult for those lacking the coordinates to find the delivery. For those with the coordinates and the means to reach them, the retrieval was child's play. Reentry into an occupied system was somewhat more difficult, but that was the responsibility of the receiving party. All in all it was relatively safe and highly profitable work. Somewhat less than respectable to the Eng—akin to smuggling, according to the League—but there was little they could do to stop it.

In many cases the League and Ojinate had no incentive to stop it, as they often employed Freeman merchants as private contractors when plausible deniability was desired.

The *Golden Parachute*'s crew thought nothing of a pickup in the void between stars, this being standard practice. What they were unprepared for, however, was a rendezvous with a League vessel and the sudden, brain-splitting pain that rendered them unable to defend themselves. The next thing they knew they were in the brig and a new crew, all Leaguemen, operating the *Golden Parachute*.

"And Merchant Roche?" Aoife asked. She hadn't touched her caife.

"Still in command," Ciarán said.

"Amazing."

"Indeed." Ciarán took a sip of caife. "Shall I continue?"

"Shall I brain you?"

"I would prefer not, Merchant Captain."

"Then continue."

"Right," Ciarán said. "This is where it gets strange."

"Wait, though. The timeline makes no sense."

"It didn't to me either, at first. I thought the prisoners were saying they left Ambidex in a hurry *after* our run-in with them. But this actually happened much earlier, which explains something Captain Swan and Mrs. Amati both told me."

"Which is?"

"That they could see one Truxton merchant going rogue but not an entire Truxton crew."

"I would agree with that."

"So now I'm thinking that this upside-down mutiny took place before Roche hijacked the *Last Stand*'s cargo, and Roche had the Truxton crew held in the brig the entire time. Then, loaded with whatever he stole from *Last Stand*, Roche proceeded to Gallarus before returning to Ambidex, where we encountered him."

"And how do you explain Roche's merchant apprentice being on Ambidex at the same time we were, and being in the slave pen here when we arrived?"

"It took us forever to get here. Roche could have returned to Gallarus and dropped Seamus off. He had plenty of time to do that twice over."

"And what does this Seamus say?"

"I haven't asked him yet."

"I assume the Merchant Academy still teaches classes on facial recognition, and that you have taken these classes."

"They do, and I have. I'm actually better with voices than faces, but . . . you really don't care about that."

"I care about the *Golden Parachute* crew we encountered on Ambidex."

"Not a single one of them with the exception of Seamus was in that slave pen. Carlsbad, Maura, and Ko Shan confirm that this is their assessment as well."

"Amati and Swan were with Truxton for many years."

"They don't recognize any of the prisoners. And Amati didn't recognize any of those on Ambidex either, with the exception of Merchant Roche."

"I see. Continue."

"Right. According to the prisoners, Merchant Roche sold his crew to the Huangxu on Gallarus Four in exchange for weapons, ones of Huangxu design useful only to Huangxu vassals such as the Invincible Spear Bearers of Imperial Wrath. The best weapons the Huangxu had, and they agreed to the deal. The prisoners said they watched Leaguemen load these goods.

"Here the story might have ended as it pertained to us, but one of the prisoners overheard a conversation between Merchant Roche and Young, in which Roche transferred the device we captured to Young along with information that *Quite Possibly Alien* would be calling at Gallarus Four, and that the entire crew would be susceptible to the device's effects."

"Is that so?" Aoife said.

"It is, Merchant Captain." Ciarán found his mug empty.

"Did Merchant Roche offer any . . . compensation for Young's betrayal of us?"

"All we have," Ciarán said. "But for one thing."

"*Quite Possibly Alien.*"

"Exactly."

"What would make Roche believe that all of us would have implants of League design?"

"In the case of crew, I don't know. In my case, I believe he was informed of this fact by his merchant apprentice."

"Who assumed you had an implant?"

"Who was certain of it." Ciarán felt himself flush. "He overheard me make the appointment, while we were roommates. I meant to get one. I understand they are quite useful—"

"An implant sharpens edges. It does not forge the blade."

"So I've heard. But anyway, I couldn't go through with it. Having a . . . foreign device stuffed into my skull." Ciarán shrugged. "I do well on standardized tests, so people just assumed I'd gone through with the procedure. I didn't tell anyone."

"Until now."

"You already know. Seamus didn't. Doesn't."

"This merchant apprentice is amongst the prisoners."

"He's the one who overheard Roche's conversation."

"And he overheard this conversation because . . ."

"Because he was party to the conspiracy until recently," Ciarán said.

"But when his good friend Ciarán was endangered his conscience got the better of him. Even though he was fine with selling his crewmates into slavery."

"He's not evil. He's . . . Seamus. And bailing out is the sort of thing Seamus would do. Deciding at some point the next step is a step too far. That definitely isn't out of character. Participating in the slave trade definitely is. I'm not even certain he was on board the *Golden Parachute* until quite recently. We graduated in the same Academy cohort."

"And what of this device?" Aoife said. "The one used on us."

"Devices. Seamus says Roche has hundreds of them."

"That is very bad of Merchant Roche."

"But not as bad as selling his crew into slavery."

"Not his crew. Truxton's. The Merchant Roche is insane."

"Seamus is of this opinion, Merchant Captain."

"I would like to meet this merchant apprentice."

"Carlsbad is taking him to the infirmary. Natsuko assures me she is prepared." Prepared to strip Seamus's mind open just as Ciarán's had been. To poke around in his secrets against his will. Only this time it would be illegal. Seamus wasn't under contract to Aoife nic Cartaí.

"You hate this." Aoife leaned forward, elbow on the table, and placed her chin in her palm, her gaze glued to Ciarán's.

"Like lungs hate vacuum."

"Then stop me." Aoife drew a circle on the table with her fingertip. "If you say to me, 'Do not do this, it is evil,' then I will not do so, and any information we might have gained to protect ourselves will have been lost."

"It's illegal. And morally abhorrent."

"Then be my conscience." Aoife leaned back and crossed her arms. "Perhaps I've lost perspective. You are newly acquainted with evil in one of its most recurrent forms. If you say what I propose to do is comparable, then I will believe you, Ciarán."

"It's not even close, but—"

"I propose to chemically interrogate every one of the prisoners if necessary," Aoife said. "With or without their consent. In gross violation of Freeman laws and custom. In violation of our *most fundamental* laws and customs. This may further damage some of the prisoners. The Huangxu may have pushed past the point where some prisoners could suffer permanent damage."

"I understand, Merchant Captain."

He did understand. Now. It might just as easily have been

Ciarán in that cell. Aoife and Maura in that . . . pleasure room, Ciarán forced to listen, powerless and crumbling with every tormented scream, every satisfied grunt and demented laugh.

Aoife slammed her fist on the table. "Say it is evil!"

"It's the opposite. It's your duty. Under the circumstances."

Aoife nodded. "No court in the Federation would see it that way. Truxton might himself, but he would not admit to that in public. It would be easier to space them all when I'm done."

"For the record? That would be evil."

Aoife chuckled. "It would." Her fingers brushed against the overseer's rod beneath her belt. "It is merely a matter of time before it will be you in such a cell, Ciarán. It will be Ko Shan. It will be Natsuko screaming for mercy. Or some other horrid end you will witness between now and the moment of your own death. That will be your fate."

"I know." The wider world wasn't at all what he expected.

"Such is the nature of our business. I have imagined my death thus a thousand nights. These are fates one may contemplate with dispassion, fates one may steel oneself to bear without disintegration of the soul. One imagines that those who live as prey inevitably find their way to heaven."

"You're a predator," Ciarán said. "With a crew of predators."

"Nearly so," Aoife said. "We are sheep who have had enough of wolves."

"Protecting the flock?"

"In no way. Defending ourselves. Wolves do not fear us. Our comrade sheep do not love us. We must see to our own salvation. There are no shepherds in the wider world. Only sheep and wolves, and those creatures for whom wolves are as sheep. We aspire to be neither predator nor prey. There must be some middle ground. We need only survive long enough to stumble upon it."

"That makes sense."

"We Cartaí women were raised as wolves." Aoife placed her hand on Ciarán's wrist. "You must speak up when my fangs show. In my worst nightmares I am not strapped to a table, Ciarán."

"You're strapping others down."

Aoife pulled her hand away. "And enjoying it. Heaven is closed to such a one. I am certain of it."

"Then I'm almost afraid to tell you the rest." Ciarán shifted in his seat.

"But more afraid not to."

"That is so. Seamus reports that Merchant Roche will return to Gallarus Four to collect *Quite Possibly Alien*."

Aoife grinned a toothy grin. "Will he?"

"I expect so. In three days. Seamus isn't a liar."

"That is it? The revelation you feared?"

"Not quite." Ciarán studied the surface of the table. He had to trust the merchant captain. She needed full information. He did not want to see her or any of his shipmates in a Huangxu slave cell or worse. Ciarán needed allies, and if not the merchant captain, then whom?

Ciarán placed his hands, palms down, on the table and took a deep breath. "I have translated a number of documents not entered into the ship's log. Ones . . . of a sensitive nature."

The smile disappeared from her face. "Do tell."

"It would be easier to show you."

"Then by all means show me."

There was no turning back from this. Ciarán hoped he wasn't making a horrible mistake. "Sxipestro."

"I am here," *Quite Possibly Alien* said.

"Make yourself known to Aoife nic Cartaí."

"I am here, Merchant Captain."

Aoife lurched back in her chair.

"The part of the ship you've been dealing with is the . . . nervous system part," Ciarán said. "This is the ship's minder."

"A ship's minder?"

"Like the ship's brain."

"The ship's weapon would be more accurate," *Quite Possibly Alien* said. "A weapon you do not wish to see used, Merchant Captain."

"I don't?" Aoife glared at Ciarán.

"You do not," *Quite Possibly Alien* said. "But I fear you shall."

AOIFE STRODE down the corridor with such haste that Ciarán had to work to keep up. "So nice of you to enlighten me." She bent her fingers into one of the two hatch cipher locks and glared at Ciarán. "I am gratified that I have earned your trust."

Ciarán worked the second cipher lock and tugged on the hatch. "It was the part about sheep. You've never seen any sheep, have you?"

"I've read of them. I've seen images. They are peaceful."

"They're also stupid as can be, blind followers, and if it weren't for shepherds there wouldn't be a sheep left alive anywhere in the world."

"What sort of pitiful creature would depend on another for its safety?" Aoife strode off toward the next blast door. "There must be a class of sheep that understands what is necessary and sees it is done. Perhaps you are unfamiliar with sheep such as these."

Ciarán shook his head. "I am unfamiliar with such sheep, Merchant Captain."

Ciarán's dad had tried raising sheep once, but that didn't last a year. Macer's dad had scores of sheep. There were no sheep like

Aoife described. She held an idealized vision, a schoolgirl's picture of fluffy clouds of wool, of prancing lambs in springtime sunlight. She would be one of these happy creatures if the world were a safer place.

In this world Aoife placed herself between the dark woods and the blissfully ignorant flock. She could deny it if she liked, could put it down to self-preservation, but there was no need to stray so near to the darkness were that true. Aoife was fooling herself, just as Ciarán fooled himself.

He didn't rescue damsels in distress for the damsel's sake. He did it for his own. He couldn't stomach turning a blind eye to suffering. Aoife was the same, whether she admitted it or not.

If that made you a pirate, then so be it.

It was better than the alternative.

"You have not seen everything in the wider world, Ciarán mac Diarmuid." Aoife tapped on Natsuko's hatchway. "There are such sheep. There must be."

"I believe you, Merchant Captain." Ciarán donned the respirator required for survival in the medic's carbon dioxide–rich infirmary. He tried not to flinch as the decontaminant spray began to fall from the deckhead. "I will not doubt you again."

"See that you don't." Aoife banged on the infirmary hatch.

SEAMUS WAS SEATED on an examination table. He was dressed in clean utilities but there was something wrong with his face. Even with a respirator on it was evident he was smiling.

"I would like you to submit to chemical interrogation," Aoife said. "Purely for information as it relates to threats to this vessel and crew. Do you consent to this?"

Seamus nodded, his gaze latched on to Ciarán's. "Whatever Ciarán says." He brushed invisible lint from his sleeve. "Ciarán

and I were roommates. Back before, um, back before, um."
Seamus kicked his heels against the table pedestal.

"Well?" Aoife glanced at Ciarán. "What does Ciarán say?"

"Ciarán and I were roommates," Seamus said. "Weren't we,
Ciarán? Back before, um, back, you know . . ." Seamus began
to cry.

"I think you should refuse," Ciarán said. It was what the real
Seamus would do. If he ever recovered from what Roche had
done to him, Seamus would want that. To remain defiant.
Ciarán knew Seamus almost as well as he knew Macer. If Seamus
were in his right mind, he wouldn't submit to such a request.

"I refuse," Seamus said. "Ciarán knows what's best for
Seamus. Ciarán and Seamus were roommates. Once upon a
time. Before . . . um. Before . . . um, before . . ."

"Do it," Aoife said.

Natsuko tapped her palm against Seamus's shoulder, and he
babbled on for a while longer before lying back on the table with
his eyes open.

"You are not making my life any easier," Aoife said.

"Your fangs were showing," Ciarán said.

"Barely."

"He's ready." Natsuko adjusted an intravenous drip.

"I can't watch this. Seamus wouldn't want me to." Ciarán
started toward the compartment hatch.

"You will sit here and witness every single interrogation,"
Aoife said. "You will be able to attest in court that I did not . . .
delve."

"Natsuko can do that."

"She did, for your interrogation." Aoife kicked a chair
toward Ciarán. "Freemen will be more willing to believe you.
And you would survive a forced chemical interrogation, should
one be ordered by the court. Natsuko would not."

Ciarán sat, and Aoife pulled her chair near his. "If you think

I relish this . . . opportunity, then you will soon be disabused of the idea." Aoife pulled out her hand comp and scrolled through display after display of questions before she spoke into the transponder adhered to Seamus's ear.

"What is your name?"

"Seamus mac Donnocha."

"Where were you born?"

"Trinity Station, Freeman Federation."

"How old are you?"

"Twenty-one standard years and some days." Seamus's forehead wrinkled.

"That is sufficiently accurate." Aoife held her hand over the transponder. She glanced at Ciarán. "Settle in, Merchant Apprentice. This is going to be a long day. And a longer night."

Ciarán adjusted his breathing apparatus and eyeballed the chronometer.

"Next question . . ."

29

Ciarán yawned and took the mug of caife from Aoife's hand. He'd fallen asleep in his chair. The crew was assembled, jammed together at one end of the mess. Ciarán hadn't been listening to the merchant captain. He'd heard every word she now recounted firsthand.

There were many details learned but nothing planet-shattering in the stories they'd extracted from the prisoners under chemical interrogation.

Hess scribbled on his hand comp, modifying a standard Freeman merchant vessel's layout to match the details of the *Golden Parachute* gleaned from the prisoners.

Mrs. Amati studied her own hand comp, scrolling through the inventory of weapons Roche had purchased, as well as those stacked in *Quite Possibly Alien*'s boat bay, and comparing them to the Huangxu manifest she and Ko Shan had retrieved from the battered hulk buried on Gallarus Four.

The remaining Invincible Spear Bearers of Imperial Wrath were indeed in cold storage in their ruined vessel. They were either deserters, as Mrs. Amati said, or cashiered and disposable.

When the superluminal drive of their vessel failed they eased it gently down the gravity well over the course of months.

Carlsbad had studied the Huangxu records as well. He was convinced that Roche had offered the Huangxu soldiers the use of Truxton's *Golden Parachute* in exchange for *Quite Possibly Alien*.

The only new fact came from Seamus. Roche's cargo for Ambidex Station was still on board the *Golden Parachute*, including an FFE full of League implants, a redesign, and from a new supplier.

"Transshipped from DP-ENA2345-92," Ciarán said.

"A League origin designator." Maura tapped the designator into her pilot's hand comp. "It's . . ."

"Contract system," Agnes Swan said. "Second moon of the ninth planet."

"Right." Maura looked up from her hand comp. "The cockroach is horning in our contract!"

"Blast." Hess's fingers tripped over his hand comp's display. "He say which FFE it was? According to your buddies there's supposed to be a dozen on the mast."

Freeman vessels were constructed of a forward section where piloting and freight handling functions were performed, the boat bay was located, and the crew lived. A separate propulsion section at the stern housed the superluminal drive and primary engineering control. Between was the mast, a long spine from which Freeman Freight Expediting containers, FFEs, were suspended in concentric rings. Twelve FFEs was a light load for such a vessel. An unprofitable load, unless the freight contained was extremely compact or extremely valuable. Even then, merchants tended to work up a full mast, three score containers in all. Sixty self-powered, environmentally controlled containers that could be dropped into orbit, unloaded at a station, or shot down the gravity well of a planet to land under their own power.

Getting them back up the well required a rail gun to hammer them through the atmosphere until they were able to settle into orbit under their own power.

Quite Possibly Alien had a mast but it was grafted on, single-ended, a straight, vestigial tail that clashed with the alien curves of the vessel's hull. There wasn't a single FFE on it, and there probably hadn't ever been. *Quite Possibly Alien* resembled a Freeman merchant vessel for appearances only.

"Does it matter which container holds this cargo?" Ko Shan asked.

"Maybe not," Hess said, "but if we knew what was in the other cans and how he's stowed them it might tell us something."

Ko Shan frowned at Hess. "Like what?"

"Something we don't know," Carlsbad said.

"What possible use could such knowledge be?" Ko Shan wasn't backing down.

"Knowledge is an end in itself," Carlsbad said. "To know—"

"If we knew how the mast was loaded, we'd know where it was easiest to snap," Ciarán said.

Everyone was staring at him.

"It doesn't matter unless the vessel is in close proximity to a larger mass." Or if an FFE was fired up while still on the mast. Ciarán closed his eyes. "It's happened, by accident. And it's what could have happened to *Last Stand*. Except we studied it in the Academy, and no one is so stupid anymore."

"No Freeman merchant is so ignorant," Aoife said.

"Roche is no Freeman," Maura said.

"He's not much of a merchant either," Hess said. "My granny could rustle up more than twelve cans out here."

"What do you expect?" Maura said. "He's one of Truxton's blow-ins."

Konstantine glared at Maura. "Like me."

"And me," Amati said. "A blow-in."

"I didn't mean that—"

"I served Truxton for more than a decade," Swan said. "He is an estimable man, Freeman or not."

"Then you explain it," Maura said.

"Can our sensors determine this vulnerability?" Ko Shan asked. She tapped Ciarán on the sleeve and repeated her question.

"Freeman sensors can't." Ciarán yawned. "It's why cargo masters are usually second-in-command on Freeman vessels. A live load is a dead crew. But you know all this."

"Freeman merchants know this," Aoife said. "There are only three Freemen on board."

"Thirteen," Natsuko said. "Counting the prisoners."

"An inauspicious number," Swan said.

"Ciarán."

"Um?"

Aoife kicked Ciarán's chair. "Wake up."

"I'm awake." Ciarán scrubbed his palm over his face.

"Engineer Hess and I will interview the cargo master of the *Golden Parachute*. The merchant apprentice will review *Quite Possibly Alien*'s sensor documentation with Sensorman Ko."

"I will." Ciarán used his hands against the tabletop to stand.

"Keer-on hasn't had an hour of rack time since before we first made planetfall," Mrs. Amati said. "Merchant Captain."

"Is this true?" Aoife stared at Ciarán.

"Maybe," Ciarán said. "I need to think."

"Pilot Kavanagh," Aoife said. "Take the merchant apprentice to his cabin and tuck him in."

"I'd like nothing better, Merchant Captain."

"Tuck him in alone," Aoife said.

"Come on." Maura wrapped her arm around Ciarán's

shoulders. "I'm to take you back to your cabin alone and tuck you in."

"Tuck him in alone, Navigator," Ko Shan said. "I will need him fresh and lively in but a few hours."

Mrs. Amati bellowed, "Maura Kavanagh!"

Ciarán's eyes popped open. Maura was pressed against Ciarán, hip to hip, arm around him. She jerked away like Ciarán was on fire.

Mrs. Amati lowered her blowgun. There was a yellow sleepy dart stuck in Ciarán's shoulder. He pulled it out and studied it.

Maura helped Ciarán to a chair. "Great. Somebody hold him up and I'll get a fast-pallet."

Ko Shan raced over and propped Ciarán up.

Maura pointed her finger at Amati. "I owe you, you old bag of—"

"Wisdom," Amati said. When she grinned, both her human teeth and her League-augmented incisors gleamed. "Old bag of wisdom, girl. Now go get that freight mover and hustle back. Your plowboy paladin needs his beauty rest."

"*Our* plowboy paladin," Ko Shan muttered.

Ciarán blinked, his throat dry. Mrs. Amati must be putting hallucinogens in her sleepy darts now. He was hearing things. It was strange. Very strange. Ciarán yawned. Very . . .

CIARÁN SCREAMED and jerked upright in his bunk. "Blast and Fire!" Someone was gnawing Ciarán's leg off.

Natsuko. She'd placed her rebreather mask on Ciarán's bunk so she could use both hands to saw away on Ciarán with a force abrader.

"You wail like a baby," Natsuko said. "These bandages must not be neglected so long. They wither and die."

Ciarán flipped the covers back and tried to pull away. "Where are my clothes?"

"In the recycler," Natsuko said. "Calm down. My work is nearly done."

Ciarán glanced around his cabin. "I'm to meet Ko Shan first thing—"

"Over here." Ko Shan waved from Ciarán's worktable. "I started without you."

Ciarán fumbled with his bedding. "Natsuko, let go!"

Natsuko slapped a pair of bandages over the pulse-rifle burns. They writhed, muttering their thankfulness for the opportunity to serve. "Quit your squirming, Merchant Apprentice." She twisted Ciarán's leg and applied a third bandage. Natsuko packed her bag. "You Freemen and your modesty. You have nothing I have not seen before."

Maura stepped into the cabin carrying fresh utilities. "Just more of it."

"He is tall for a Freeman," Ko Shan said. "Well proportioned."

Maura tossed the utilities on the bunk. "I guess. If you like them that way." Maura grinned.

Natsuko took a long pull from her rebreather. Today's version was gold as usual, and shaped like a smiling mong hu. Her sides heaved.

"You're laughing!" Ciarán roared. "Get out! All of you!"

"We are to work together," Ko Shan said.

"On the bridge," Ciarán said. "In five."

"In thirty," Aoife said. She leaned in the hatchway.

"He looks like he's going to salute," Maura said. "Ten hut, Apprentice."

"Get out all of you," Aoife said. "In the mess, Merchant Apprentice. In five minutes."

AOIFE SAT BEFORE A VAST BREAKFAST. Mr. Gagenot laid out another plate as Ciarán took his seat.

Ciarán's face burned. "It's not what you think."

"Do you have sisters?" Aoife said.

"Brothers," Ciarán said. "Three." His mouth watered. He couldn't remember when he'd eaten last.

"You have sisters now," Aoife said. "Keep it that way."

"I wasn't—"

"What do they say on Trinity Surface? Something about fishing and ponds."

"Don't angle in the family pool." It felt as if his ears were on fire. "It's a tasteless joke. It refers to first landing days, when . . . I mean, no one nowadays . . ."

"I recall the context. This advice is not merely a matter of genetics, but of group dynamics."

"I didn't do anything."

"Rescuing damsels. That is doing something."

"They're not damsels. And I didn't rescue them."

"Is that so? Maura on Trinity Station. Carlsbad and Konstantine at Ambidex. Amati is a different matter altogether. She assures me she did not require rescue but that your exploits saved her considerable . . . exertion. It is a long walk from Gallarus to Freeman space."

"See? I didn't do anything. And I'm not—"

"This list is incomplete. You neglected Hess on Gallarus and Konstantine also on Gallarus, rescuing her a second time."

"That was just luck."

Aoife plucked her overseer's rod free and tossed it onto the table. It lay there, powered up and glowing. "This is not a lucky charm. Any child can master its controls. Any fool can teach a child. One might disassemble it, study its parts, comprehend its ugly perfection, and still be ignorant to the most important aspect of its nature."

She stared at him.

Ciarán refused to meet her gaze.

"You understand this aspect?"

He nodded. He understood. Now.

"It does not work alone. It needs a firm hand to wield it and a heart of cold iron to bear it. These are facts not taught in the Academy."

"They aren't, Merchant Captain." They were learned when there was nothing between your friends and harm but you and that thing.

Ciarán didn't want to think about that ever again.

"This list remains incomplete."

"No, I don't think so," Ciarán said. The smell of breakfast gnawed into his brain. If he didn't eat something soon he was going to feel sicker than he already did. And if he did eat something he'd probably just toss it back up.

"I have yet to mention the only damsel in distress that could bend the crew's attention to you with such fervor."

"Is that ham?"

"Ciarán. You will look at me."

Aoife was not smiling. Her turquoise eyes saw him. Saw everything about him.

"When we have dealt with our current inconveniences, I will begin to train you in the proper use of this weapon." She brushed her fingers against the overseer's rod. "We will settle down to normalcy, and I will tutor you in those matters you will need to know to sit for a merchant's license. This will not be easy. Our ways aboard *Quite Possibly Alien* are unconventional, but we are a merchant vessel. Everything you need to learn in order to be a merchant may be learned here."

"And then?" Ciarán felt as if his entire body were made of glass. That Aoife nic Cartaí might shatter him with a sound.

"And then Merchant mac Diarmuid may find his own vessel. And then we may speak of this matter again if this remains your wish. No insult is offered or intended."

"I understand."

"I believe you do, Ciarán."

"What if I like this vessel?"

"Then I will be honored to see you stay and glad for your company. But I can offer you nothing more . . . personal in nature."

"I see. Thank you."

"Thank me? For what? Allowing you to save my life and the lives of my crew?"

"For being straight with me. For sparing me from embarrassing myself. For treating me like a man and not a boy just now."

He could feel her studying his face even as he refused to meet her gaze. She didn't speak for the longest time.

"As you say, Merchant Apprentice." Aoife jammed the overseer's rod beneath her belt. It clicked home with an air of finality. "Ko Shan awaits you on the bridge. Do not tarry."

Ciarán began piling brown bread, butter, and cheese onto a to-go plate. A plowman's lunch, his dad called that. "I'm on the run after loading up." He was too keyed up to eat it now, but he'd be hungry later. At least he hoped he would.

Aoife paused at the compartment hatch. "Ciarán."

Ciarán picked up the heaping plate and stood. He kicked his chair beneath the table. "Merchant Captain?"

"You are many things, but I assure you. No one on this vessel confuses you with a boy. Word of a merchant."

30

I t was good to have the merchant captain back in charge. They had less than three days to prepare for an attack and very little information to work from. Mrs. Amati suggested they just drop an asteroid on the Huangxu ship and get on with their business.

Mrs. Amati wasn't Freeman.

Or Voyager. The look on Carlsbad's face said that his people weren't the sort to turn the other cheek either. Both Aoife and Maura were of Freeman first families. Even if they were estranged from their kin, there was still the family honor to think of. Merchant Roche had done violence against a Cartaí. And a Kavanagh. He would pay, and he would do it here and he would do it in less than three days.

When Ciarán finished going over the sensor manuals with Ko Shan, they both knew a lot more about *Quite Possibly Alien*'s capabilities. *Quite Possibly Alien* shipped a number of micro–sensor satellites as well as a retractable sensor array, a kilometers-long tail of instruments that could be extended from the hull. They also knew that detecting minute stress imbalances in a

Freeman merchant vessel's mast from thousands of kilometers wasn't one of them.

"I'll keep looking," Ko Shan said.

She would too. The crew of *Quite Possibly Alien* were unconventional but they were good at their jobs, and they didn't quit when the task turned hard. Thorough. Meticulous. All the things Ciarán wanted to be someday.

Ko Shan would eventually figure out a way to measure the strain on the mast of a remote vessel, but it would take her more than three days to work it out.

Ciarán was to meet Mrs. Amati in the boat bay and he was running late. He belted in just as the League shuttle lifted.

"I still think we should put the prisoners onto the planet," Mrs. Amati said.

"Can we call them something else?" Konstantine said. "Survivors? Refugees? They're Truxton crew."

"Prisoners," Amati said. "Until we know what they are for certain. In any event, we'd still be keeping them in the specimen lab."

"You mean sick bay," Konstantine said.

"Next door to," Amati said. "But through another set of double biolocks."

The specimen lab was aired up and all the cage doors were unlocked and all the isolation field generators powered down. The plain old mechanical isolation still made the prisoners nervous. They weren't in solitary confinement, but they were cut off from all the familiar aspects of shipboard life.

The ancient League had no idea what a survey vessel might run across, so they prepared for every eventuality. There was no way to get to the rest of the vessel from the specimen lab without trekking through the carbon dioxide–rich atmosphere of Natsuko's infirmary. Without respirators, no one would make it to the main biolock. Without the proper access codes, there was no way any specimen was getting out of that lab alive. Ciarán didn't like that, but he understood it. Amati was right.

Seamus wasn't acting like Seamus and none of *Quite Possibly Alien's* crew knew the other prisoners. Agnes Swan had been a Truxton captain for many years, and she didn't recognize a single one of them. That was what she said, anyway, but Ciarán couldn't tell if she was telling the truth. It didn't matter. Ciarán had begun trying to think like a merchant captain. There was only one sensible thing to do.

"If we call them prisoners we'll keep thinking of them as a threat," Ciarán said. "As long as they're on board they are a threat, no matter how small. Better to be safe."

Ciarán's weight shifted against the crash harness as Hess plunged the shuttle toward the surface of the planet.

"Sure," Konstantine said. "Safety first. Hess's motto."

"I thought 'Try power cycling it' was Hess's motto," Amati said.

"You may be right," Konstantine said.

The crash harness dug into Ciarán as Hess slowed the shuttle and settled it down with a thump.

Aoife was first out of her harness. She popped the hatch to the cargo bay as Hess lowered the ramp. Carlsbad and Wisp followed her to the edge of the ramp. The glassfield was still liquid, popping and crackling as it cooled, the hot atmosphere blasting through the open hatch reeking of spent propellant and superheated silica. Carlsbad deployed a cooltube without taking a step onto the surface. The pair disappeared into the pale tunnel. Wisp trailed after them.

"That's unusual." Amati gripped her weapon. "'Safety first' is the merchant captain's motto. She's not supposed to go jetting off onto the surface without me."

"Wisp is with her." Ciarán began unlocking fast-pallets.

"Right," Amati said. "That's fine, then." She shouldered her weapon and trotted down the ramp.

Ciarán was still unloading by the time Hess had the shuttle squared away. Hess brushed his hair back from his forehead and scratched the back of his neck. "About Amati's exo."

"The exoskeletal armor you agreed to repair." Ciarán flipped the fast-pallet's gravity field setting to "let's roll."

"Yeah. It's fixed. But it's not exactly League standard anymore."

"Will Mrs. Amati like it?" Ciarán began shoving the fast-pallet down the ramp. Hess followed along.

"Oh yeah. I had to scrounge for parts. It's like one hundred and thirty percent quite-possibly-alien whoop-ass now."

"But it works?"

"Comes with a lifetime guarantee."

Ciarán shoved the fast-pallet out onto the glassfield. "Right."

"Saw you smile there, merchie. She'll like it, Ciarán."

"I have no doubt."

"Good. Now let's get these instruments set up so I can figure out how this brain-frying little pinhole works." He twirled Young's implant-jamming device between his fingers.

CIARÁN AND HESS strung a full-spectrum net of sensors across the glassfield well away from the shuttle while Aoife and Carlsbad explored the buried Huangxu vessel and its contents. Wisp and Amati were out of sight, Konstantine in the shuttle monitoring communication and sensors. They were all linked through the communication nodes in their implants, all but Ciarán and Wisp.

Hess launched a handful of micro–sensor drones to augment the two-dimensional array of sensors strung across the glassfield.

"That's done," Hess said. "Now we're going to back up and you're going to key this monster on." He handed Ciarán the jammer.

For the second time ever Ciarán was glad he hadn't had the guts to have his head cut open and something alien jammed inside.

Hess began walking toward Ciarán from well outside the measured range of the device. He'd made it less than a step inside the maximum-range radius they'd plotted before he screamed and fell to his knees. Ciarán keyed the device off and Hess staggered to his feet, shaking his head. He limped over to Ciarán. "Strip the nut, I'm not doing that again."

"I don't see why you did it in the first place."

"Because we didn't know if what we're measuring is the thing that screws with our implants or not."

"What else could it be?"

"Anything. But we don't need to know if what we're measuring is what's doing a number on us. We only need to know that the range of whatever we're measuring and the maximum range of whatever is causing the effect are roughly the same. On this planet. On a glassfield." Hess looked skyward. "On a cloudy day."

"I see."

"You don't feel anything at all?"

"I'm getting hungry. But I don't think—"

"Hang on." Hess had the absent, listening-to-a-comms-channel look League implant users sometimes wore. When he spoke again his voice had lost all humor. "Truxton's *Golden Parachute* has arrived early." Hess began trotting toward the shuttle. Ciarán began to follow but Hess waved him away. "Run and tell the merchant captain. Her comm's not working inside the Huangxu vessel."

"Amati is closer. She could—"

"She's inbound. We're going to need the major here."

Ciarán turned to go. Amati had pointed out the entrance of the tunnel to the Huangxu ship on the overflight.

"Ciarán," Hess said.

"Engineer?"

"If you hear screaming coming from over this way, don't let Carlsbad or Aoife come near."

"I won't, Engineer Hess."

"Don't come yourself either."

"You could lift. If there's no way to intercept you before you reach *Quite Possibly Alien*—"

"Major Amati's not abandoning the merchant captain on the surface. It's not her way."

"Is this still a merchant operation?"

Hess chewed his lip. "Yeah."

"Then you'll lift if you can make it. That's an order."

"Right. If we can make it."

"You can make it."

"Go on now, Ciarán. Get to the merchant captain and stay put until the shooting stops."

CIARÁN WORKED his way down the fissure near the edge of the glassfield. Beyond it was what Gallarus Four had been before ships had begun to land—one endless black sand dune after another. He should have checked to see if there was water nearby, or shelter, or any place to hide other than in the Huangxu vessel.

Amati had found the vessel but she'd had to sweat the location out of a prisoner. Now all of *Quite Possibly Alien*'s crew knew the coordinates. If Hess and Konstantine and Amati had the sense to lift, there wouldn't be any prisoners to sweat the location out of. Unless Young had revealed the location of the hidden vessel to Roche, anyone left behind on the planet should be safe there.

It wasn't easy to find the entrance to the ship. Ciarán missed it three times before he literally stumbled into it.

Ciarán doubted Hess would tell Amati his lift order, and he doubted that she'd follow it. The sound of the shuttle lifting took him by surprise. His hands slipped and he fell the final two meters to the bottom of the crevasse. He was still scraping himself up when Wisp trotted over and rubbed against him. Ciarán scratched Wisp behind the ears before he began limping toward the black mouth of the tunnel that led to the Invincible Spear Bearers of Imperial Wrath's flightless vessel. He hoped that he'd missed Carlsbad and Aoife on their way back to the shuttle and they'd managed to lift as well.

Aoife and Carlsbad weren't in the Huangxu vessel. Wisp growled, her fur standing on end as they searched.

The Huangxu vessel was dimly lit, with a layout similar to a Freeman merchant vessel. In place of FFEs were flex-bulkheaded cargo holds, interconnected, ugly smelling, pliable, and disturbingly . . . alive. The vessel showed signs of recent occupation but otherwise seemed abandoned. He wondered if Young and his soldiers had bunked elsewhere.

Ciarán took a quick look around, calling for Aoife and Carlsbad, not liking a single thing he smelled, saw, or heard. Instruments whispered to him, begging for the opportunity to serve. The stale air reeked of dry rot. The hatch locks caressed his hands and thanked him for choosing them. They wished the master good fortune, calling after him and imploring him to return this way. The cargo holds were the worst. They cooed and sighed when Ciarán entered. The cryo console moaned in ecstasy when Ciarán touched it and scrolled through the log. The luminaries shivered when he keyed them awake, worshipfully inquiring if the great lord wished more or less illumination.

Ciarán wanted less. Aoife and Carlsbad weren't on board, but there were nearly a thousand Invincible Spear Bearers in cold storage. The luminaries wept when he switched them off, begging to let them serve again, soon. Wisp hadn't stopped growling since they set foot in the vessel.

Once outside, Ciarán sucked in a great lungful of Gallarus Four's chill air. It was growing dark as he climbed out of the fissure and began to trot across the glassfield, Wisp at his side. Wisp was beginning to settle until the sound of a shuttle shoving through the atmosphere tore across the sky.

A Freeman longboat punched through the clouds and plummeted toward the glassfield near the Huangxu slave pen. Wisp raced ahead, and Ciarán would have called to stop her if he dared.

It wasn't *Quite Possibly Alien*'s longboat.

The longboat landed in a cloud of superheated gas. A cooltube licked out like a pale and bloated tongue. Armed men began to muster beyond the glassfield, half a score of them.

Ciarán recognized Roche's bony form. Ciarán had a chance of getting closer while the glassfield below the shuttle continued to vent steam into the atmosphere.

He trotted as close as he dared, hoping the waste heat from the shuttle's landing would hide his infrared signature. Ciarán's blue utilities were nearly as dark as the glassfield itself, and the light was failing.

Roche and his men were headed for the slave pen. Ciarán inched closer. If he kept the slave pen between him and the men he might be able to creep closer still. Ciarán moved slowly. It was motion hunters that saw in twilight. His dad said that, and if his dad said it then it was true. Ciarán's feet wanted to run for the cover of the slave pen's blockhouse. Keeping to a slow walk was an act of will. He'd be harder to see if he crawled, but he didn't like the idea.

Roche and his men clustered around the entry to the slave pen.

Roche had something in his hand. Not a weapon. Ciarán was almost there when a man inside the blockhouse began to scream. Roche and his men ducked through the slave pen's door. They were inside for quite some time, and the screaming didn't stop. When they came outside, they were dragging Carlsbad with them. Carlsbad writhed on the glassfield where they'd dumped him, clutching at his head. They were beginning to search the area now that they'd finished inside. It wouldn't be long before one of them spied Ciarán crouched behind the corner of the blockhouse.

Roche swept his arm about, pointing. *Spread out*, his gesture said. *Search*.

One of the men shouted. He began to turn toward the blockhouse.

He would see Ciarán. His plasma rifle swung up and then the muzzle jerked skyward with a blast of fire and the man was down and thrashing, his dying sounds drowned out by Carlsbad's screaming.

Wisp bowled into another man who dropped his weapon, clutching his thigh and collapsing before a mad confusion of fire lashed out in all directions.

The fallen man's screams cut off as a plasma beam struck him in the face and kept sweeping on.

Carlsbad's screaming didn't let up.

Ciarán ducked inside the slave pen. He had to do something. He needed a weapon. Outside, the weapons fire tapered off, then stopped.

Carlsbad's voice was growing hoarse, his screams not nearly as loud as they'd first been.

Ciarán padded into the medical lab. There had to be something. He'd seen a long pipe in there earlier when they'd packed up the autodoc for shipment.

The autodoc was powered up. That shouldn't be. Someone had blackened the control panel but they'd done a rushed job.

Ciarán's heart hammered in his chest. He cleared the panel and worked the controls as silently as possible.

Someone was inside. Heavily sedated. Vitals normal, the autodoc's display said. Ready for the next casualty. Ciarán eased the body out. He glanced over his shoulder.

Carlsbad's screams had stopped.

Ciarán began to hoist Aoife's sedated form over his shoulder. He stopped and pulled her overseer's rod free. He tucked the terror weapon beneath his belt before he lifted the merchant captain gently in his arms and began to creep toward the blockhouse door.

The sound of a longboat lifting tore through the night. Ciarán waited for his eyes to adjust to the darkness.

Plowboy Ciarán mac Diarmuid would have charged out into the dark and straight into the arms of whatever forces Roche had left in his wake. Merchant Apprentice mac Diarmuid hunkered in the entry to the slave pen listening to Aoife's steady breathing and waited for reinforcements.

Once he might have run toward the shout in the night and the frantic sound of begging.

Ciarán had seen evil in the wider world. He had responsibilities now. When Wisp stuck her bloodied muzzle into Ciarán's palm, he scratched her behind the ears until she purred.

"Good girl." Ciarán stood. He had a lot of work yet to do tonight. He needed to get started.

31

A oife smiled at Ciarán. He brushed a lock of golden hair from her forehead and she blinked.

"She lives," Old said. The Ninth Cohort Captain of the Invincible Spear Bearers of Imperial Wrath stood on his tiptoes and peered over Ciarán's shoulder. They were in a dimly lit decantation chamber aboard the Invincible Spear's ship, a claustrophobic space sized for children. The hatch was open, and from the corridor the sound of metal pounding metal and the smell of frying circuitry drifted in. He tapped Ciarán on the shoulder with his spear. "Will she honor our deal?"

"She will." Aoife's brow furrowed and the smile vanished from her face. "What is this deal?"

"The usual," Old said. "Transit off this planet in exchange for pain and death for our foes."

Aoife braced herself with both arms and shoved herself into a sitting position. She swung her legs over the rim of the decantation table. Ciarán steadied her until her glare forced his hand away. When she stood, she did it without help.

"It will be done," Aoife said. "Word of a merchant. Now describe the particulars. As briefly as possible."

"Roche has Carlsbad," Ciarán said. "Amati, Konstantine, and Hess lifted on my order."

"Go on," Aoife said.

"That's it," Ciarán said.

"What of the ship's cat?"

"On patrol," Ciaran said. The Invincible Spear Bearers and Wisp didn't get on. Ciaran had glimpsed her twice as she disappeared and reappeared in the shadows.

"And our allies?"

"The Invincible Spear Bearers." Ciarán glanced at Old. The cohort captain bore a striking resemblance to Young. There were only sixteen versions of the Spear Bearers, but Ciarán hadn't learned that until he'd begun to decant them.

"How many?" Aoife said.

"All of them," Ciarán said. "About a thousand."

"Nine hundred and ninety-one," Old said. "Forty-three are . . . unaccounted for."

"Weapons?"

"Two surface-to-air batteries," Old said. "Nine hundred and ninety-one spears. One of our batteries is . . . missing. Missing also are all of our projectile and energy weapons."

"Is that so?"

"It is so." Old spat on the deck. "We each bear our burdens as we must, Merchant Captain. Yet we remain unvanquished."

"I suppose we do," Aoife said. "Spears?"

"Largely ceremonial weapons," Old said. "Such as the ceremonial weapon your executive officer carries." Old nodded toward the overseer's rod beneath Ciarán's belt.

"I see," Aoife said. "Largely ceremonial."

"It is common knowledge," Old said. "Amongst the living."

"Common, but not particularly accurate," Aoife said.

"With age comes accuracy," Old said. "Or death."

"And what of your . . . missing comrades?"

Old shrugged. "Mistakes are made. Malfunctions occur. Our vessel is unreliable, its . . . programming susceptible to . . . corruption. One might, for instance, arrange to modify the order of decantation. Were one a worthless licker of Erl boots, a craven, Ojin-caressing weakling whose honor is no greater than that of a worm, whose sense of duty is as stunted as his faculties of reason, whose . . . concept of self extends no further than his juvenile flesh. Such a one could cause difficulties. Such a one might sully the name of the Invincible Spear Bearers of Imperial Wrath. Such a one would of course be worthy of a death in a fiery hell, he and his conniving conspirators. Such would be justice."

"Were such a one to be devoured twitching and screaming by a mong hu?" Aoife said.

"We would of course be indebted to the bright tiger and all those who share his house."

"Her house."

"Doubly so then," Old said. "Most certainly."

"Transit off the planet to where?" Aoife said.

"Some place without sand," Old said. "We are not particular so long as there are foes and pay. Some sand would be acceptable, we suppose, but a predominance of sand would not be acceptable. Unless the pay was high and the foes worthy. But not too worthy. Unless we had more weapons or access to a macrofabrication unit or units. Then any foes would be acceptable provided the pay is appropriate and we have sufficient time to produce suitable weapons in quantity. We live to serve."

"I see," Aoife said.

"Your executive officer assured us of your gifts for discernment," Old said. "At length."

"Is that so?"

"At length," Old said. "Most certainly. Doubly so, if we may be so bold. And then doubly so again, for fear we did not truly appreciate the gravity of his words."

"May I speak with my . . . executive officer in private?"

"We have prepared a cabin for such a contingency," Old said. "I trust you will find it to your liking, and if for any reason you do not, you will make your dissatisfaction known to the vessel and any deficiencies will be remedied immediately."

"Will you show this cabin to me?"

"Immediately," Old said. "We will escort you, Merchant Captain."

AOIFE GRILLED Ciarán for every bit of information he possessed. She didn't seem to care if Old and his crew monitored their conversation or not. They surely did; the Invincible Spear Bearers were enamored with monitoring and recording. Ciarán had reviewed hours of recordings before he instructed the cryo chamber to begin reviving the Huangxu soldiers. Those recordings included Roche's visits and his conversations with Young, as well as private discussions between Young and his troops. As Old said, Young had arranged to be decanted first, usurping the chain of command.

"I've been in contact with *Quite Possibly Alien,*" Ciarán said. This was the part Ciarán didn't want Old to hear, but Aoife insisted he continue. "Roche has deployed an array of microsatellites around the vessel."

"Satellites with implant jammers."

"The vessel's shielding blocks the transmissions."

"And a longboat's would not," Aoife said.

"Ko Shan doesn't think it would. The League Planetary Occupation Shuttle definitely doesn't."

"So they're trapped."

"They might flee the system," Ciarán said. "But I couldn't give that order."

"Jump the vessel within the system."

"Tried. The jammers get carried along in some way."

"Jump into the photosphere of the star," Aoife said.

"Hess thinks that would destroy the satellites."

"Then why has this not been done?"

"Because I ordered the ship's captain not to," Ciarán said. "Roche has Carlsbad. As long as he thinks we're bottled up, he might not use him for leverage."

"Roche will chemically interrogate Carlsbad."

"Sure. I would."

A smile flashed across Aoife's face and disappeared. "And he will learn that Carlsbad assaulted me and hid me in the autodoc."

"That was quick thinking on Carlsbad's part."

"He blackjacked his superior officer."

"From the bruise I'd say he hardhanded his superior officer," Ciarán said. "I don't think Carlsbad carries a blackjack. Anyway, Roche can negotiate for the ship any time. But I'm guessing he'd like to have you as well, and he'll send people down to get you soon."

"He could just destroy the slave pen from orbit. Drop an FFE on it, or—"

"I don't think so. I reviewed the Spear Bearers' surveillance recordings. It wasn't Young and his people running that slave pen."

"Wasn't it?"

"It was Merchant Roche. The Huangxu were merely custodians."

"Slave keepers." Aoife's eyes blazed.

"But not slavers. Accessories, but not principals. A fine distinction, I admit, but—"

"There is no distinction. What of the women prisoners?" Aoife's fingers clutched for the overseer's rod. The one she would be unable to wield with a jammer beaming pain through her implant into her brain. Unable to defend herself. Her face said that this was a new concept for Aoife nic Cartaí.

"Roche and some of his new League crew. During interrogation we weren't asking the right questions."

"I didn't wish to delve. Those we captured were not complicit in these abominations. This we determined. Anything else seemed immaterial."

"It should have been," Ciarán said. "But we jumped to conclusions regarding the Spear Bearers."

"Not without good reason based on experience. The prisoners are contained?"

"They were. But now I can't raise *Quite Possibly Alien* on the comm."

Aoife was silent for a long time. She chewed a fingernail. "So you woke these Huangxu to field a force."

"Not really." Ciarán didn't know how Aoife was going to take what he had to say. "I thought Roche might get desperate and chuck an FFE onto the Spear Bearers' ship. I don't know how he thinks." Young hadn't revealed the vessel's location, but Carlsbad knew it. If Carlsbad knew it, Roche would know it in time.

"And?"

"I reviewed a lot of surveillance records." Ciarán shrugged. "If the Spear Bearers aren't really people, they do a pretty good job of impersonating them when no one is looking." Ciarán watched Aoife.

"They only appear to be children."

"I know that." Ciarán had seen enough to know what these

Huangxu were. Not children, and not friends. Perhaps not even trustworthy allies. But they were people. No one deserved to die in their sleep, without a chance to fight back.

"How do you propose we live up to our end of the bargain? Assuming we prevail."

"I had Hess walk me through the diagnostics of the Huangxu superluminal drive. It's a standard Templeman unit. Hess says he can fix it if we can take Truxton's *Golden Parachute* without blowing the engineering end of the mast."

"I see." Aoife paced the compartment. "And because of my implant, I'll be useless in this conflict."

"Worse than useless. A liability."

"And how do you propose to take Roche's vessel?"

Old tapped his spear on the compartment hatch. "We beg your pardons, Merchant Lords, but the foe approaches. We are tracking them upon entry and they appear to be responding to pattern."

"One moment, Cohort Captain." Ciarán pulled Aoife's overseer's rod free.

"We live to serve." Old disappeared into the corridor.

"I propose to take Roche's longboat," Ciarán said. "The Spear Bearers have no implants."

"And after that?"

"I'll improvise." Ciarán held the overseer's rod out to Aoife. "Can you give me a crash course in how to use this? I only remember how to extend a whip and drop the field."

Aoife's gaze met Ciarán's. He had no idea what she saw there. If he were to look in a mirror he'd have no idea what he would see either.

"There is no turning back from this," Aoife said. "Once begun you will never be the same man again. This is not the tool of a paladin."

"I know. But right now it's the only tool to hand. I can't just sit by and watch."

"But that is what you propose I do. You make an unconvincing pirate, Ciarán mac Diarmuid."

"Pirate apprentice. And I'm not proposing anything. You know the facts as well as I do. Help me do what I need to. I beg you."

Aoife's gaze bored into his. "Freemen do not beg."

Ciarán thought of Annie Blum and the boy he used to be, what now seemed like a lifetime ago. He laughed. "That's the face of the story, lassie."

A grin crept across Aoife's face. "Spoken like a true pirate apprentice." Aoife held out her hand. "Now give me that weapon."

"And you'll show me how to use it."

"A little, but we won't have much time."

Ciarán didn't like the look on Aoife's face as she turned the weapon over and over in her hands. "And we won't have time because . . ."

"Because you will be otherwise occupied."

"Doing what?"

"Offering to betray your comrades and sell me to this man who trades in flesh and pain." Aoife nic Cartaí pinned Ciarán with her gaze. "We will go together to instruct Merchant Roche in pirating. Word of a merchant."

32

F or people who hated sand, the Invincible Spear Bearers had a way with it. Old and his spearmen bored a tunnel beneath the glassfield almost silently, the boring device shoving along, compacting the sand into a tunnel and fusing the walls as it moved. They all wore respirators and Ciarán and Aoife marched to the rear, well away from the working end of the device. It was a strange item, a crew-operated borer controlled by four spear-bearers working as a team.

"A breaching device," Aoife said. "These Huangxu were designed to penetrate the hulls of League military vessels and turn their corridors into galleries of certain death."

"That doesn't sound good."

"They are all but obsolete. Abandoned by the Empire, destined for scrap."

"They're people," Ciarán said.

"They are tools of empire. That they are people is not a commonly held belief."

"I don't care. I couldn't just leave them to die."

"Spoken like a merchant. This is how we live. Repurposing. They appear to have some remaining utility."

"That's not—"

"It is," Aoife said. "The wider world is filled with such as these. Castoffs. Out of place, remnants clinging on despite their lack of purpose. They make lives for themselves but they are not self-guiding. They live to serve. Their services are no longer needed."

"The services they were made for. They're people. They can learn to do something else if they want to."

"They don't want to. This is what they were made for. Bringing death and pain to their foes."

Old trotted back along the tunnel toward Aoife and Ciarán. He smiled when he saluted the merchant captain. "We are beneath the foe's vessel undetected. What shall we do, Merchant Lords?"

"What you were made for, Cohort Captain."

"As you wish," Old said. "It will be done. We live to—"

"Don't breach the hull of the vessel," Aoife said. "We need it intact."

"We hear, Lord."

"What about prisoners?" Ciarán said.

"We are not made for taking prisoners," Old said. "Death or pain. It makes no difference to us."

"Don't kill the wounded," Aoife said.

"We rarely do. We prefer their hearts beating. You will watch and learn, Merchant Lords. We know many ways to die now. With age comes wisdom." He trotted away, a smile on his face.

Ciarán swallowed. "What does he mean?"

"He means that if these are people, Merchant Apprentice, they are not the sort you will wish to wake again."

"At least they're on our side," Ciarán said.

"They aren't," Aoife said. "Not in the long run. You will need to see that for yourself."

CIARÁN HELPED Aoife from the tunnel. The fighting had been brief and one-sided. A half dozen of Roche's crew were lined up on the glassfield, obviously dead. Two more were nursing superficial wounds, a pilot and copilot, those who surrendered without a fight. One of the spear-bearers was also dead, and the surviving spear-bearers gathered them up and piled them with the dead from Roche's crew.

Aoife pulled her overseer's rod clear and held it out for Ciarán to observe. "This is not an intended purpose for the device, but you may find it useful at times." She shook out several centimeters of the monomolecular whip and held it stiff in the containment field. "See how this is done?"

"I do." Ciarán watched Aoife's fingers manipulate the studs on the device. It was that or look at the mangled bodies of the dead.

Aoife marched over to one of the dead, Ciarán trailing in her wake.

She bent and gripped the corpse by the chin, turning the man's head so that his neck and the back of his head faced up. "Watch now." Aoife shifted a finger and the containment field fell just as she plunged the still-stiff whip into the man's skull.

Bile rose in Ciarán's throat as Aoife thrust her bloodied fingertips against Ciarán's chest. "Attend me!"

Ciarán looked.

Silver gleamed in Aoife's fingers beneath the blood.

"An implant," Aoife said. "One presumably impervious to the effects of that infernal device." She shoved the overseer's rod into Ciarán's hands. "Collect the rest."

Ciarán swallowed and gripped the hideous weapon in both hands. "It's blasphemy." Handling the dead. Defiling the dead.

"You haven't seen blasphemy yet. Now do it. We need to discover if their implants are all the same."

Two of Old's soldiers began dragging the man's corpse away. The pair disappeared into the tunnel with the body.

"What are they doing with him?"

"Do I need to spell it out?" Aoife said. "We need to finish here and lift before we're invited to dinner. It is perilously rude to refuse the victory feast, Merchant Apprentice."

Another pair dragged their own dead toward the tunnel.

"We need those implants," Aoife said. "As evidence and as finished goods to reverse engineer. This is not the time for custom to rear its ugly head."

"It's wrong." Ciarán glanced at the overseer's rod in his hand. "I caused this."

"Do not wake the dead. That is our way. But you've awoken them, Ciarán, and nothing can be served by joining them for a meal. Now get to work. I will interrogate the prisoners."

THERE WERE SIX IMPLANTS, all seemingly the same. Ciarán wiped his hands on his trousers again and again. The stain persisted, would persist as long as he lived.

Old clapped his hand on Ciarán's shoulder. "To the victor go the spoils, Merchant Lord. That is our way as well."

"I—"

"You are a lord, and true to your word. We share this."

"I'm not sure I'd give you that."

"This is said of you Freemen also. That a Freeman never gives. This is our way as well. We are kin in spirit. We know this now."

Aoife finished with the prisoners. She frowned at Ciarán and Old. "I need one pilot."

"As the Merchant Lord requires," Old said. "We will discover which of these vanquished is most tractable."

"Do that," Aoife said. "My . . . executive officer and I must make haste. I regret we cannot tarry."

"It is to be expected. We will raise a cup in your honor, and wait for our deliverance from this hell of sand. Death and pain to our foes."

"Indeed." Aoife tossed an implant jammer to Ciarán. "These seem to be quite a bit more common than I like."

Ciarán stared at the device in his hand.

"You have the implants?"

"I have them, Merchant Captain."

"When Old finds us a pilot, we shall go."

"What of the other survivor?"

"These creatures hunt a Cartaí and her crew." Aoife held out her hand for the overseer's rod. "There are no survivors in such a case."

"Aoife—"

"Do what must be done. Bleed over it later. This is our way, Merchant Apprentice. It always has been our way."

"But—"

The copilot's screams grew louder as a pair of Old's soldiers dragged him into the tunnel. A bleak-eyed man in Truxton orange followed their bitter progress.

"Pilot, attend me. You will do as I say," Aoife said. "You will do as I say or you will wish you were that one."

The man stared at Aoife, his eyes wide.

"Nod in acknowledgement or I will have you change places with the other pilot."

His tongue stuck in his throat.

"Old!" Aoife shouted. "Take this one and bring me the other."

"It will be done, Merchant Lord," Old called out. He gestured for his men.

"No," the man said. "No. I'll do it. Whatever you say."

"I said nod in acknowledgment."

The man nodded, again and again. He was still nodding as Aoife shoved him onto the pilot's seat. "Lift as if your life depended on it."

Ciarán was going to be sick.

He'd done this. He'd raised the dead. He'd leashed himself to Old and his crew of cannibals.

They were human. Were people. He knew that. But they weren't people he wanted to know. Let alone be allied with. He licked his lips, that iron-cold taste in his mouth stronger again, a taste that didn't ever go away. Not anymore. Not since he'd killed his first Huangxu Eng.

His first human.

It didn't get any easier. Maybe that was better than if it did.

It had to be.

Wisp bolted up the cooltube and past the cargo hatch. She circled once and settled in on the crash couch, purring.

They were all aboard. Everyone but Carlsbad. Ciaran dogged the hatch. They would free Carlsbad. The merchant captain would see to it.

"Belt in," Aoife said. "Now it gets ugly."

"I can't raise them," Ciarán said. *Quite Possibly Alien* was still in orbit, still where she was supposed to be but not answering any hails.

It was an uncomfortable longboat ride, a jerking affair with the pilot's hands shaking on the controls and Aoife belted into the copilot's seat, overseer's rod in her fist.

Ciarán leaned over her shoulder and worked the communications equipment. Soon it would be apparent to Roche that the longboat deviated from its course, that it was bending to meet *Quite Possibly Alien*. Surely Roche knew there was a problem.

The comm squawked three times before it began to scream. "Roche wants to talk to us," Ciarán said.

"How nice." Aoife's gaze remained glued to the piloting display. She unbelted. "Let me by."

The pilot's gaze followed the merchant captain until it brushed up against Ciarán's. Ciarán pulled on his hardhands and eased into the copilot's seat.

"I'd hate to have to hurt you," Ciarán said.

The pilot didn't look like he believed Ciarán.

It was true. He hated having to hurt anyone, yet he did it again and again. There was no excuse. No excuses.

Aoife belted into one of the crash seats in the cabin. "Ignore my discomfort," she said. "Take us through this array of jamming devices." She pulled the crash belts tighter. "Quickly."

Ciarán didn't look back when Aoife's screams began. The great eye of the boat bay opened and blinked once before they were through, the longboat jammed in with centimeters to spare.

"Made it," the pilot said.

His body stiffened.

Aoife's screams turned to sobs the instant the boat bay iris closed.

Ciarán turned to check on the merchant captain and the pilot moved, fast, faster than any man should be able to move.

His fingers found Ciarán's throat and began to squeeze.

Ciarán fumbled for the crash belts holding him to the seat.

The pilot squeezed harder. "Die," the pilot said, his voice the sound of a machine, his eyes black and bottomless, not human eyes at all.

Ciarán found the belt latch and pulled as he twisted, jerking free from the copilot's seat and tumbling into the cabin.

He twisted but the pilot was too fast.

The pilot's fingers encircled Ciarán's neck and squeezed.

Ciarán balled his left hand into a clenched fist, the power-up gesture for his hardhands. He drew his arm back and slammed the field-reinforced glove into the pilot's temple. He felt bone snap.

The pilot's viselike grip tightened.

Ciarán powered up the right glove, grasped the man's forearm in both hands, sucked in a great breath, and yanked. The pilot's grip faltered, and Ciarán spun away, but the pilot was on him, one arm dangling. Ciarán slammed his knee into the pilot's chest and crabbed backwards away from the man, surveying the damage.

The pilot's arm had snapped, a compound fracture, bone jutting white and jagged. His head was caved in from ear to eye socket and tilted to one side. Still he advanced. Blood bubbled on the pilot's lips. "Die."

A blue line licked around the pilot's throat. Aoife nic Cartaí let the containment field fall, and the line turned red, blood fountained, and the monomolecular whip retracted into the overseer's rod, ready for another strike.

Ciarán glanced away but not before slick blood splattered his face, warm and clinging.

Aoife shoved the overseer's rod into Ciarán's hands.

"Get the implant."

She began working the longboat hatch.

Ciarán followed the blood trail.

When he found the pilot's head, the thing's lips were still

working, a mechanical wheezing without a man's lungs to power it. "Die. Die. Die."

"You do that," Ciarán said.

He gripped the overseer's rod in both hands and went to work.

"THIS ISN'T EXACTLY how I envisioned my apprentice cruise." Ciarán worked both cipher locks on the boat bay blast door and waited for Aoife's command. She'd scoured the League shuttle and only come up with Ciarán's borrowed vibraknife. She held it at arm's length as if it were poisoned. Her other hand gripped the overseer's rod as if it were born to wield it.

"It's not over yet," Aoife said. "Now open the hatch."

Nothing nasty came through. The corridor looked no different than it had ever done.

"Sxipestro," Ciarán said.

"I am here," *Quite Possibly Alien* said.

"Where is the crew?"

"In the isolation lab," *Quite Possibly Alien* said. "They are contaminated."

"By what?" Aoife said.

"Malevolence of an unknown nature," *Quite Possibly Alien* said. "As are you, Merchant Captain. You must report to the isolation lab immediately. Should you resist—"

"This is absurd," Ciarán said. "Release the crew and—"

"Merchant captain?" *Quite Possibly Alien* said.

"I won't resist," Aoife said. "Is there a cure for this contamination?"

"It appears so. For some."

"We proceed to the lab," Aoife said.

"That is wise," *Quite Possibly Alien* said.

"What of the prisoners?" Ciarán said.

"Contained for now."

"What about Carlsbad?" Ciarán said. "Has Roche been in contact?"

"Carlsbad is dead," *Quite Possibly Alien* said. "As is Roche. They just don't know it yet."

"You can't—"

"I can," *Quite Possibly Alien* said.

"But—"

"You understand my nature and my duty, Ciarán. The contamination must be stopped before it spreads."

"Show us," Aoife said.

33

Ciarán adjusted his respirator and tried to keep from hyperventilating. The entire crew of *Quite Possibly Alien* lay stretched out on examination tables, their eyes closed, their breathing regular but shallow. Only Natsuko was without a mask. The stillness of her face robbed her of the pure animal attraction she normally exuded. She seemed more human, as if Ciarán were seeing past her otherness for the first time. It wasn't so hard to imagine her as kin, and if not a sister, a cousin of sorts.

The others were the same. Konstantine, Ko Shan, even Mrs. Amati didn't seem the strange specimens Ciarán had seen when he'd first met them.

They were people, his comrades, and they were not moving. Only Mr. Gagenot looked as if he belonged on an examination table, his body long, and thin, and pale as a corpse. Hess looked like he was sleeping, his self-confident frontiersman's smirk still pasted to his face.

Agnes Swan was another matter altogether. She was stretched out on an examination table, the thin cloth of a sheet covering her lanky frame. She looked every bit a Huangxu Eng and then some. Out of the loose-fitting Imperial skinsuit she was even more alien that he had imagined.

"She has wings," Ciarán said.

"A recent development," Aoife said. "A mark of the Imperial line, and not a fact Agnes would like spread about.

"Showing her age, Ciarán. The wings begin to come in after the fourth decade of life."

Only the emperor and his close relatives had wings. Pops said so. He even showed Ciarán a recording he said was smuggled out of the Celestial Palace, the vast orbiting construction that was the core of the Huangxu Eng empire. Ciarán thought that he was watching a pair of angels until he realized what they were doing. Copulating in free fall, a tangle of limbs and wings. Ciarán decided the recording was a hoax.

Now he wasn't so sure. "Ship's Captain Swan is a blood relative to the Huangxu emperor?" That was a big deal in the Hundred Planets. The biggest deal, really. It meant she hadn't been elevated to Eng through service to the empire, but rather engineered to rule from before her birth.

"She has not denied it," Aoife said. "Now her body betrays her secrets." Aoife brushed Agnes's hair from her forehead. "I believe she sees this relationship as a mark of shame."

"As you see," *Quite Possibly Alien* said, "they live. The corruption has been removed."

"Their implants," Ciarán said.

"The infestation," *Quite Possibly Alien* said. "Within the implants. Their implants act as host to a parasite most vile. It spreads within the implant, altering the implant's nature and deepening the implant's integration with the victim."

"Wake my crew," Aoife said.

"Who performed the . . . removal operation?" Ciarán said.

"They will each wake within the next two hours," *Quite*

Possibly Alien said. "Though it may be some time before they are fit for duty."

A device on the deckhead Ciarán had taken for a luminary moved. It extended eight multijointed limbs and began to stride across the deckhead. It stopped above an unoccupied examination table and extended two limbs from its jet-black carapace. Multilobed manipulator fields flickered blue at the end of its limbs.

"I performed the operation," *Quite Possibly Alien* said. "The service drones are quite adept at manipulating matter. You will now submit to this procedure, Merchant Captain. Please disrobe and lie upon the table. The process is quick."

"But painful," Aoife said.

"More painful than quick."

"The implant is in her skull," Ciarán said. "Why does she have to disrobe?"

"To monitor her vital signs and to assess how far the infestation has spread."

"But the infestation is in her implant."

"It is *seated* in her implant. From there it spreads its tendrils into blood and tissue, into organs and bone. The longer the infestation is allowed to spread, the more difficult it becomes to root out."

"I was thinking about it like software," Ciarán said. "Are you saying it's hardware?"

"It is unlike anything I have ever experienced. Likely not a human invention."

The service drone moved silently, its fields extending and shifting shapes, now a force blade, now an injection needle.

"Delaying won't make it any less painful, Merchant Captain."

"Show me the prisoners," Aoife said.

"Are you sure this . . . operation is necessary?" Ciarán said.

"They are contained," *Quite Possibly Alien* said. "You may observe and decide for yourself as to necessity."

The prisoners moved toward the specimen lab's viewing ports when they noticed Aoife and Ciarán. Their eyes were red-rimmed and hollow, their faces slack from lack of sleep. Ciarán looked for Seamus but didn't see him. A bone-thin man keyed the compartment-to-compartment comm alive. "Let us out," he said. "This is inhumane, to hold us like animals. We've done nothing—"

Aoife pressed the mute button on the local comm. "Show me what it is I'm to see."

"As you wish," *Quite Possibly Alien* said. "I have modified the atmosphere within the confinement area. The prisoners will begin to lose consciousness."

The prisoners clutched their throats and fell to their knees. One dropped like a stone, his forehead striking against the bulkhead as he fell.

"Stop it!" Ciarán shouted. He could see Seamus. Seamus knelt, hands on his thighs, panting. His gaze met Ciarán's before it faltered. Seamus collapsed on the deck near the center of the compartment. He didn't seem to be breathing.

"It is done," *Quite Possibly Alien* said. "Now watch."

One by one the prisoners rose. The man who had struck his head bled profusely from a scalp wound. He didn't appear to notice.

Each of the prisoners seemed normal enough until Ciarán got a look at their eyes. They were black and bottomless, like the pilot's eyes on the shuttle.

One of them noticed Ciarán. Then another. They leapt against the viewport and hammered their fists, their mouths all silently shaping the same word again and again.

The viewport was field-reinforced. If it were possible for them to escape, *Quite Possibly Alien* wouldn't risk this display.

Aoife keyed the mute control off and the chorus of shouting voices flooded the infirmary.

"Die die die die die—"

"It's rather like a zombie holo," Aoife said.

"Except they're not dead. Only unconscious." And this was real. Ciarán touched the mute. "Remove their implants."

"They are too tightly entwined," *Quite Possibly Alien* said. "These new implants appear crafted to speed the integration between parasite and host. The parasite has had weeks or months to spread its tendrils and gain control. "

Aoife elbowed Ciarán and nodded toward Seamus. "Your friend is acting differently."

"That one is playing dead," *Quite Possibly Alien* said. "Watch."

A spider-legged remote drone dropped from the deckhead and prodded Seamus with a blunt-ended field. The blue tracer outlining the field glowed brighter where it touched, but Seamus didn't seem to notice. His eyes didn't open.

The drone's field reconfigured into a force blade. The blade scythed toward Seamus. Seamus dodged, faster than a man should be able to.

Seamus was quick, and agile, and impossibly competent. He had been as long as Ciarán had known him.

Except Seamus was supposed to be unconscious.

"Could he have a rebreather or a—"

Seamus opened his eyes and stared at Ciarán.

Ciarán didn't recognize the dead-eyed thing staring back.

It wasn't Seamus.

It stood and skirted the drone. The remaining prisoners stilled and grew silent. They backed up as Seamus approached the viewport.

He placed his hand against the containment field, his fingers splayed. When he spoke, it was Seamus's voice. "Not half bad, eh, Plowboy?" Seamus's lips twisted into a grin.

That wasn't Seamus in there. It couldn't be.

"This one has achieved a level of integration that the others lack," *Quite Possibly Alien* said.

"What is it?" Ciarán said.

"Most definitely alien," *Quite Possibly Alien* said. "Most definitely a threat. A contagion that propagates through League implants. A parasite that supplants the volition of the host and, in time, enslaves it."

"Remove it," Ciarán said.

"I lack the power and skill. Killing the host is the best I can do."

"That's not good enough. That's—"

"Is the contagion contained?" Aoife said.

"On this vessel," *Quite Possibly Alien* said. "It remains loose in this system. It may be loose in the wider world."

"Every League citizen over the age of five has an implant," Aoife said.

"And most Freemen," *Quite Possibly Alien* said.

"Most space-born Freemen," Ciarán said. "I doubt there's a hundred people with implants on Trinity Surface."

"In any case, it's not just our problem in Gallarus system," Aoife said. "It's the end of civilization."

"The end of the League unless it is stopped," *Quite Possibly Alien* said. "Civilization ended long ago."

"You are mistaken," Aoife said. "And we will stop this. Somehow."

"I will do what needs to be done, Merchant Captain," *Quite Possibly Alien* said. "Whatever needs to be done."

"Here is what you will do," Aoife said. "First you will get this parasite out of me. Until such time as I am able to resume my responsibilities, you will consult with the Merchant Apprentice before doing anything irreversible."

"I do not take orders from humans. To do so would defeat my purpose."

"No one is ordering you to do anything," Aoife said. "Consult first before you act. This is not so much to ask. Do what you must, but as a last resort. Not as a first option."

"I am—"

"Quite possibly alien." Aoife pointed through the viewport. "Some small part of those within remain human. Until that spark dies this is our affair, not yours."

Seamus smiled at Ciarán. The thing inside him did.

"Ciarán?" *Quite Possibly Alien* said.

"Hold them, and leave them be," Ciarán said. "If they're contained they can't harm us."

Aoife's face was very pale. Her hand seemed to want to stray to the base of her skull where even now a terrible nightmare was at work, conspiring to steal her very self.

"And should they break free?" *Quite Possibly Alien* said.

Ciarán couldn't hide behind vague phrases. As if by not saying the words it became something different, something less bleak and soul destroying.

Something cowardly. And craven. And self-deluding.

"Remove their implants," Ciarán said. "Even if it kills them."

"Spoken like a merchant." Aoife turned and stalked away.

If this was what it meant to be a merchant, Ciarán had made a bad career choice. He wasn't meant for this. No one was.

Aoife began to disrobe. "You're needed on the bridge." She tossed her overseer's rod to Ciarán.

"I am," Ciarán said.

"And you're in command. Whether you like it or not."

"I am. And I don't."

"Welcome to my world, Merchant Apprentice." Aoife hopped up onto the examination table and pulled the thin sheet over her. "Now stop gaping and get to work. One would think you've not seen a woman before."

"I—"

"Silence!"

Ciarán felt his face twist into a grin. That was the merchant captain, not the thin slip of a girl whose fingers shook as they kept straying toward the base of her skull.

"That's better. You're in command, Ciarán. Don't tear the gasket."

"I am in command, Merchant Captain." Ciarán jammed the overseer's rod beneath his belt. "I'll try not to screw up."

"Merchants don't try."

"I know," Ciarán said. "They do."

Merchant apprentices screwed up. Regularly, like clockwork. He'd have to pretend to be something else for the duration, and see how that worked out. Once Aoife was back in charge, he could go back to screwing up if he wanted to.

34

E very five minutes, the hail from Truxton's *Golden Parachute* repeated.

Ciarán hadn't listened to it yet. There was no point. He studied the low-resolution sensors. Roche's vessel appeared in the same position relative to *Quite Possibly Alien*. There was no discernible activity on the planet's surface.

Wisp rubbed against Ciarán and hopped up into the piloting seat. She circled three times, padding, before she settled in for a nap. Most of her hung off the edge of the seat, her legs dangling in a way that probably look comfortable to another cat. She used to sleep amongst the overhead struts of their loft on Trinity Station in the same loose-limbed pose. Those days seemed like ancient history now, even though it hadn't been that long ago.

Ciarán might nap as well. He couldn't operate the vessel without assistance. He couldn't flit over to Roche's vessel and rescue Carlsbad. Not without backup.

Freemen prided themselves on their independence. On their self-sufficiency. It was ridiculous, all the posing and posturing. There might be one in ten thousand who could perform all the functions required to operate a superluminal vessel. Even then, the merchant ships weren't designed for single-handing. Even the most skilled needed help. Trustworthy help.

They didn't teach this at the Academy. You had to learn it yourself.

The crew of *Quite Possibly Alien* was a set. A mismatched set, but a set nonetheless, each crewman an integral part of a cobbled-together machine that needed all its parts to function.

All of them. Carlsbad. Aoife. Everyone else.

Everyone but Ciarán. He was a stand-in for the merchant captain. There was no doubt that Amati could perform that role, but *Quite Possibly Alien* was a merchant vessel, and according to Freeman custom and law a merchant was always in charge. Even if that merchant was only a merchant apprentice on his first cruise, trying to take it all in, pretending to know what he was doing.

No one was fooled. Least of all Ciarán.

Ciarán turned when the bridge hatch opened. "It's about time—"

Agnes Swan dropped into the captain's seat. "Is it?"

Ciarán swallowed. "Aren't you going to tell me to get off your bridge?"

"Would you go?" Swan began cycling through a series on her display. Ciarán recognized the repeated screens of communications, sensors, engineering, duplicates of those on each of the consoles around the bridge.

"I wouldn't."

"I don't like you. Freeman whelp."

"I'm not surprised. I don't much like myself most of the time."

"It doesn't show." Swan settled her display on the communications screen "Quite the opposite, in fact."

"That I like myself too much?"

"Arrogant. A common character flaw amongst you Freemen. Have you answered these hails?"

"I have not. And I don't think I'm—"

"Why not?"

"Because I just don't think so. How do I appear arrogant?"

"Why haven't you answered the hails?" Swan shifted so that she could face Ciarán. "Or shall we discuss you, Merchant Apprentice? Shall we ignore the wider world and explore your precious self?"

"I have not answered the hails, Ship's Captain, because I have not listened to them. I have not listened to them because I cannot act without the assistance of this crew. I might, however, upon hearing these hails, feel compelled to act should they threaten harm to a comrade. This would definitely not be a wise course of action."

"Instead you choose ignorance, believing that your conscience would not be burdened and your unbridled self would not act unwisely, even knowing wisdom."

"That's right. So educate me. What would you do?" Ciarán shifted so he could give the Huangxu Eng his full attention.

Swan leaned forward in the captain's seat. She frowned at the displays. She started to speak but stopped. Her gaze met Ciarán's and it was cold as space.

"The same, though for different reasons."

"So I did the right thing."

"No." Swan's fingers danced across the displays. "We shall listen together. Then we shall argue. I will express my position and you will speak against it."

"But—"

"This is how right decisions are determined."

"By the Huangxu Eng?"

"No," Swan said. "By those who would be wise."

"Oh," Ciarán said.

"Just don't sit there, fool." Swan leaned back in the captain's seat and winced. "Begin the playback."

"I will."

"On the main display."

Ciarán rerouted the communications display. "Done."

"Pay close attention, Freeman whelp. I expect a reasoned argument."

The bridge hatch cycled and Maura limped through. "I have the mother of all headaches." She looked from Swan's face to Ciarán's then back again before she turned to step back through the hatch. "I don't need this."

Swan smiled at Maura and motioned for her to sit. "My headache is your headache, Navigator. Let us learn its dimensions."

Roche stared back from the display. He was larger than life size, as was the image of Carlsbad strapped to a table in the *Golden Parachute*'s infirmary. When Roche smiled, only his lips moved. His eyes were dark and dead. "Your man wants to say a few words, yes."

Carlsbad turned his head and spat on Roche's boots. "I want to cut out your black heart and—"

Roche pressed a button on the device in his hand. Carlsbad writhed against the straps holding him to the table. His screams were ragged and hoarse. Roche had to raise his voice to be heard.

"It is quite painful, yes?" He nodded to himself. "But so easily remedied."

Roche picked up a device and pressed it to the base of Carlsbad's skull. Carlsbad's screams grew louder before they turned into a breathless pant. Blood drained onto the table as Roche pressed a button and the device ejected a silver object onto the table. Carlsbad's implant.

"This mercy may be yours," Roche said. "In exchange for the vessel *Impossibly Alien* and the feckless hide of Eefa McCarthy. I offer an additional reward for her alive, yes, but it does not need to be so. Dead or alive, yes. It will do. "

Roche retrieved a box from his pocket and opened it with care. He drew forth another silver object, larger, more curved than the implant he'd removed from Carlsbad's body. He placed the object on Carlsbad's chest. It was just like the ones Ciarán and Aoife had removed from the dead on Gallarus.

Carlsbad pulled against the straps holding him to the table.

"This is the part I like best," Roche said. "Yes!"

The implant glowed blue and began to crawl slowly up Carlsbad's chest. Carlsbad twisted but the device refused to slow or deviate. It clung to his chest, to his throat, to his neck. It worked its way up a bloody trail to the raw slash where Carlsbad's implant had been and began to burrow in. Carlsbad stiffened and screamed again and again.

His cries abruptly cut off.

"Your man has a few words for you, yes." Roche unstrapped Carlsbad and pulled him into a seated position.

Carlsbad stared back from the display, his eyes black and dead. When he spoke, it didn't sound like Carlsbad at all but a mechanized parody of the man.

"Die."

"Now you will do as I ask and you will be spared."

"Die."

"Yes." Roche grinned. "Yes. Spared."

"Die."

"Or not. You have until this time tomorrow to decide. Do as I ask or . . ."

"Die."

"DID YOU SEE THAT?" Maura was practically shouting. "That yoke moved!"

It moved and Ciarán and Aoife had brought a carry-sack full of them back on the stolen longboat. And *Quite Possibly Alien* had already done half of the job, removing the original implants to make room for the new ones.

"I've got to get to the boat bay," Ciarán said.

"I'm coming with you," Maura said.

"No you are not," Swan said. "No one is going anywhere."

"We brought implants back with us," Ciarán said. "If they can move, they could be loose on the vessel."

"They don't move very fast," Maura said.

"They would not need to," Swan said. "If we were asleep, or otherwise incapacitated."

"Like in the infirmary."

"They can't open the boat bay blast doors," Maura said. "Or the biolocks."

"I don't remember if we closed the boat bay hatch," Ciarán said. "We were in a hurry."

"Whose idea was it to remove our implants?" Swan said.

"Sxipestro," Ciarán said.

"I am here," *Quite Possibly Alien* said.

"Whose idea was it to remove the implants?"

"Mine."

"Have you been monitoring—"

"Always."

"And?"

"Mistakes were made. I will find these alien devices."

Maura jumped when the overhead lighting crashed to the floor. She pulled a force blade from somewhere when the light fixture began to scuttle toward the hatch on eight multijointed limbs. It extended two of its limbs and worked the hatch before disappearing into the corridor.

Ciarán peered out. Hatches up and down the corridor were opening and more drones stepped out, dogging the hatches behind them.

"Now the overhead lamps are turning into huge black spiders?" Maura said. "I must still be out cold. This has to be a dream."

"A nightmare." Swan's gaze drilled into Ciarán. "What is this, Sxipestro?"

Swan's face paled when *Quite Possibly Alien*'s ship's minder spoke in Swan's head, and in Ciarán's.

"I am here, Ship's Captain."

Swan dropped back into her seat with a wince. "You are," she said. "But what in all the heavens are you?" She looked at Ciarán.

"Sxipestro?" Maura said. "What's—"

"I am here, Navigator."

Maura collapsed into her seat. "I'm losing my mind. Now I'm hearing voices inside my skull."

"I can explain," Ciarán said.

"Then explain why the ship's cat is chasing a giant mechanical spider down the corridor," Maura said.

"Wisp?" Ciarán turned and looked just as Wisp's tail disappeared through the hatch. "Wisp!"

Ciarán stepped into the corridor and pulled the overseer's rod free. He managed to take one step before Maura tackled him.

"No you don't," Maura said. "We stick together. Two or more, we can't—"

"One of those things could get into Wisp and—"

"The cat's not human." She rolled off Ciarán as another drone sprinted past. "The implants—"

"We don't know what the implants can do," Ciarán said. "They can move, and if you think an implant in one of us is dangerous imagine one in a—"

"A genetically engineered killing machine. The most perfect weapon ever devised." Swan stared down the corridor.

"No it's not." Maura brushed herself off.

"I assure you," Swan said. "Mong hu were engineered—"

"Sure they were," Maura said. "But it's not the most perfect weapon ever devised." The force blade flicked to life in her fingers. "I am."

"You see, Merchant's Apprentice?" Swan said. "Freeman arrogance. It—"

"It's not arrogance if you can back it up," Maura said. "Now are we going or staying?"

"Staying," Swan said.

"Going," Ciarán said. "We can argue later."

"I disagree, Freeman whelp. We should stay—"

Ciarán turned to Swan. "Is this a merchant operation or not?"

"Merchant all the way," Maura said. "All your best pirates are merchants."

"This is so," Swan said. "But—"

"Argue later," Maura said. "Now come on."

35

"You have to admit, Ciarán," Maura said. "We may be unorthodox but we're entertaining." She leaned against the boat bay blast doors while Swan peeled out of her skinsuit. "Good idea dropping the gravity in the bay."

"It was *Quite Possibly Alien*'s idea." Ciarán tried not to stare at Swan.

"I have not done this before," Swan said.

"Get naked in front of an audience?" Maura said. "It helps if you have a few drinks in you."

"You know very well what I mean." Swan grimaced and shook out her wings.

How Ciarán had ever mistaken a Huangxu Eng for an angel . . .

"My eyes are up here, merchant boy," Agnes said. "Those are standard issue. Nothing novel, I assure you."

"But perky, Ship's Captain. Very perky for a woman your age. Look how red Ciarán's face gets when I say 'perky.'"

"Enough," Swan said. "I will attempt to—"

"Pirates don't attempt," Maura said. "We do."

They were wasting time. Wisp needed them. Now. "I—"

"Shush, Ciarán," Maura said. "Perky." She chuckled when Ciarán looked. She laughed when he blushed again.

"I will soar above the longboat hull and proceed to grid search the bay for the mong hu. If I sight it—"

"Her," Ciarán said.

"I will point to her and keep pointing so that you can locate the bright tiger. We retrieve her and we return to the bridge. It is agreed."

A drone scuttled by, limbs moving silently.

"Agreed," Ciarán said.

Most Huangxu Eng lived their entire lives in free fall. They designed themselves to suit their environment. All the Eng did. Engineers in flesh, the Eng crafted themselves and those that they created into task-specific configurations. The Eng were slave-makers who perfected themselves first. That's what Pops said.

When Agnes Swan leapt and began to soar, Ciarán could believe it. She was built for low gravity. Crafted for flight. Everything about her lithe body declared it.

She began to search.

"Agnes is prickly as they come," Maura said. "But if you need someone at your back, she's your man." She craned her neck. "Straight up, I wish I could fly."

"With the gravity set this low, you almost can." Ciarán clung to the hatch.

"Right," Maura said. "You're liable to be useless. I remember your graduation blastoff."

"I've been practicing. With Mrs. Amati."

"And now you're dangerous?"

"Less so."

"No, I mean—"

"She's pointing. Come on." Ciarán pulled out the overseer's rod and powered it up. He pushed off.

Wisp was in the aft inboard section of the boat bay. She was nose down, ignoring Agnes Swan, ignoring everything but whatever she had trapped beneath her paw.

She batted the thing and pounced on it again. It tried to worm away. She dropped her nose toward it, scenting it.

"Wisp!"

Wisp looked up at Ciarán's shout.

The thing began to scuttle away.

Ciarán shouted for Maura to stand back, but she ignored him. He held the overseer's rod over his head and let the monomolecular whip spool long. He'd only have one chance before the scuttling thing disappeared beneath the shuttle.

He swung the rod. The whip lashed out. As it struck the implant, Ciarán let the containment field fall on the first meter of the whip.

The blast knocked him off his feet.

He tumbled across the deck before smashing into the longboat's landing gear.

Ciarán shook his head and scanned the deck for Maura.

She was crumpled up beneath the League shuttle.

Wisp trotted over and licked Ciarán's hand. She was purring.

Swan hopped down from atop the shuttle. She was holding her arm tight against her side. She winced as she landed. "Whatever you did, don't do it again."

Ciarán's ears rang. "I won't, Ship's Captain."

"See that you don't, Freeman whelp."

The boat bay deck had fractured, spidery lines radiating from the blast point.

Maura struggled to her feet. She peered down at the

shattered decking. She kicked a chunk free. "It's not just pure evil jammed into your head!" she shouted. "It's a bomb!"

"You're shouting," Swan said.

"What?"

"You're shouting!"

"You're whispering!"

"I'm—"

Ciarán nabbed Maura by the elbow with one hand and palmed a ball of augustinite with the other. The two most perfect weapons ever devised trailed in his wake. "Let's go. We need to warn the others."

"I'll dress on the bridge." Swan cradled her arm. She eyeballed Ciarán. "I may need help."

"Perky!"

Ciarán's face burned. He could see now why Aoife had learned to school her face into a perfect mask of bland disinterest. Her crew was certifiable.

If he was going to pretend to be a merchant, that was a skill he was going to have to develop.

Soonest.

Right after a cold shower.

Swan leaned in close after Maura pulled free from Ciarán's grasp and ranged ahead, always staying in sight. "She jokes because of Carlsbad. They are like brother and sister beneath the skin."

"I see," Ciarán said.

"Carlsbad is supremely competent," Swan said. "Extremely . . . dangerous. If such a fate could befall a Voyager—"

"Then no one is safe."

"No one."

"The wider world is more terrible than I imagined."

"Now you know," Swan said. "This is why we do what we do. To make a terrible world less so."

"So far that hasn't worked out."

"It will. In any case, it is a sin to live in ignorance."

"I didn't think I was living in ignorance."

"The ignorant never do."

"I've not gotten a lecture from a naked woman before."

"A certain sign of ignorance," Swan said.

"Inexperience," Ciarán said. "Ignorance is different."

Swan was silent for a long time.

"You should seek another posting, Ciarán mac Diarmuid. On another vessel."

"Have I offended you? Because if I did I'm—"

"No. But ship's captains have a rule. We do not angle in—"

Ciarán's ears burned. "In the family pool. I know."

Swan peered at Ciarán from under her feather-light brows. "We do not angle in the merchant captain's orbit. That is the rule."

Ciarán nearly stumbled.

"No angling. No matter how much we are tempted."

Ciarán swallowed. "Right."

"You will help me dress. And we will resume our argument. Fool."

"I will, Ship's Captain."

"I know you will. As you say, ignorance and inexperience are not the same. One we may remedy. The other is a sin."

36

Konstantine sat in the mess and sipped caife from a disposable mug. "I feel . . ."

"Broken." Hess kicked a chair out for Ciarán and went back to thumbing on his hand comp.

"Worse than broken. Dead-like. Deadish. Is that a word?" Konstantine grimaced. "Listen to me. I'm talking like Maura Kavanagh. I hate this."

"It ought to be a word." Hess tossed the hand comp onto the table and threw his hands up. "Stuff I just thought about and knew is all gone. I can't even find what I'm looking for in the ship's database. Half the stuff I know was in my implant."

"So you're not *the* engineer anymore," Ciarán said. "You're just an engineer. Now."

"Not hardly, merchie man," Hess said. "I figure it's like being shipwrecked with nothing but a plasma cutter and a set of spanners. I could still build a macrofab. It would just take a blistering long time."

"We don't have a lot of time," Ciarán said.

"Yeah." Hess picked up his hand comp and began scrolling through the displays. "I know."

"It's Major Amati that has to be feeling it the most," Konstantine said. "Her kit depends on an implant for its interface."

"Think about it," Hess said. "All the decent weapons in the League depend on an implant. One day you're the trigger finger of a nearly invincible fighting machine and the next you're just some hyper-augmented rando chucking stones at the advancing horde."

"Unless you're unconscious, or brain-dead." Konstantine said. "And slaved to the horde-master." Her brow wrinkled. "There has to be a horde-master? Right? Find the kingpin implant and destroy it."

"It could be a distributed consciousness," Hess said. "Kill the horde-master and some protocol just elects another one. Like nodes in an ad-hoc network. It would be more resilient that way. Harder to kill."

Ciarán didn't want to think about that. "Amati's augmentation depends on an implant?"

"No," Hess said. "But all the stuff that plugs in and needs a fast targeting solution does. Just about everything she uses to do her job."

"Except the blowgun," Ciarán said. And her fists. And knives. And clubs. Anything, really, could turn out to be a weapon in Amati's hands.

"Yeah," Hess said. "I guess."

"Glad I didn't get a piloting net," Konstantine said. "At least I can still pilot."

"Your reaction times will be shot," Hess said. "Mine are."

"Mine weren't ever any good. I tell you one thing I don't miss."

"What's that?" Hess looked up from his hand comp.

A sleepy dart buried itself nose deep into Konstantine's disposable mug.

The pilot blinked and turned to face the far end of the table where Amati, Ko Shan, and Natsuko had stopped chatting.

Amati pocketed her blowgun and smiled, half human, half machine. "She won't miss Major Amati listening in on everything she says."

"Right," Konstantine said. Caife dripped onto the table.

"Half crippled I'm still twice as nasty as anything you ever met," Amati said. "So quit your bellyaching and work up. We're not beat."

"Didn't say we were," Hess said.

"Good." Amati flexed a mechanized fist. "Huangxu don't have implants. We have the weapons we bought for trade."

"The leftovers they didn't sell to Roche," Hess said. "The rubbish."

"Rubbish that only works in Huangxu hands," Konstantine said.

"Keer-on," Amati said, "didn't your child warriors give you one of their ceremonial spears?"

"They did," Ciarán said.

"Run and get it. I think it's time for a little refresher."

"Couldn't you just beat me with your fists? I—"

"This isn't playtime. I mean a real demonstration."

"I need someone to go with me," Ciarán said. "We're to stay in pairs or better."

Mr. Gagenot set a fresh pot of caife on the table. "Will Gag will go with Ciarán mac Diarmuid."

"Go on," Amati said. "Seeing is believing. We need some believing right about now."

"I will," Ciarán said.

Amati slid a handheld comm down the table. "Take that. Something you can't handle pops up you just call."

MR. GAGENOT WAS silent all the way to Ciarán's cabin. Spidery drones scuttled about, but Gagenot simply stepped over or around them as if their strangeness didn't even register on him.

Ciarán scooped up the spear and turned. Mr. Gagenot blocked the hatch. He was tall and pale as death, his skin stretched tight against his skull. Ciarán jerked his gaze away when he realized he was staring at the bang-stick scars on Gagenot's neck and throat.

"We're ready to go," Ciarán said.

"Will Gag remembers." Gagenot held his hands in front of him, fingers spread, palms toward his chest. His head dipped as he studied his hands. "Will Gag knows more about Contract Nine. About the lab."

"I remember. You made a joke. You said that if you told me more you'd have to kill me."

"Will Gag knows no jokes." Gagenot turned his hands over slowly, studying the backs of them.

Ciarán's grip tightened on the spear. "You didn't tell me more."

"Will Gag didn't tell then. Will Gag is telling now. Will Gag remembers the Others lab."

"What other lab?"

"Will Gag worked on the riders. Will Gag did not like the Others lab. Will Gag tried to tell about the Others lab." Gagenot jerked his chin up, showing Ciarán his scars. All of them. "Will Gag earned these."

"I'm confused. Why are you telling me this now?"

"Will Gag doesn't have to kill you now." Gagenot's gaze met Ciarán's. "Will Gag is free of the rider."

"I'm still not getting it. What is a rider?"

Mr. Gagenot pointed at Ciarán's bunk. A silver object wormed its way beneath his pillow.

"Will Gag sees a rider."

The thing was buried under his pillow. If he'd come back to his bunk alone . . . Ciarán crept forward and placed the tip of the spear under the pillow.

Mr. Gagenot's giant fingers wrapped around Ciarán's wrist. "Will Gag will handle the rider. Will Gag remembers the riders."

Gagenot released Ciarán and shoved his hands beneath the pillow. A silver and blue implant struggled to escape his grasp.

"Careful," Ciarán said. "It's a bomb."

"Will Gag knows bombs. Will Gag remembers riders are not bombs." Gagenot manipulated the implant in his fingers. Ciarán couldn't see exactly what he did, but when he held the implant out for Ciarán to see, it was a dull gray. "Will Gag remembers the power-down sequence for the riders. Will Gag worked on the riders."

"You made these things?"

"Will Gag worked on many things." He pocketed the device. "Will Gag sees." A tear ran down Mr. Gagenot's face. "Will Gag remembers."

"Can you teach others how to work the power-down sequence?"

Gagenot didn't speak. He stared at his hands.

"Mr. Gagenot?"

"Will Gag can teach. Will Gag can show how to find the riders."

Ciarán nodded. At last. A lucky break. "Sxipestro," Ciarán said.

"I am here."

"Mr. Gagenot can show us how to find the riders. The implants."

"Excellent," *Quite Possibly Alien* said.

"I'm bringing him to the bridge."

"If you wish. Introduce us and I will debrief him on the way."

"Good idea." Ciarán stepped through the hatch. "Come on, Mr. Gagenot."

"Will Gag comes."

"Say the word 'Sxipestro,' Mr. Gagenot," Ciarán said. A drone scuttled by.

"Will Gag says Sxipestro."

"I am here," *Quite Possibly Alien* said. "I am here . . . I am . . . Ciarán, what is he?"

Gagenot jerked to a halt. "Will Gag hears demons in Will Gag's head."

"The victualer," Ciarán said. "Ship's cook."

"No. That is what he does. This is not what he is. Bring him to the infirmary. Immediately."

"What's wrong?"

"Bring him," *Quite Possibly Alien* said. "NOW!"

"Mr. Gagenot?"

Gagenot stood frozen to the spot.

He blinked.

He blinked again.

"Mr. Gagenot?" Ciarán tugged on Gagenot's sleeve.

Gagenot took a stumbling step toward Ciarán.

Ciarán tugged again.

Gagenot took another step. It was more than half the length of the ship to the infirmary. Ciarán tugged again. And again and again.

KO SHAN SKIDDED into the corridor, Natsuko racing along behind her.

"Agnes told us to meet you," Ko Shan said. "We're supposed to get Mr. Gagenot to the infirmary."

Ciarán wiped the sweat from his eyes. "Then get a grip on his other sleeve."

"Perhaps a fast-pallet would be better," Natsuko said.

"Right." Ciarán tugged again and Mr. Gagenot took another step. "Get one, and hurry."

Ko Shan took off for the boat bay.

"Both of you!" Ciarán shouted. "Stick together!"

"He doesn't look like he will be much help to you," Natsuko said. "Should you be attacked."

"I have a spear." Ciarán shook the murderous thing. "Now go."

"But—"

"Are we really going to stand here arguing?"

"I go, Merchant." Natsuko took a deep breath from her mask and ran after Ko Shan.

"Merchant Apprentice," Ciarán said, but by then Natsuko had disappeared down the winding corridor.

Ciarán gripped Mr. Gagenot's sleeve and tugged. Natsuko and Ko Shan returned with the fast-pallet just as Ciarán shoved Mr. Gagenot into the infirmary biolock.

The four of them piled into the biolock was a tight fit. Ciarán couldn't move without rubbing up against Ko Shan or Natsuko. Decontaminants began to rain down.

Ciarán adjusted his respirator and fitted one to Mr. Gagenot. "How do I know if this is working?"

Natsuko checked Ciarán's work. "If he doesn't tumble over, it's working."

"I hate this biolock," Ciarán said.

Ko Shan smiled up at Ciarán and popped her respirator on. She was pressed tight against him. "I find it quite invigorating."

"It has its appeal." Natsuko chuckled silently behind her mask.

Natsuko did something on her hand comp. The inner hatch popped open.

"Quit playing around," Ciarán said. "And tug."

Ko Shan tugged.

"Not on me."

"My mistake, Merchant." She grabbed Gagenot's sleeve and pulled.

"No!" Natsuko dropped her mask and rushed away.

"What's wrong?" Ciarán said. Gagenot was clear of the lock. Ciarán tugged the hatch closed and dogged it.

When Ciarán turned, it was obvious what was wrong. Aoife nic Cartaí was in a cryo chamber. It was already beginning to frost up.

"Mistakes were made," *Quite Possibly Alien* said. "It seems that—"

"What did you do!" Ciarán rushed to Aoife's side. "Why is she turning blue?"

"This is normal," *Quite Possibly Alien* said. "There was no choice. Her implant is quite . . .

different than these others."

"Who are you talking to?" Natsuko said.

Ko Shan punched Ciarán in the arm. "Ciarán?"

"Look, both of you," Ciarán said. "Just say 'Sxipestro.'"

They did so.

"I am here, Medic."

Natsuko flopped into a chair.

"I am here, Sensorman."

Ko Shan leaned against an examination table, panting. "What the—"

"Perhaps now that the doctor is here there may be

alternatives. The removal of the merchant captain's implant is beyond my skill. I may have . . . caused harm."

"No." Ciarán shook his head. "No."

"I'm a medic," Natsuko said. "Not a doctor."

"Dr. Gagenot," *Quite Possibly Alien* said.

Mr. Gagenot blinked. He blinked again.

"The cook?" Natsuko said. "He's brain damaged. The Huangxu Eng—"

Ciarán's voice was very low, so low he barely recognized it as his own. "What did you do to her?"

"He has sensory and communication damage," *Quite Possibly Alien* said. "His memory persists."

"That's horrible," Ko Shan said. "They tell us that the bang sticks rob the intellect, they—"

"They appear to do this. However the intellect remains intact."

"So Mr. Gagenot is normal?" Natsuko said.

"I doubt he ever was normal," *Quite Possibly Alien* said. "I am communicating with him now."

Ciarán pressed his fingers against the viewport of the cryo chamber. The cold seeped into his hands, his arms, his heart. "What did you do to her? You will answer me."

Quite Possibly Alien said nothing for the longest time.

"Her implant cannot be removed. It defends itself against this."

"Then leave it. Get her out of that chamber."

"She puts the crew at risk. She cannot be allowed to run free."

"But—"

"She is not dead. This is not irreversible."

"Then reverse it."

"I won't."

She looked so cold. Ciarán pulled his gaze away. "What am I supposed to do?"

"What you must," *Quite Possibly Alien* said. "What we must. Horrors are loose on this vessel. In this system. Perhaps in the wider world. What is one life against that?"

He pressed his fingers to the glass. "Everything."

"I thought better of you, Merchant Apprentice."

"As did I," Natsuko said.

"And I," Ko Shan said. "The merchant captain left you in command. She trusted you to do what is necessary."

"I can't," Ciarán said. He was just a merchant apprentice. He wasn't prepared. No one was. Only Aoife—

"Will Gag remembers Aoife nic Cartaí."

"What?"

"Will Gag sees Ciarán mac Diarmuid."

"No."

"Will Gag sees Ciarán mac Diarmuid."

"No." Ciarán ran for the biolock. The decontaminants rained down. He tore the respirator off before the second lock cycled, lungs burning. Ciarán closed his eyes and pressed his palms against the bulkhead. He let his body slide down. He buried his head in his hands.

He couldn't do this. He wasn't a merchant captain. He wasn't even a merchant. He was barely a merchant apprentice. He could not, would not, be responsible for these people's lives. He would get them all killed.

He needed to get Aoife to Freeman space, and medical attention. They could return to Gallarus space after she was safe. Except there was Carlsbad. They couldn't leave without him.

They'd rescue Carlsbad. Somehow. And then they'd go. All he needed was a plan, and he already had most of one.

He felt a sharp stab on is finger. When he glanced at his

hand he discovered a silver device had crawled up his sleeve. A rider.

He tried to shake it off but his arm wouldn't move. When he tried to stand his legs wouldn't work. The rider crept forward, up his sleeve and onto his shoulder. He couldn't brush it away. It must have injected him with some sort of paralyzing agent. It was on his neck. He tried to shout but his lips wouldn't obey him. When it tore into his flesh all he could do was scream.

And then Ko Shan was with him, one hand grasping his, the other on his neck, and then she had something silver, bloody and wriggling in her hands. Her fingers danced; he couldn't see clearly, but the device turned a dead gray. She pocketed it. "Gagenot showed me how."

Ciarán couldn't move. He couldn't even nod in thanks.

Ko Shan tucked her feet beneath her and pressed her back against the bulkhead beside him. She leaned forward and touched Ciarán's cheek lightly with her lips. "We're supposed to stick together. Merchant's orders."

After a while Ciarán could move his fingers. He could move his arms. He pressed Ko Shan's fingers in his. "Merchant's orders."

37

It was a sullen crew gathered in the mess. Ciarán looked them over, trying to find one face that said it would take orders from a merchant apprentice.

"We'll go ahead with the merchant captain's plan," Ciarán said. "With modifications."

Agnes Swan spoke. "And that plan is?"

"I'm to betray the trust of the merchant captain and crew. Selling the merchant captain to Roche, letting his men on board *Quite Possibly Alien*. Taking the merchant captain on board Truxton's *Golden Parachute*.

"And then?" Maura said. "What did Aoife have in mind?"

"I don't know," Ciarán said. "She didn't say."

"Roche will not believe you will do this," Ko Shan said. "No one would."

"He will if Seamus tells him," Ciarán said.

Ciarán would let Seamus escape. Would help him steal a longboat. When Seamus returned to Roche he'd carry a story about Ciarán's mistreatment. How Aoife nic Cartaí's merchant apprentice detested life amongst these pirates, and how he was willing to betray them all for a chance on a Truxton ship.

It wouldn't be too hard to fake. There was a time when, given the offer, Ciarán would have done just that. That would be the deal, Ciarán and his pet cat, a Truxton contract, in exchange for betrayal.

"After every horror you've seen?" Swan said. "What sort of fool would believe you'd be so gullible?"

"He is that gullible." Maura stared at Ciarán. A brief smile flicked across her lips. "He was, anyway."

"One look at him and you can see he is no longer a fool," Swan said.

"Maybe you can see that, Ship's Captain," Ciarán said. "But that's because you didn't know me before I stepped on board. Seamus was my roommate for three years. He knows what I'm like—I mean, what I was like. And that's what he'll see. He'll be convinced, and he'll convince Roche."

"And then?"

"And then the gullible merchant apprentice and his plush little kitty will go visit Merchant Roche."

"Roche has seen your cat murder his crew," Maura said.

"He hasn't. He's heard his crew call out from the darkness. No one that saw Wisp survived the encounter."

"Why would this Seamus do such a thing?" Swan said. "He was imprisoned by Roche and destined for a slave's fate."

"He was," Ciarán said. "I'm still thinking about that one. There's a way, but I'm not exactly sure how to play it." Ciarán could feel it, though. There was some way to use what he knew about Seamus and the rider that controlled Seamus when it could.

"In any event, this isn't a workable plan," Amati said. "You don't have the firepower or the skills to take a vessel, much less operate it if you did."

Ciarán brushed past Amati's objections. "When you learn of my treachery you will abandon ship and flee to the planet. The bulk of Roche's crew will attempt to seize *Quite Possibly Alien*."

"Aoife would not do that," Maura said. "Abandon this vessel."

"She's incapacitated, not in charge," Ciarán said. "Seamus will see her in cryo and tell Roche. The filthy Huangxu Eng coward Agnes Swan is leading the desertion of the ship."

"This is a wish, not a plan," Swan said. "It cannot work. Eng captains do not abandon their commands. Even filthy cowards, were there such a one. I assure you."

"Do they follow orders?" Ciarán said.

Swan grimaced. "Yes."

"Then think up an order Aoife would give that would cause you to abandon ship," Ciarán said. "And execute it."

"That's—"

"That's an order."

Swan stared at Ciarán for the longest time. "It shall be done, Merchant."

"Merchant Apprentice."

Swan nodded. "As you wish." Half a grin flashed across her face and disappeared. "Freeman whelp."

"What about the merchant captain?" Natsuko said. "Will we take her to the planet?"

"She'll be with me," Ciarán said. "As soon as she's off *Quite Possibly Alien* I can bring her out of cryo."

"Her implant makes her useless," Amati said.

"She can be quite distracting," Ciarán said. "With all eyes on the merchant captain I may be able to—"

"So now we're down and out on Gallarus Four," Hess said.

"Not quite," Ciarán said. "Could you strip the parts from this vessel to repair the Huangxu ship?"

"Sure, but it would take time," Hess said. "And break our superluminal drive."

"How long?"

"I don't know with half my brain cut out."

"If you can fix the Invincible Spear Bearers' drive, then you've a way up out of the gravity well. With over nine hundred troops designed for hull breaking."

"Armed with spears," Maura said.

"But without implants," Ciarán said. " Mrs. Amati, would you care to demonstrate what these spears can do?"

"Maybe later," Amati said. "Quantity has a quality all its own, spears or not. Plus we can take the weapons we have here with us. The ones we bought from them."

"Who's going to defend this vessel?" Maura said.

"Sxipestro."

"I am here."

"Please show the crew your defenders."

Three spidery drones piled through the hatch. Then three more. And three more. They brandished blue-bladed force knives at the end of their articulated limbs. More drones kept coming.

"Creepy," Hess said.

Konstantine shivered. "It does change how I look at lighting fixtures."

"That's enough." Natsuko took a long pull from her mask. "Your point is made."

"The drones work on the exterior of the hull as well as inside," Ciarán said. *Quite Possibly Alien* had additional defenses that only worked outside the hull. Ciarán hoped she wouldn't have to use them. "No one is taking our ship. Word of a merchant."

"Word of a merchant apprentice," Swan said.

Ciarán's fingers strayed to the overseer's rod. "Right."

"There are too many moving parts," Hess said. "Too much to go wrong."

"Then we'll improvise," Ciarán said. "I'm open to suggestions. Come up with a better plan and we'll execute that."

They were silent.

"Right." Ciarán felt a lump in his chest, had felt it from the moment he had seen Aoife in the cryo chamber. He didn't like what he was becoming, but it was better than what he'd be if he did nothing. "It is all too much. Carlsbad. The merchant captain. This ends here and now."

"You're going to get yourself killed," Amati said. "You need someone to go with you. To watch your back."

"Impossible," Ciarán said. "No one would believe that I'd . . ."

"Stoop to befriend one of us," Ko Shan said.

"It is unlikely that such a one as Ciarán mac Diarmuid would associate with pirates," Natsuko said. "Let alone come to esteem even one of this crew."

"Unless he was bewitched by her smoking-hot bod," Maura said. "And her energetic—"

"Ciarán mac Diarmuid isn't like that," Ciarán said. "He's . . ."

The mess was silent.

"He's . . ."

"Well?" Swan said.

"I don't know what he is," Ciarán said. "Anymore."

"Will Gag sees Ciarán mac Diarmuid. Will Gag will go with Ciarán mac Diarmuid."

"Thank you, Mr. Gagenot," Ciarán said. "But it is too dangerous."

"Perfect," Hess said.

"It works," Amati said.

"Yes," Swan said. "Mr. Gagenot would be the only one of us the plowboy paladin would befriend."

"And rescue," Maura said. "From Aoife nic Cartaí and her evil crew of pirates."

"No," Ciarán said. "I won't—"

"He goes," Amati said. "Or you stay. No arguing, Speedy."

Ciarán didn't like the look in Amati's eyes. Eye. Her augmented eye was studying Mr. Gagenot.

"Right," Ciarán said. "Let's get to work."

38

Ciarán watched Seamus through the specimen lab viewport. He looked like he'd been through hell, red-eyed and emaciated, but his cockiness was back.

"I have to get off this vessel," Ciarán whispered into the comm. "They're blaming me."

"Blaming you for what?" Seamus moved closer to the comm.

"For saddling them with all of you. It's just a matter of time before I'm in there with you. Or they space me. Or they space us all."

"I thought you and the merchant captain—"

"She's not in charge anymore. She's in cryo. The Huangxu Eng, Agnes Swan, the ship's captain—"

"Mutiny?"

"What do you think? Who's going to take orders from Merchant Apprentice Ciarán mac Diarmuid? You've seen these people—"

"I didn't get a good look at them." Seamus's brow wrinkled. "At least, if I did I don't remember."

"You don't want to get a good look at them. Amati's half

machine, Gagenot's like a walking skeleton. There's not another Freeman on the vessel outside you and your comrades, Maura, and me."

"Maura. The Kavanagh who came and got you. At graduation."

"That one. She's—"

"I know what she is," Seamus said. "Guys like you have to see for yourself."

"I've seen. If I let you out, do you think you and your comrades and I could . . ."

"What?"

"Take Roche's ship?"

"I don't. And neither should you."

"Well, think about it," Ciarán said. "Because I wouldn't put it past Swan to take us all into Huangxu Eng space. I don't want to end up in a slave pen."

"You don't." Seamus was quiet for a while. "Could we take this ship?"

"Not a chance. We could take a longboat. Maybe get down to the planet—"

"Then what? Rot on Gallarus Four?"

"I don't know," Ciarán said.

"Let me think about it," Seamus said.

"Right."

CIARÁN HATED MANIPULATING SEAMUS. It wasn't Seamus's fault that he had some sort of monster jammed into his skull.

They weren't exactly friends, Seamus and Ciarán, but they knew each other. Seamus wasn't half bad, but he was far from good. If anyone Ciarán knew was likely to fall in with pirates, it was Seamus. In a way he had, for Roche was clearly a pirate of the worst sort. Roche appeared upright in Freeman space, but out in the wider world he was another thing entirely. And Seamus had gone along right up until the time it looked like Ciarán was going to wind up in Roche's clutches.

That was what Seamus said under chemical interrogation. That didn't sound like Seamus, though. It sounded like the thing jammed in Seamus's head pretending to be Seamus.

If Ciarán ignored what Seamus said, and trusted what he knew about Seamus, then there had to be some other reason Seamus was in that slave pen.

He just didn't know what it was. Yet.

"I THINK WE CAN DO IT," Seamus whispered. "But I need to talk to Roche. Privately."

"I don't see how I can arrange that," Ciarán said.

"Then you need to talk to him. Can you do that?"

"I think so. So long as I don't have to be on the comm for long. These people are paranoid and—"

"I know it. But you can do it? Get a message to Roche?"

"I can," Ciarán said. "I will."

"Good." Seamus grinned. "Then here's what you tell him . . ."

CIARÁN DRESSED in his most ragged utilities. He clipped his merchant apprentice pips to his collar and settled into Aoife nic Cartaí's office chair.

It wouldn't be hard to play the part of traitor. He felt every bit of one settling into that seat. Aoife's living quarters remained as cold and impersonal as a prison cell. Except for the single flowering bulb resting in a shallow basin of polished stones.

Ciarán pulled his gaze away and keyed the comm on.

Roche glared back from the display. "You! Nic Cartaí's toy boy. What do you—"

"Seamus mac Donnocha said there's something you should know."

Roche's eyes narrowed. "That ingrate—"

"He says he surrenders."

"He surrenders. To whom?"

"I don't know. He said to tell you, 'Ixatl-nine-go.'"

A smile flashed across Roche's face. "And you are telling me this because?"

"I want out," Ciarán said. "A place for me on a Truxton ship. A place for Seamus and for me."

"Why would I possibly care to do this?"

"Because in exchange I'll get the crew to abandon *Quite Possibly Alien*. And I'll bring you Aoife nic Cartaí."

"This is a boast and a lie, yes."

"It isn't. I will do this, in exchange for what I ask. That and safe passage for me and my cat to Freeman space."

Roche stared at Ciarán. "If you can do this I will uphold my end of the bargain, yes."

"Swear," Ciarán said.

Roche smiled. "Safe passage for you and your pet. A place for you and for the mac Donnocha boy on a Truxton ship. Word of a merchant. Yes."

Ciarán nodded. "Right. Look for us in your longboat."

"I'll believe it when—"

Ciarán flicked the comm off. Now came the hard part. "Sxipestro."

"I am here, Merchant Apprentice."

"I need to get Seamus off the ship."

"Not alive you don't," *Quite Possibly Alien* said. "Tell Roche he died in the escape. I will provide the body and you may load it onto the longboat."

"Do no such thing," Ciarán said. "I—"

"He stays until we discover some way to separate him from the infestation. He stays or he dies."

"You are beginning to irritate me."

"Only beginning?"

"Are you going to stop me from moving Aoife to the longboat?"

"So long as she is in cryogenic storage she is no concern of mine."

"And If I take her out of cryo?"

"You do not want to do that."

"Can we put Seamus in cryo?"

"It might well kill him. So yes, if you wish."

"Right. We'll leave him locked up and compound the lies." And Ciarán would just have to live with the betrayal of a friend.

"WHAT DID YOU DO?" Amati kicked the pile of parts that was once a set of League exoskeletal armor.

Hess scratched his chin. "Well, first I removed all the broken parts, then I—"

Amati picked up the command helmet. "It is grotesque."

"Do you need an implant to work it?" Ciarán said.

"I could work it if all I had left was my little toe," Amati said. "A Leagueman in an exo is the most perfect weapon ever devised. You've turned my deadly beauty into a black-and-blue clown suit."

"I'm telling you," Hess said. "It don't look like much but it's good to go. Extra whoop-ass included free of charge. It's got a—"

"Lifetime guarantee. I know. My granny's heard that one." Amati eyeballed the flat black mass of panels and actuator rods. "No harm in trying it on."

"If you say so." Hess took a step back.

"You've run the diagnostic?"

"Yeah."

"And?"

"Good to go, Major. As far as I can tell."

Amati worked her way into the exo. She keyed the command enunciator alive. A mechanical voice boomed across the boat bay. "Stand back!"

"That's good advice, Ciarán," Hess said.

"Sounded like an order to me." Ciarán began sprinting toward the blast doors.

If Amati said to stand back, only an idiot would still be standing there, gaping up at the enormous killing machine she'd crawled inside.

"Hess!" Ciarán shouted.

The engineer began loping in Ciarán's direction.

"Sealed and certified, that turned out nice. Told you she'd like it."

"Did you have to paint a smile on the helmet?"

"Didn't have to. But it seemed like a good idea at the time. I think the fangs are a nice touch."

Amati bent and picked up a massive weapon. When it clicked home her laugh hammered against the bulkheads.

"GRAIL gun," Hess said. "Only thing I could find that works with the new power supply."

"What's it do?" Ciarán said.

"Kills stuff. What do you think it does, brother?"

"How?"

"Quick. And dirty. Don't get in front of it."

With Amati that was good advice. The best advice, really.

"I've got the drive parts ready to pull," Hess said. "Any time we need to bug out, we can."

"And you can fix the Huangxu ship?"

"I fixed that thing."

Amati leapt onto the top of the League shuttle. She jumped from there to the topside of a longboat and then up to cling to a bulkhead where it curved to become the deckhead. She clambered across the deckhead before she dropped to the deck and bounded away.

"Don't worry about my end of the deal, merchie man."

CIARÁN FOUND that conversing with *Quite Possibly Alien's* minder was the least disturbing from the privacy of his cabin. He dimmed the lights, lay on his bunk, and stared at the deckhead, gathering his thoughts. He didn't think the plan could work without the vessel's assistance. Wisp padded across the compartment and settled in where she could see the hatch.

"Here's the problem," Ciarán said. "I don't know how to operate a longboat."

"You can't have him," *Quite Possibly Alien* said.

"I can't take one of the crew. Seamus is the obvious choice."

"Obvious to you. He is infested with an alien contagion I cannot remove. It is too deeply attached."

"But it wasn't too deeply attached in Mr. Gagenot."

"His implant was of an earlier design. Less sophisticated and much less capable."

"It's not like I'm proposing to set Seamus free," Ciarán said.

"What are you doing?"

"Using him."

He was using Seamus. Using another Freeman. Not by force, but by guile. He'd be breaking a dozen laws. And turning his back on everything he'd been raised to believe.

"And when he ceases being of use?"

"I'll—"

"You'll free him. I know you, Ciarán mac Diarmuid."

"I won't let him go free. I'll keep him prisoner. I'll bring him back here."

"By your own admission Seamus mac Donnocha is extraordinarily competent and resourceful, with an ethical flexibility enabling him to take actions you are not only unwilling to take but incapable of imagining."

"That's probably true."

"It is fact. In addition, he does not act alone. The contagion appears to grant him enhanced abilities. Abilities that Seamus mac Donnocha may now consciously control."

"Or he could be under that thing's control."

"A more likely scenario."

"What's your point?"

"My point is that you are no match for such a man. You may not be able to keep mac Donnacha prisoner even if you wished to. He may well end up using *you* to flee the system and spread this contagion throughout the League."

"I know," Ciarán said. "But what other choice do I have?"

"A choice that would not occur to you," *Quite Possibly Alien* said. "One that will permit me to release him to you. Unconditionally."

"I'm listening."

"A slow-release poison. One that will grant you time to use Seamus mac Donnocha while guaranteeing he cannot escape this system alive."

"What? That's monstrous."

"But effective."

"I can't do that."

"You don't need to. I will do it."

"Well, don't."

"It has already been done."

"What? You've poisoned Seamus?"

"I've poisoned Aoife nic Cartaí," *Quite Possibly Alien* said. "Poisoning another is quite simple."

"What!"

"Calm down. There is an antidote."

"You poisoned the merchant captain?"

"At her request."

"I don't believe you."

"Then wake her and ask her, though I advise against it. So long as she remains in cryogenic stasis the poison remains inactive. But should she waken—"

"The poison wakes too."

"The poison is fatal in twenty hours. She asked that I test to verify the agent was active. This consumed two hours, and entering stasis another hour. Bringing her out and putting her back in will consume another two hours. You do the math, Ciarán."

"This is crazy."

"She does not wish to live as a slave."

"I need to think about this."

"I will offer you the same alternative I offered the merchant captain."

"And that is?"

"You may free Seamus mac Donnacha when you can guarantee the contagion he carries will not spread beyond this system."

"It's already loose in the wider world," Ciarán said.

"It may not be," *Quite Possibly Alien* said. "If we fail here, it most certainly will be. There are protocols. You ask that I violate those most deeply held to accommodate sentiment. This is why I was created. To prevent just such occurrences."

"Like you said, I can't guarantee that."

"Then, at the moment I suspect that the contagion will escape the system, I will do what must be done."

"I understand."

"Do you?"

"You'll collapse Gallarus's star," Ciarán said.

That was the terrible truth about *Quite Possibly Alien*. That was why none of the other survey ships were ever found.

The ship's minders did what they were made for. There were unseen terrors loose in the wider world. It was *Quite Possibly Alien*'s job to make certain such monsters never found their way home to League space.

"We have been in this system long enough to collect the necessary data. It won't be just those in this system destroyed.

"This star's poles are perfectly aligned. When the black hole forms, it will be spectacular. Are you familiar with the concept of gamma-ray bursters?"

"I am not," Ciarán said.

"Then look it up. More than those in this system will perish. Freeman space will be scoured of all life."

"What? That's impossible."

"Not impossible. Inevitable, should I collapse the star," *Quite Possibly Alien* said.

"That's why the merchant captain agreed to take the poison. To remove herself from the threat equation."

"That is why she supplied the poison and demanded I administer it."

"To her, but not to the prisoners."

"The prisoners are sufficiently contained, and according to the merchant captain, incapable of making decisions for themselves."

"But she was capable."

"Capable, and fully aware of the consequences of her actions."

If he took Seamus and it even looked like Seamus might escape, then *Quite Possibly Alien* would collapse the system's star. And if he did nothing, and it even looked like Merchant Roche was trying to leave the system, then *Quite Possibly Alien* would collapse the system's star. If Roche attacked them and it even looked like he might succeed, then *Quite Possibly Alien* would collapse the system's star.

He could do nothing. Wait for someone else to come up with a better plan. Wait for Roche to attack and see how it goes. Wait for *Quite Possibly Alien* to alter its threat equation based on some new variable he couldn't foresee.

"I am informed," Ciaran said. He was stuck in a broken airlock. If he stayed put and did nothing he'd run out of oxygen eventually. But if he tried to escape he'd have to work fast and execute flawlessly to avert the same fate. One was doing something, and the other was waiting for a miracle to occur. And the merchant captain had said herself that she'd regretted not acting, and that not acting had gotten people killed.

Except that wasn't exactly what she'd said. She'd said it was her own *unwillingness* to act that had gotten people killed.

If he were responsible for just himself, he knew what he would do. But if he acted now, aboard *Quite Possibly Alien*, he wouldn't be risking his own life, but the lives of the crew, and even the ship's intelligence. If what *Quite Possibly Alien* said was true, he was also risking the lives of everyone in Freeman space, including his own family and the families of everyone he knew.

Except, if he did nothing he was still risking their lives. The only difference was that no one could blame him if he made the wrong choice.

Correction, almost no one.

He'd blame himself, and keep on blaming himself, for however long it took Gallarus's star to supernova and collapse into a black hole. Which, according to the ship's manuals he'd translated, wasn't very long at all.

Ciarán wondered if this was what the merchant captain was trying to tell him in the boat bay. That the two worlds she'd spoken of were entirely in his head. In one world he could live as a crewman, or even a passenger, taking orders and executing them. He wasn't responsible.

The world of *command* was different. The choices he made would not only determine the future of his comrades and crew but define him. He could either be the sort of person that made things happen or the sort of person that things happened to.

If that were true then there really wasn't any choice to make. He'd stepped through that hatch the day he told his dad he'd applied to the Merchant Academy. That being Seán mac Diarmuid's son wasn't enough, and an entire planet's gravity not strong enough to hold him.

"Sxipestro," Ciaran said.

"I am here," the ship's minder said.

"So am I."

Ciarán remembered what it felt like when he stepped off the longboat on Gallarus Four, and looked skyward, and felt the light of another planet's star upon his face.

One miracle was enough for one life.

He wasn't waiting for another.

39

Separating Seamus from the others in the specimen lab turned out to be easier than Ciarán expected. Seamus's comrades parted to let him through to the hatch. A pair of prisoners spat on his boots.

"Turncoat," one of them said. "I hope they space you for the slaver's pet you are."

"Dirt," another said as Seamus passed. "Just our luck they'll let this filth go and we'll rot until Truxton wrenches us loose."

"What are you going to do with him?" a man said. His borrowed utilities hung on his body as if they were made for a man three times his size.

Ciarán had to look twice to be certain. Those were his old utilities, the ones he'd come on board wearing.

"It's up to the merchant captain," Ciarán said.

It would be once he got her off the ship and out of cryo.

"You know he's a betrayer," the man said. "Trust him not." He nodded twice to himself. "Trust him not."

"I won't." Ciarán was through trusting first and asking

questions later. Even Seamus hadn't earned his trust. He wasn't part of *Quite Possibly Alien*'s crew.

Ciarán handed Seamus a respirator and pointed. "This way."

"How long do we have?" Seamus said.

"How long until what?"

"How long until these pirates find out you've left me loose?"

"I imagine they know by now. We have a head start, though. It's an indirect route from here to the boat bay, but it's marginally faster."

If they went the direct way they'd run into Mr. Gagenot waiting in the ship's mess.

Seamus shivered when the biolock began to rain on him.

"Your comrades seemed glad to see you gone," Ciarán said.

"Can you blame them? I helped Roche prepare them for sale."

"Seamus—"

"You don't have to pretend to be surprised. You've always known what I am."

"I didn't think you were a slaver."

"Neither did I. But it was either that, or join them in the cell."

"Which you ended up doing anyway."

"Yeah, well. Things don't always work out like you want them to."

The lock hatch cycled.

"No one ever changes, Ciarán." Seamus started through the lock. "I'm still all bad. You're still the gullible plowboy, still expecting people to turn out to be something they never will be."

"I thought it might be the implant." Ciarán rushed Seamus along. "If it made you do that—"

"So you know about iXatl9GO. How'd you find out?"

"The merchant captain. Roche has an implant jammer—"

"It's not a jammer," Seamus said. "It's an uploading device. It reprograms League standard implants. Makes the prisoners easier to handle."

"That's not what it did. It crippled everyone—"

"That's the first stage. Once the upload is complete, they stop screaming." Seamus stopped at the blast door. "You get used to the noise."

Ciarán worked the locks and swung the door clear. "I doubt that."

"Well, you probably wouldn't. Get used to it, I mean," Seamus said. "This ship creeps me out."

"You get used to it."

"Used to this? I don't think so."

They paced along the corridor, whispering.

"So you didn't have the guts to go through with it either," Seamus said.

"Go through with what?"

"Getting an implant. I lied about it, but I didn't figure that you'd—"

"I didn't lie. I just didn't say."

"That's lying. It gets easy, you know, the lying. Roche gave me this implant. It . . . changed things."

"Gave it to you, or forced it on you?"

"It doesn't matter."

"We'll get it out of you," Ciarán said. "When we get back to Freeman space—"

"You really believe Roche is going to live up to his word? And it's not that easy. Getting iXatl9GO out of me."

Ciarán worked the next lock. Seamus stepped through.

"Why are there so many blast doors?" Seamus said.

"That was the lab part of the vessel. *Quite Possibly Alien* is a survey vessel. They didn't know what they'd find, so all the labs and the specimen areas can be locked off from the ship proper. The whole section can be dumped if there's an . . . outbreak."

"So now we're on the ship proper." Seamus's gaze met Ciarán's.

"We are," Ciarán lied. "It's the fastest way to the boat bay."

"But not the safest."

"That would take too long."

Seamus shook his head. "You really are as gullible as ever."

Ciarán shrugged. "Look, we can stand here and catalog my faults or we can try to escape. I know which I'd prefer."

"Lead on, Plowboy."

Ciarán began to trot. Seamus had no problem keeping up. That was no big surprise. Seamus had no problem doing anything.

Ciarán worked the blast door locks and Seamus stepped into the boat bay.

Seamus pointed at the longboats. "Which one?"

"Roche's. It's powered up and the boat bay window is expecting it."

"You could stay here. This isn't going to turn out well."

"It would be worse if I stayed."

"It's your funeral." Seamus began to trot across the boat bay.

Ciarán had to run to catch up. "I hope not." It was everybody's funeral if this didn't work.

Seamus dropped into the pilot's seat and began to run through the preflight checklist. He'd grown up on Freeman vessels and there wasn't anything about being a Freeman Seamus didn't know. He'd been piloting longboats since he was old enough to walk.

"What's in the cryo chamber?"

"Aoife nic Cartaí." Ciarán settled into copilot's seat. "Part of my deal with Roche."

"Damn." Seamus adjusted the thruster collective and the longboat lifted. "This really is a one-way trip for you."

"For both of us. We're in this together."

"Ciarán—"

"Less talk, more getting us out of here," Ciarán said.

"Sure. Whatever you say, Plowboy."

Seamus eased the longboat through the boat bay window. Once clear of the hull he plotted an intersect course for Roche's ship. He blipped the thrusters once and settled deeper into the piloting seat, his gaze scanning one display after another. Five minutes later Seamus lit up the main drive. Another two minutes passed before the communications enunciator began to scream. Seamus toggled the alarm to silent mode.

"They're hailing us," Seamus said. "Your pirate shipmates."

"So? Let them."

"Don't they have any weapons? They could blast us—"

"Blast us and the merchant captain."

Seamus laughed. "Right. You do have this planned out."

"I hope so. I really do."

Seamus settled the controls and leaned back. "What else did you promise Roche?"

"I told him I'd get the crew to abandon *Quite Possibly Alien*. So he would be able to take the ship."

"That's a laugh. He could take the ship, crew or not."

"I doubt it."

"That's because you have no idea what he has in those FFEs." Seamus's gaze met Ciarán's. "Trust me on this, Plowboy."

Ciarán's stomach felt like it was going to geyser out his throat. "What's in them?"

"Weapons. People." Seamus shivered. "The most alien damned things you are ever likely to see."

"You haven't met my shipmates."

"I don't have to. I've met *them*. The Others."

"Met who?"

"Not who," Seamus said. "What."

SEAMUS NEARLY JUMPED out of the pilot's seat when Wisp brushed up against him. "Plumpkin." Seamus rubbed Wisp's ears. "You brought your cat?"

"I did. I couldn't leave her with pirates."

Seamus frowned. "Do you have to be so damned loyal?"

"Tell me you'd leave her."

"I'd leave her," Seamus said. "I'd do anything to save my own skin." He glanced at Ciarán. "You have to remember that, Plowboy."

"What were you doing in that slave pen, Seamus? Why did Roche make a special trip to Gallarus to put you there?"

Seamus looked away. "Roche is hailing us." He hunched lower in the piloting seat.

"I think we'll ignore him. If the boat bay is open, just take us in."

"He won't like that."

"Do you care?"

"You don't understand," Seamus said. "We're putting ourselves in his hands."

"I understand that," Ciarán said. "He gave his word. Word of a merchant."

"That's not worth a damn. He's not just Roche anymore."

"What do you mean?"

"Well I'll be damned." Seamus stared at the piloting display. "There's a shuttle and a longboat dropping toward the planet. Looks like your pirate crew is abandoning ship."

"Then I've held up my end of the deal."

The longboat settled into the boat bay on Truxton's *Golden*

Parachute. Seamus brought the boat to rest without so much as a bump.

"You have," Seamus said. "Now what?"

Ciarán fished in his pocket and pulled out a razorgun.

Seamus's gaze locked on the weapon. "You—"

"Ever used one of these?" Ciarán said.

"I've not."

Ciarán stuffed the weapon into Seamus's hand. "Make sure you're close. Then just point it and pull the trigger. It does the rest."

"Ciarán—"

"Come on." Ciarán levered himself out of the copilot's seat. He checked the cryo chamber.

Aoife's face seemed peaceful. Peaceful and so terribly blue. Ciarán checked the display panel. It said the merchant captain was in the deepest depths of frozen near-death.

Wisp brushed against his hand and Ciarán rubbed her ears. "I know," Ciarán said. "She doesn't look right like this." He jammed Aoife's overseer's rod beneath his belt.

Someone began banging on the hatch.

Seamus was still staring at the razorgun in his fist.

"If Roche keeps his word you won't have to use that."

"I'll have to use it." Seamus licked his lips.

"We don't have any choice. This way we have a chance." Ciarán worked the hatch lock.

"You don't understand," Seamus said.

Carlsbad stepped aboard. His eyes were black and dead. He glanced at Ciarán, then at Seamus. Wisp brushed against Carlsbad's hand. He ignored her.

Seamus aimed the razorgun at Ciarán's chest. His finger hovered over the trigger. "I'm sorry, Plowboy."

He fired.

Seamus knew how to do everything.

Everything but how to be a pirate.

If he were really a pirate, he'd know the difference between a loaded razorgun and an empty one just by the way it felt in his hand.

"Not as sorry as I am," Ciarán said. "Wisp!"

Ciarán turned to face Carlsbad.

Seamus began to scream.

"Die," Carlsbad said. He lunged at Ciarán.

Roche was just beginning to climb on board.

Ciarán ducked beneath Carlsbad's arms and slammed the hatch closed.

It took two hands to dog it.

Carlsbad had both his hands around Ciarán's neck. He squeezed and kept on squeezing.

Ciarán's fingers fumbled toward the overseer's rod. He pulled it free.

"Die," Carlsbad said. "Die."

Ciarán's knees struck the deck.

Carlsbad hammered Ciarán's head against the hatch.

The overseer's rod slipped from Ciarán's fingers and rolled across the deck.

Blackness swam before Ciarán's eyes.

He gripped one of Carlsbad's wrists.

Then the other.

Hardhands were a weapon. Carlsbad carried them.

Stars swam before Ciarán's eyes.

Carrying hardhands wasn't enough.

You had to put them on.

"Die," Carlsbad said.

Unless you'd never taken them off.

Ciarán couldn't breathe. He had to do this. Now.

Darkness swirled around him, threatening to pull him in.

Ciarán squeezed his hands into fists about Carlsbad's wrists. Bone snapped when the field-reinforced gloves sprang to life.

Ciarán sucked in a great breath of air then another.

"Die," Carlsbad said.

He hammered on Ciarán with his elbows, his hands useless.

"Wisp!" Ciarán said.

"No!" Aoife shouted.

She pressed her overseer's rod against the base of Carlsbad's skull. Blue fire exploded from the weapon.

Carlsbad slumped to the deck as Ciarán crabbed backwards.

Ciarán kicked against something. A razorgun, still in Seamus's fist. Seamus's severed forearm ended in a mess of torn flesh and mangled bone.

Aoife stood beside Carlsbad's inert form, overseer's rod in her hands. The blue dye on her face was smeared. Her eyes blazed.

"Get Carlsbad into the cryo chamber and crank it down." She slid into the pilot's seat. "Then get a tourniquet on the hostage's arm."

She pointed to a crash seat where a bloody Seamus held the remains of his gun arm in his lap.

"Don't come near," Seamus said. "You wanted to know why I was in that slave pen. I was there because that's what *It* wanted. I can't stop iXatl9GO. No one can. It owns me." He blinked. When his eyes opened again, they were black and dead.

He began to stand.

Ciarán gripped Seamus by the neck and sank his fingers in. He shaped the glove's field into a blade and struck.

It was there, the thing that thought it owned his friend.

Ciarán closed his fingers and began to withdraw the field.

Seamus's scream died in his throat.

Gleaming silver writhed in Ciarán's fingers. He gripped the

rider as Mr. Gagenot had shown him and worked the power-down sequence. It lay dull and gray in his bloody fingers.

Ciarán dropped to his knees.

Seamus slumped in the crash seat, his head at an odd angle. His eyes flicked open and closed. They opened again. He was trying to say something.

Ciarán leaned in close, his ear brushing Seamus's lips.

"Die." Seamus coughed. "I die."

He lurched again, his fingers tightening on Ciarán's sleeve.

"I die free."

"Seamus—"

"Belt in," Aoife said. The longboat jerked. "Now!"

Ciarán belted Seamus in and slid into the copilot's seat. They had what they came for. Carlsbad. All they had to do was escape.

"I hope they can't see in," Aoife said. The longboat began to accelerate.

Ciarán turned to look at Seamus.

"Attend me!" Aoife said.

"These controls regulate velocity. They work thus."

The longboat sped up and slowed down.

"These control direction."

The longboat pitched and yawed.

"Why are you—"

Aoife clutched her hands to her head and began to scream.

The longboat slammed against the deck. It gouged it way across work-scarred ceramic.

Ciarán gripped the controls.

Aoife's screaming grew louder. She pitched back and forth in her seat.

Two longboats had cleared the hull. Outbound, to take *Quite Possibly Alien.*

The boat bay doors began to close.

Ciarán slammed the longboat into a bulkhead before he got it under control.

People were scrambling about in the boat bay.

Ciarán saw him.

Roche.

Roche glared at the longboat, implant jammer in his fist, his eyes gleaming black and bottomless.

The boat bay doors continued to close.

Aoife's screaming grew louder as the longboat slewed toward Roche.

There was one thing they told you never to do.

Every Freeman knew.

They drilled it into every spacer at the Academy.

Ciarán hadn't really listened.

He was a merchant, not a pilot, but still, even a merchant knew.

Ciarán jockeyed the longboat's controls until it was pointed between the boat bay doors.

They continued to close.

Ciarán searched the control panel.

When Ciarán looked up, his gaze locked with Roche's. Ciarán felt his lips peel back from his teeth as his index finger descended.

Roche's eyes grew wide and he took a step, then another.

He could run if he wanted.

It wouldn't do any good.

Aoife's screaming changed pitch.

Ciarán's finger found the main drive ignition stud.

He kept on pressing until the world exploded.

40

S moke filled the cabin. Ciarán shook his head and glanced down at the longboat's copilot's console. Most of the telltales were red. Those that weren't red were yellow. The scent of smoldering plastic warred with the odor of hot ceramics.

Ciarán's finger hovered over the fire-suppression control. At least two different materials were burning somewhere in the longboat.

"Don't." Aoife unbelted from the pilot's seat and ducked into the cabin. She said something else but Ciarán couldn't hear her over the ringing in his ears.

"I need your help," Aoife said. "The cryo chamber is intact."

Wisp pushed past Aoife. She butted her head against Ciarán's dangling palm.

"There might be a problem." Ciarán gestured toward his leg. If he didn't look closely it didn't hurt as much.

The auxiliary console had broken loose and shifted, pinning Ciarán in place. That was bad enough, but some sort of support bracket had shoved through his right thigh. It didn't hurt too much until he tried to move. He figured he was in shock.

Aoife flicked the overseer's rod alive, letting the whip wind around the bracket. When she let the containment field fall the bracket sheared.

The part still embedded in Ciarán's leg felt as if it were on fire.

"Can you stand?"

"Shouldn't someone be piloting?" Ciarán's head spun. The smoke was growing thicker.

"Do you even have the slightest understanding of physics?"

"Not really," Ciarán said. "I didn't think that—"

"We're jammed partway through the boat bay force window. We're still on Roche's ship. Largely."

Aoife ripped the cover off the piloting station med cubby.

"I thought—"

"No more improvising." She yanked a stimpac out of the cubby and tore the packaging open. "That's an order."

Stimpacs were League tech. Like a numbing agent and stimulant in one. Oversized ones like the one in Aoife's hand were dangerous and probably illegal, but at least they didn't thank you for using them like Eng medpacs.

"Roll up your left sleeve."

Aoife slapped the stimpac against his flesh, right above the wrist. At first it seemed bulky, like it would get in his way if he tried to use his left arm, but the medical device seemed to flow around his wrist and up his forearm.

"Now try to stand."

He tried.

Aoife slapped a second stimpac onto his right arm and he tried to stand again.

This time Ciarán could, with help. He limped into the cabin. His gaze swept across Seamus's lifeless form. It felt as if everything decent inside him was shattered. That he might fly apart at any minute if not for the stimpac's numbing.

"Work the hatch." Aoife operated the controls of the fast-pallet under the cryo chamber.

Ciarán worked the hatch. Wisp rushed through the hatch before Ciarán could stop her.

Aoife coughed. "Stand clear."

Ciarán hopped aside. Smoke poured from the hatch. Flames licked out from under the piloting console.

Aoife ducked back through the hatch and gripped Seamus under one arm. "Are you going to help me or not?"

"What are you doing with his body?"

"Trying to keep it alive," Aoife said. "Now help me lift him onto the cryo chamber."

"But—"

"Hurry," Aoife said.

Ciarán gritted his teeth and lifted. His leg burned like hellfire but he could deal with that later.

Seamus was alive.

THE BOAT BAY WAS A SMOLDERING, mangled mass of junk. Ciarán searched for Roche's body but couldn't find it.

"Let's see about getting out of here," Aoife said.

"If we can get Seamus to the infirmary—"

"We're going to the bridge." Aoife tossed Ciarán a razorgun and a charge pack. "If it moves, kill it."

"I will," Ciarán said. He could worry about what that made him later. "The infirmary is on the way to the bridge."

It was on the way to the bridge on every Freeman vessel but one. On *Quite Possibly Alien* it was hidden deep within the belly of the beast.

On Roche's ship it would be right next to the boat bay.

Truxton merchants were known for returning to the ship somewhat worse for wear.

"Bring them," Aoife said. "But keep your weapon ready."

"I will," Ciarán said.

"I have no doubt." Aoife strode across the boat bay toward the exit. Ciarán followed, shoving the cryo chamber on its fast-pallet before him, Seamus's limp body stretched atop the device. Around them, mangled wreckage smoked and burned.

The boat bay blast doors were sealed.

"Not cipher locks," Aoife said. "Bio."

"Let's try something," Ciarán said. He bit his lip until it bled as he hoisted Seamus upright, face toward the biolock. His leg screamed for mercy. "Hold his eyelid open."

"I have a better idea." Aoife brandished Seamus's severed hand. "There could be a dozen biolocks between us and the bridge. We're not trundling your man all the way there."

The lock recognized Seamus's thumbprint.

"Arm yourself," Aoife said.

Ciarán lowered Seamus gently atop the cryo chamber again. He gripped the blast door controls in one hand, razorgun in the other. "Ready?"

"Do it," Aoife said.

There were no monsters waiting behind the blast doors, just a straight ceramic-composite corridor that looked oddly geometric to Ciarán's quite possibly alien sensibilities.

There was something untrustworthy about the directness of the corridor, as if it forced its will on the world instead of bending to meet it obliquely.

Four hatches lined the corridor in ugly symmetry.

"That should be the infirmary." Aoife worked the biolock.

Ciarán shoved the hatch open.

He recognized the compartment. It was the one where Roche had tortured and enslaved Carlsbad.

The compartment was unoccupied but it did have an autodoc. Ciarán nestled Seamus inside the autodoc while Aoife checked the cryo-chamber's display.

"Carlsbad's vitals are stable."

"Seamus's aren't." The autodoc display told an ugly story. Twenty percent chance of survival. Brain damage a near certainty. The list scrolled on.

Ciarán jerked his gaze away.

Aoife fished in storage cabinets until she found what she was looking for. "Get up on the exam table."

"We need to—"

"Have it your way." Aoife kicked Ciarán behind the knee.

He collapsed to the deck with a thud.

"This is going to hurt." She gripped the bracket jutting from his leg and pulled.

Ciarán might have screamed then. He wasn't sure. When he could see again, Aoife was bent over him, slapping a pair of emergency medpacs to life. They wriggled and whispered in their eagerness to serve.

"I hate that," Ciarán croaked. His throat was dry.

"They are rather fawning. But the Huangxu medpacs work better than the Ojin versions. Can you stand?"

He could.

"Can you walk?"

"I can."

"Good. To the bridge, then."

"Where is everybody?"

"I hope we don't find out," Aoife said. "But I fear we shall."

THE BRIDGE REEKED of charred flesh.

Roche hunched over the piloting console, his back to the

open hatch. How he managed to stay upright was a mystery. His left side was a dripping, roasted ruin. He looked cooked alive. But still he moved.

He punched coordinates into the navigation computer.

"Step away from the console," Ciarán said.

Roche continued to work the console. His ruined fingers strayed toward the superluminal drive control.

Ciarán leveled the razorgun and fired.

Roche lurched into the console.

His fingers spasmed.

He gripped the drive control.

Roche was going to jump the ship out of the system.

Quite Possibly Alien was going to collapse the sun.

Everyone in Freeman space was going to die.

Ciarán fired again.

Roche's fingers twitched one final time.

The superluminal drive engaged.

41

A nd failed.

     Ciarán's heart was beating so hard he expected to see it tear through his utilities and flop out onto the deck. When it didn't, he limped to the console and powered the superluminal drive down.

Aoife stepped over the body and swung into the captain's seat. "I take it that ends the crooked career of Merchant Roche." She began repeating piloting console displays onto the captain's console.

"Right." Ciarán turned the body over. The left side of Roche's face was gone. A gleaming silver monster squirmed deeper into the gore. Ciarán balled his hand into a fist, activating the field-reinforced glove.

He knelt.

"Don't remove it," Aoife said. "See if you can deactivate it in place. Annie will want this one intact."

Ciarán worked the power-off sequence. "Who?"

"Anastasia Blum. Our patron."

"What?"

"Come now, Ciarán. Surely you don't think we do this sort of thing for fun."

"Wait a minute—"

"She didn't think you were ready," Aoife said. "Not for this."

"I'm not," Ciarán said. "But Annie said you were pirates, that I didn't want to ship with you. That I'd become—"

"What you have become."

"Right." Ciarán stared at the wreckage of Aengus Roche. "Right."

Ciarán had done that. Done that to a man. No man could have survived that. Roche had become something else. Something not human.

That couldn't be. That had to be an excuse.

An excuse for what Ciarán had done to a man.

"We are not merely sheep," Aoife said. "And we are not wolves."

"We're creatures that prey on wolves."

"Perhaps. I prefer to think of us as sheep who have had enough."

"Annie said *Quite Possibly Alien* is mad."

"She'd have to be," Aoife said. "Otherwise she would surely destroy us all for what we have become. The League, the Eng, even we Freemen. We are all of us impossibly alien to her."

"But we're human."

"We might yet prove to be. One works toward this goal."

"But—"

"Attend me, Merchant Apprentice. You may bleed later."

"I will, Merchant Captain."

"I expect you will. See here. Roche has dumped the FFEs into the star. He has plotted a course."

"To Contract Nine," Ciarán said.

"Specifically, to an orbit around the second moon of Contract Nine."

"What's wrong with the superluminal drive?"

"I believe Engineer Hess is what is wrong with it," Aoife said. "This console reports that the engineer and Maura Kavanagh are in command of the aft section."

"I sent them to the planet."

Aoife leaned over the console and frowned. "They altered course when some fool ignited a longboat's primary drive within the hull of a starship. An improvisation on their part, according to Agnes Swan. The sort of improvisation the merchant apprentice had authorized, and demanded of his comrades, according to Engineer Hess."

"I didn't demand anything."

"I believe you have set an example. One that appears to be contagious."

"Oh. That's—"

"You are a bad influence on my crew."

There was no point in arguing with the merchant captain. She had her war face on.

"What of the other Leaguemen on board?"

"No longer on board," Aoife said. "Amati has shown some small number the exit. The bulk of Roche's crew is currently engaged in a futile attempt to commandeer *Quite Possibly Alien.*

"It seems as if Merchant Roche has been pirating under a false flag. His Leaguemen wear armor emblazoned with the name of our own vessel."

Aoife scrolled through screen after screen of data.

"What about the poison?"

"Natsuko has the antidote. We're to meet her in the ship's infirmary soonest."

Ciarán leaned against the piloting station. "And that's it?"

"It is not." Aoife swiveled so that her gaze met Ciarán's. "This is a Truxton ship. Unless Roche has sold the spares on board, one could build a Templeman drive entirely from ship's stores. Hess will restore *Quite Possibly Alien*'s drive and repair the Invincible Spear Bearers' vessel.

"You will take *Quite Possibly Alien* to Contract Nine. Take the Spear Bearers if you feel the need. It is my suggestion that you do so."

"But—"

"No buts," Aoife said. "I will take this vessel and the prisoners to Freeman space. I will take Carlsbad as well. And I need Konstantine. The rest are yours."

"*Quite Possibly Alien* won't let you leave the system. Not with your implant in place."

"We have reached an accommodation."

"What sort of accommodation?"

"The sort that does not concern you. We have an agreement. It will be met and all will be forgotten."

"Then what?"

"This contagion is not limited to one system. Ko Shan reports that Roche's records are quite detailed. And quite explicit. We may be able to stop the spread of this abomination. But only if we act swiftly."

"You'll need Engineer Hess," Ciarán said.

"I am an engineer. All nic Cartaí daughters must be in order to rise. What I truly need is to be in two places at once. Even a Cartaí captain cannot accomplish that alone.

"Carlsbad, Konstantine, and I will meet you in Contract space once our responsibilities are discharged and Carlsbad is fit for duty. It falls to you, Ciarán, to carry out the terms of our contract to the letter."

"But—"

"To the letter and nothing more. I do not subscribe to the belief that a contract once executed becomes a sacred object. But the sanctity of a merchant's word is the bond that holds the Federation together."

"I understand, Merchant Captain."

"Do nothing . . . innovative. Unless you have to. That is an order."

"I'll have to."

"Of course," Aoife said. "But this way we both know what is asked of you."

"You need Wisp with you," Ciarán said. "If you end up in court you'll want all the trappings of a merchant captain."

"I don't care about that."

"You don't, but other people do. They need to see you as you are."

"And how is that?"

"Stronger than them. More resolute. Willing to fight."

"Is that all?"

"It is not, Merchant Captain. You have socially redeeming qualities as well. I suggest you keep them on a short tether. You don't want to get a good reputation."

Aoife laughed. "As you wish, Merchant."

"Merchant Apprentice."

"We'll see about that," Aoife said. "I will leave a course of study. You must attend to it when you may."

"I'm in no big rush to change things."

Aoife rose. "Is that so?"

Ciarán smiled. "It is, Merchant Captain."

"That makes one of us."

His heart stopped when his gaze met hers.

"I am informed, Merchant Captain."

She laughed. "You are many things, Ciarán mac Diarmuid. Informed is not the word I would choose to describe you."

"Oh. For a minute there I thought you were . . ."

"That I was what, Ciarán?"

"Never mind."

She placed her hand on his sleeve. "Please. Enlighten me."

"Okay." He studied her eyes, searching them for some faint reflection of what she couldn't help but see in his. "Do you know the difference between ignorance and inexperience, Merchant Captain?"

Her pupils dilated.

And Aoife nic Cartaí blushed.

"I see," Ciarán said. "You do know."

She pulled her gaze away. "In theory I do."

"Same here," Ciarán said. "I—"

"Ciaran, please don't—"

"Hear me out."

"Very well."

"Could you maybe prop me up a little? These stimpacs are depleted. I'm pretty sure my knee is about to buckle again."

"I could just slap another stimpac on you and send for a fast-pallet."

"You could do that. But I know which option I'd prefer."

"And you believe your preferences somehow matter to me."

"I'd like to think so. But I guess we'll find out."

Merchant Captain Aoife nic Cartaí stared at him, seeing who knows what.

"We will," she said.

42

Ciarán mac Diarmuid hobbled along, imagining his future. How every journey aboard *Quite Possibly Alien* began with a fiery plunge into the heart of a star, halted for a breathless moment of calculation, and then launched headlong into the bottomless terror of a superluminal leap into the unknown.

"I expect a full report from Contract space," Aoife said. "Once you have news."

Ciarán nodded. He leaned against his Merchant Captain, trying to match her stride, his pirate lips perilously close to her own.

Count on it.

ABOUT THE AUTHOR

Patrick O'Sullivan is a writer living and working in the United States and Ireland. Patrick's fantasy and science fiction works have won awards in the Writers of the Future Contest as well as the James Patrick Baen Memorial Writing Contest sponsored by Baen Books and the National Space Society.

www.patrickosullivan.com

Made in the USA
Las Vegas, NV
13 September 2022

55229689R00187